DANCE OF SUBMISSION

Jane's eyes opened wide. She shook her head and glared at McGivern, wondering if she should beg him for some compassion. It was bad enough having to suffer this degrading punishment. She didn't want to be gagged as well. 'Please. No,' she whispered. 'Not that.'

His reply left her cold. 'I might as well gag you,' he explained. 'I'm tired of listening to your pathetic lies and unacceptable excuses.'

'But I . . .'

Jane got no further. The hard rubber ball was pressed against her teeth and although she struggled not to take it into her mouth she was left with no other option. Her jaw was forced wide open and the straps were fastened at the back of her head.

By the same author:

THE BLACK ROOM
THE BLACK GARTER
AMAZON SLAVE
FAIRGROUND ATTRACTIONS
THE BLACK WIDOW
THE BLACK MASQUE

DANCE OF SUBMISSION

Lisette Ashton

This book is a work of fiction.
In real life, make sure you practise safe sex.

First published in 1999 by
Nexus
Thames Wharf Studios
Rainville Road
London W6 9HT

Typeset by TW Typesetting, Plymouth, Devon

Printed and bound by
Cox & Wyman Ltd, Reading, Berks

ISBN 0 352 33450 9

One

'Welcome to the castle, my friends. Welcome to the home of every depraved dream you've ever held, to a haven where the rules of the outside world no longer intrude. Welcome to paradise.' McGivern flashed a grin at each of the guests.

Beside his seat at the head of the banqueting table, a naked slave knelt on all fours. A long, dark fringe hung over her face, loosely masking her identity. The mounds of her arse were at hand height and he casually slapped his palm against one cheek. The echo of flesh striking flesh resounded from the stone walls, yet the slave remained silent. As she accepted the smack to her bottom, McGivern saw that her fringe didn't even sway.

He grinned to himself, delighted with her servility.

'This island holds a unique geographic position,' he went on. 'It rests in the overlapping coastal waters of three separate countries, none of which enforce their jurisdiction. We're just out of the English Channel but not quite in the Atlantic Ocean. Mainland Europe is far enough away to be out of sight but close enough so that supplies can be affordably delivered.'

'We know where we are,' Frankie told him. 'We managed to get here without you holding our hands.'

McGivern frowned, unhappy with the interruption and bristling at her disparaging tone. In a didactic voice, he said, 'As a result of its unique location, this island is unfettered by any laws of human rights or alleged obscenities. Inside this castle, the owner may do whatever they please, however it pleases them.'

1

He allowed his guests a moment to contemplate this before continuing.

'Ownership of the castle is not just a prestigious honour. It is ideally suited to people like us: people with an absolute need for privacy. This castle is far away from the sneers of the righteous but, at the same time, the dungeons offer endless opportunities to the imaginative. Trust me when I tell you that this building is kingdom come for people with requirements like ours.'

'Can the speech, McGivern,' Frankie broke in. 'Where's my bloody money?'

His frown returned. 'I'll be coming to that in good time. I have other points to make first and you're going to let me make them.'

She glared at him and he glowered back, unintimidated by the steel in her ice-blue eyes. Frankie was absurdly pretty for a dominatrix. Even with her menacing scowl and the skull-and-crossbones tattoo on her upper bicep, she still looked truly beautiful. Her mane of long, dark hair glistened in the morning light and McGivern realised the tresses were her only concession to femininity. He watched her fling the dark locks back from her face as she concentrated her wrathful gaze on him. The combination of prettiness and masculine authority made for a heady meld that was almost irresistible.

Her leather waistcoat was cut low, revealing a deep, inviting cleavage. The hem of her matching mini displayed her upper thighs and his gaze was drawn to the sight. In spite of her contemptuous sneer, and the thick Havana jammed between her teeth, he had to concede that she was desirable.

Studying the tops of her legs, he wondered what it would be like to dominate her. He didn't entertain the thought for long, but the idea of enjoying her submission brought a wicked sparkle to McGivern's eyes. Holding her gaze with his own defiant smile, he reminded himself that she was a distraction he couldn't afford right now.

His palm still rested on the slave's bare backside and he stroked her cleft as he stared at Frankie. Whilst the slave's arse remained rigid, the dewy lips of her labia parted at his touch. Her intimate wetness warmed his finger.

'Make your point, then tell me where my money is,' Frankie hissed. Wisps of cigar smoke accompanied each word. 'I'm not renowned for my patience, especially where so much cash is concerned.'

He considered taking issue with her curt tone. McGivern wasn't used to being spoken to in such a way and he wanted to remind Frankie that he was an equal, not an unbroken initiate. The words hovered at the back of his throat before he resisted the urge to vent them. Let the others fight for dominance, he warned himself. He was in a position where he could look down on their struggles. With a massive effort, he forced a smile and vanquished the urge to berate her.

Including himself, there were only three people in the banquet hall that mattered and they all shared the same perverse tastes in pleasure. Frankie was a celebrated slave-breaker and dominatrix, as was Simon, draped casually over a seat opposite hers.

Simon was studying McGivern warily but so far he had said nothing. He wore an ornate ring on the little finger of his right hand, an oval of blue and green azurite set in a long gold mount. Whilst listening to McGivern's speech, he had toyed with the stone, but it was the closest he came to showing an unsettled composure. He occasionally raked manicured fingernails through his long, blond hair but otherwise he was simply pensive and watchful, exactly as McGivern had expected.

Of course, there were other slaves in attendance, but they were just trimmings, no more important than the gold cord sash on the purple drapes. Clad in a uniform of fishnets and leather, they lined the walls with a sumptuous display of near-naked flesh. Their presence added a finishing touch to the air of perverse perfection he had been striving for.

And there was also Jane, the platinum blonde solicitor, blushing furiously and avoiding everyone's eyes. Her dark grey suit, with its cinched waist and short skirt, set her out

3

of place amongst the slaves and masters. The clothes were an attempt at sexiness for the respectable confines of an office but, in the castle, that image didn't work. She seemed intimidated by the nudity of his slaves and repulsed by the lecherous glances of his guests. Her gaze was fixed nervously on her lap where her fingers twisted together. When she did dare to look up, her eyes were wide and her cheeks were painfully crimson. McGivern took solace from the fact that, for the moment, she was mercifully silent.

Mentally dismissing her, he decided she was on the same level as the slaves. She was there for a purpose but she was expendable and, if he chose, she was ultimately replaceable.

'I'm sure we've all known about this castle since beginning our careers in the perverse. It has an enviable reputation and ownership has always been regarded as the ultimate goal for the successful master or mistress. Today I'm going to give you the chance to become the owner of the castle.' McGivern held up a silencing finger, aware that Frankie was about to assail him with another outburst, and determined to make his point first. 'Today I'm going to offer you the chance of proving your mastery and this castle will be the prize.'

Frankie sat back in her chair, wafting cigar smoke with a careless hand. 'You've finally intrigued me,' she growled. 'What's the pitch?'

His smile was fleeting. He raised his hand again and brought it down hard against the slave's backside. This time, the slap echoed ferociously around the banquet hall and he saw the solicitor recoil, as though she had received the blow. Unaware that he was doing it, McGivern sneered at the woman. 'I'll explain the "pitch" in my own good time. First, I insist that you watch the dance of submission.'

He snapped his fingers and two of the attendant slaves rushed from the walls. They had been given their instructions before the guests arrived and McGivern wasn't surprised to see them working exactly as they had been told. The slave by his side was hauled unceremoniously on

4

to the table and, for the first time, McGivern noticed her identity. The dark fringe of hair was brushed back from her face and he recognised her as number three, the most willing and servile of his minions. His confidence soared when he realised she was going to perform the dance. Number three wasn't only beautiful, she was also pliant enough to give a marvellous show for his guests.

The summoned slaves were armed with brimming buckets, brushes and cloths, as well as the other paraphernalia he had insisted on. A grey ghost of steam wafted from the water's surface and McGivern watched as one slave pushed a brush into the pail and began to build a lather. Working quickly, she created a creamy foam then pressed the brush against number three's backside. With uncaring movements, she began to work the bristles briskly up and down.

Spread across the head of the table, number three remained silent. McGivern could see her fingernails biting hard against the oak surface but it was the only sign of discomfort she allowed her body to express. Through the veil of her fringe, he saw that her face was sanguine as the bristles scrubbed against her sex.

McGivern swallowed, the sight inspiring a delicious stiffness between his legs.

With the cleaning completed, the attendant slave dropped her scrubbing brush into the bucket and wiped away the remnants of lather with a sodden cloth. The end of her finger played against number three's anus before sliding inside. It was unnecessary and gratuitous behaviour, done purely for the slave's own excitement rather than for cleaning or preparation. If there hadn't been guests in attendance, McGivern would have castigated the trio for their self-indulgence. Instead, he simply coughed, allowing the sound to carry the implications of his displeasure.

The seditious slave glanced up then snatched her finger away. Seeing the fury in McGivern's eyes, she lowered her gaze and went back to the task she had been given. After dropping the cloth in the bucket, she rubbed caressing

5

hands against number three's bare arse, spreading the cheeks wide apart.

McGivern turned his attention on the other slave as she began to prime the enema. She had donned a pair of latex gloves for the operation and the ends of her fingers were already glistening with preparatory jelly. She worked her fist slowly up and down the shaft of the enema's pipe, lubricating it fully as her colleague began to fill the bag.

Their joint concentration would have been warming for a lesser individual but McGivern didn't have the time to waste on such indulgences. He was confident enough to let the slaves perform their duty while he captured the interest of his guests.

'The dance of submission is the litmus paper for servility,' McGivern explained. He climbed out of the throne-like chair he had resided in and began to strut around the banquet table. 'Any slave who can perform the dance properly should be deemed well and truly servile. Any master who can make a slave do the dance should be considered more than worthy of that title.'

Number three released a small groan and McGivern turned to study her. The cheeks of her arse were wide apart and her anus was a taut circle. She had muttered her protest as the enema's tip started to probe the centre of her arsehole.

McGivern's face was a mask of indifference as he watched the pipe plunge inside. Slowly, the slave began to massage the enema bag, working it into a shrinking ball. She squeezed soapy water through the intrusive shaft, using harsh clenching motions. As an undercurrent to the room's silence, McGivern heard the squirt of bubbling liquid flooding into number three.

As she had with the brushing, number three remained unmoved by this latest violation. Her eyes were closed but not squeezed tight shut, as McGivern had expected. Her body was stiff but, aside from the herculean bracing of her buttock muscles, she showed no signs of her discomfort. She continued to gouge her fingernails against the table, and McGivern saw her knuckles were whiter now, but it was the only visible reaction she allowed.

6

The final rush of soapy water was squirted from the enema.

Number three glanced up at him and, for an instant, McGivern thought he saw a flicker of despair cloud her eyes. It was only a fleeting image, barely glimpsed as she cast her gaze away from his, but he felt sure he had seen it.

His erection hardened.

Dragging himself away from the scene, McGivern strutted around the table and addressed his guests. 'I don't doubt you're familiar with the dance and its many variations, and I know you both believe you could demand it from your own subordinates. But before I move on to my "pitch", I want you to see how I have it performed.' He had reached the foot of the table and saw that his props were waiting for him. After draping a sheet of white linen over the end of the table, he retrieved a short, stubby mace from the chair and sat down.

Jane placed a hand on his arm. Her body was shaking and, when he looked into her pallid face, he saw her blue eyes were wide and fearful. 'I don't think I should be here,' she began in a trembling voice. 'Could I please be excused?'

'No.'

'But I really don't want to see this,' she hissed. 'And . . .'

'Tough,' he snapped. Brushing her hand away from his arm, he made a point of ignoring her. The timid solicitor's outburst was an irritation that he could have done without at this crucial moment. He glared at the three slaves at the head of the table and snapped his fingers. Music began to play from a hidden tape recorder and McGivern tried to let the pleasant sounds help his confident mood return.

He had elected to use *Salome's Dance of the Seven Veils* as the backing track for this performance. While he wasn't a great lover of German opera, the piece had seemed appropriate for the dance. An orchestral flurry preceded number three's tentative steps on to the table and McGivern cast his gaze from Frankie to Simon as he tried to gauge their moods. Everything rested on their acceptance of the challenge he was about to lay down. Their enjoyment of the dance was the key to that acceptance.

7

They were staring at number three with expressions of obvious intrigue and, in his heart, McGivern knew that the pair were hooked. There were still a lot of variables, he reminded himself. There was always the potential for catastrophe – but their interest had been caught and that meant the main hurdle had been overcome. Feeling sure that things were going to go well, McGivern settled himself back in the chair.

Number three stood at the head of the table, her nakedness revealed to them all. Her young, slender body was attractive to the point of perfection and McGivern knew his guests would be excited by her tattoos and intimate piercings. Aside from the celtic band around her left bicep, she wore an ornate number three over her right breast. The tattoo was a character from some illuminated calligraphy, drawn in garish crimson with gold and black trimmings. The lower curl of the number followed the edge of her areola. The tattoo's spectacular artwork was almost enough to draw attention away from her body jewellery.

Her pert breasts were pierced through the nipples. Between her legs, clearly visible because her sex had been freshly shaved, the glimmer of ball closure rings glistened slickly. She looked like the embodiment of servility and, as he admired her, McGivern's smile broadened.

The enema pipe was pulled from her anus and the two slaves returned to their position at the walls. Number three stared at McGivern with sultry brown eyes, patiently awaiting his instruction.

He waited until the overture had finished before clearing his throat. The taped orchestra began to whisper the rhythm of Salome's dance and McGivern nodded at his slave. 'You may begin,' he declared.

Number three needed no other command. Swaying her body with the music, she began to dance towards the foot of the table. She bobbed and arched with careless grace. Her slender arms stretched out, and then she embraced herself as she spun around and around before pirouetting. Throughout the dance, her face was a mask of composure, occasionally hidden by her unruly fringe.

McGivern watched with hawk-like scrutiny. He could see subtle signs that her resolve was already threatening to weaken. Beads of sweat had erupted on her forehead and her eyes were touched by an unspoken plea for release. He wasn't surprised by her anguish, aware of how difficult the dance was from the moment he had devised this variation. He hadn't been misleading his guests when he said it was the ultimate test of servility but, although number three was struggling to contain herself, McGivern felt confident that she would perform the dance exactly as he expected.

She spun slowly at first, building her actions in time to the quickening pulse of the music. With graceful steps, she avoided the bottles and glasses that littered her stage.

In spite of her seemingly lithe movements, McGivern could see she was exerting a tremendous amount of self-control. The cheeks of her arse were stiff with tension and he knew she was trying to ignore the release that her bowel craved. He smiled wickedly, aware of the torment she would have to endure before he allowed that.

He glanced at his guests and saw they were now properly hooked. They studied number three with appreciative awe as she danced over their wine bottles and made her way down the dining table. Frankie's cigar was forgotten, the vile-smelling stub no longer smouldering between her fingers. Her attention was wholly captured by the slave's dance.

McGivern congratulated himself for having known that this display would appeal to her. She was a cruel dominatrix with a reputation for enjoying the kinkiest of games – and he knew that games didn't come much kinkier than this one.

Frankie licked her lips as number three spun past and, although he still had to make the bet with her, McGivern knew that she would accept the challenge.

Simon teased an acrylic fingernail against his lower lip and graced number three with a thoughtful expression. Studying him, McGivern wondered if the man found the sight of the slave exciting, or if he was simply aroused by her predicament. Simon's sexual tastes were notoriously ambiguous and McGivern hadn't known if any of his dancers would appeal to the man. He had always regarded Simon as something of a wild card and knew that if his plan did have the potential for failure, it would be because of Simon. Those fears seemed like distant memories when McGivern saw the shine in Simon's eyes. His smile was illuminated by the gleam of arousal and McGivern knew that, like Frankie, Simon was captivated.

Number three arched her back and tripped daintily across the table. She glowed beneath the admiration of her audience, writhing athletically as the music built to its crescendo. Her naked ballet was enhanced by a femininity and grace that concealed her discomfort. Wrapping her arms around her chest, she spun three times before throwing herself on to her knees in front of her master. She finished the dance in a staged pose with her arms above her head and her kneeling legs spread open.

McGivern inhaled her scent. His face was on eye level with the pierced lips of her sex and he was close enough to sense the musk of her arousal. Ignoring the heady aroma, he graced her with a critical scrutiny. From this position, he could see that she was struggling to maintain her composure. Her entire body glistened with nervous sweat and her thigh muscles trembled with exertion. Yet still her features were a mask of indifference.

'Pleasure yourself.' McGivern spoke loudly enough so his guests could hear. He stood up and made a ceremonial gesture of presenting number three with the wooden mace he had been holding. 'Pleasure yourself and, when you've climaxed, I will allow you to be excused from this room.' He held out the mace and waited for number three to accept it.

Her gaze flitted briefly over him and again he saw the flicker of desperation in her eyes. She accepted the mace and shifted position so that her legs were folded beneath her. Without needing to be told, she settled herself on the sheet of white linen and turned to face the guests.

'I don't want to be a part of this, Mr McGivern,' Jane hissed. She moved her face close to his ear and gripped his arm as she mumbled the words. 'I really don't want to be here.'

He grabbed her wrist and wrenched her hand away. Their eyes met and he glared at her with as much fury as he could muster. 'Interrupt this ceremony again and I'll show you my unpleasant side,' he growled. 'You're here for a purpose and if you have an ounce of professional integrity in that round-shouldered body of yours, I suggest you draw on it, sit down and remain silent until I tell you otherwise.'

Jane opened her mouth. McGivern didn't know if she wanted to protest or argue and he didn't particularly care. He let go of her wrist and moved his face close to hers. 'Sit down.' He hissed the warning from between clenched teeth. 'Sit down and stay quiet until I say otherwise.'

She cast him one final, fiery look then returned to her seat. She was rubbing the back of her hand as though he had hurt it.

McGivern struggled to recapture his composure, momentarily unsettled by the defiance he had seen in her eyes. It occurred to him that if she was one of his slaves, she would be a difficult one to control. The thought was no more than a passing observation and he barely entertained it as he strutted back to his throne.

Thankfully, his guests didn't seem to have noticed the contretemps. Their attention was still devoted to number three and the final act of her dance. McGivern made a mental note to thank Jane for her discretion and then forgot about it as he caught sight of his slave's performance.

The mace was a short length of wood, as thick as a man's fist at its head and as slender as a girl's wrist at the base. Its bulbous head had been carved with an intricate blend of bumps, gnarls and crevices and the implement had been lacquered and polished until it was almost a thing of a beauty. Held in number three's tiny hands, the mace looked large and menacing.

McGivern's grin widened as she teased the misshapen dome against herself. The sight of number three's pierced sex-lips always excited him. The glimmer of nine steel rings penetrated her inner and outer labia. The metal was a contrast to the suffused flesh of her pussy, making each ring seem that much more cruel. There were two through each lip and a final one behind the hood of her clitoris. Of course, the piercings through her breasts were equally arousing, but McGivern's attention was now devoted to number three's cleft and, for the moment, he had no interest in the rest of her body. This was the denouement to the dance of submission and he was determined not to miss a moment.

Number three stroked the head of the mace against herself and moaned. The sound was torn from some place between anguish and delight. With her free hand, she teased the folds of her sex apart, instinctively touching the flesh rather than the body jewellery. She quivered as the tip of her index finger trailed over her clitoris.

She was clearly aroused, McGivern noted. That much was apparent from the hue of her labia and the tremors that racked her frame. Slowly, number three manoeuvred the mace's head against her wetness. She pressed the implement over her splayed pussy lips and steeled herself for its intrusion.

As the shiver rippled through her, McGivern held his breath. She clearly needed a release from the enema's churning waters and he recognised her struggle as being nothing short of heroic. Quite how she would cope during the moment of orgasm was something he dared not contemplate. She was his most obedient slave and had never disappointed him in the past – but there was a lot at stake on this occasion and McGivern knew better than to take success for granted, especially where slaves were concerned. Trying not to think of the potential for failure, he savoured the moment's excitement and forced himself to enjoy the performance.

Number three cried out as she pushed the mace against herself. The splayed lips of her slit began to yield beneath the pressure of the misshapen dome. Her labia peeled apart and, with a rush, the gnarly head plunged inside. The tremors that shook her body were more severe this time.

12

The slave brushed a finger against the nub of her clitoris and McGivern wondered if she was already in the throes of orgasm. If she hadn't pushed herself there yet, he felt certain she wasn't far away. Swallowing thickly, he leant forward as number three pushed the mace deep into her sex.

She shivered uncontrollably as its length filled her. Her eyes were closed tight and the tendons in her neck strained like taut cables.

'She's good,' Frankie murmured quietly. There was an appreciative glimmer shining in her ice blue eyes. She licked her lips as she watched the scene.

'She's very good,' Simon agreed. He was rolling his fingers against the azurite ring as he spoke, his gaze never leaving number three.

McGivern glowed as they praised his slave, his cheeks colouring with an uncharacteristic blush. Number three's cheeks were also reddened, although McGivern doubted this was because of the compliment she had just received. Her brow was dripping rivulets of sweat and, as she worked the stubby length of the mace in and out, her hands began to shake. Small, near-hysterical cries fell from her lips when she dared to touch the swollen nub of her clitoris. Her nipples had hardened with excitement and her lower lip jutted forward in a pout of arousal. Her eyelids were almost closed in a dreamy leer and all the time she continued to frig herself with the make-shift dildo.

'Coming!' She shrieked the word as a strangled falsetto.

As one, McGivern and his guests leant further forward in their seats. The beat of his heart was synchronised with the rapid to and fro of her wrist. This was the most difficult aspect of the dance and everything he had planned hinged on the slave's ability to perform properly.

'I'm coming,' she gasped again. There was a note of urgency in her tone.

'You know what I expect of you,' McGivern said. His calm tone didn't reveal the stomach-churning thrill of his nervousness. 'You may have your orgasm.'

It looked as though she had been waiting for the words.

As soon as he had given permission, number three pushed the mace deeper inside herself. There was still enough of the shaft outside her sex for her to hold but the rest disappeared into the slippery confines of her pussy. Her posture was a balanced combination of control and elation, as she threw her head back and drew staccato fingers against her clitoris. It took little effort to push herself beyond the brink of orgasm. She screamed and held herself still as the climax started to rush through her.

McGivern held his breath as he watched.

Number three was obviously torn between opposing needs. She clearly wanted to give in to the orgasm's relief but she resisted the impulse until she could control it. Her body quaked with a twofold desire for release and she wilfully denied one urge as she tried to succumb to the other. She delayed her climax for long, excruciating minutes and McGivern saw that she was deliberately staving off the pleasure until she could be sure to contain the enema-inspired impulse. She finally submitted to her orgasm in an air that was thick with expectancy. Her guttural roar of pleasure echoed around the banquet hall.

Simon had stopped lazing in his chair. He leant over the table, no longer able to feign disinterest. Frankie chewed on the end of her cigar, oblivious to the fact that it was unlit. McGivern saw that their eyes were wide and their incredulous smiles were appreciative.

The mace was expelled from the slave's sex as the pleasure ripped through her. Her body was dripping with sweat and climactic tremors shook her. In a ragged voice, she spat guttural words of elation that rang hollowly in the castle's acoustics. Her jaw was set in a resolute square and McGivern saw that she was still exerting a phenomenal control over her body's needs.

Number three shivered and groaned, enjoying the aftermath of her climax in small, manageable morsels. Each ripple of euphoria seemed more debilitating than the last, but it was never more than she could cope with. As the final wave ebbed away, he saw that tears of effort had been squeezed from the corners of her eyes. The

14

after-echoes of her climax sparked a final tremor and she almost collapsed beneath the weight of their voyeuristic gazes.

McGivern allowed her a moment to savour her pleasure before raising from his seat. He beamed at his slave with genuine affection and said, 'Wait there.' His voice was crisp and powerful, not revealing his gratitude.

Number three struggled to her knees, nodding her willingness to obey his command. She almost stumbled as her pleasure-weary body tried to cope with the task. Frankie stopped her from falling with a steadying hand.

'There you are,' McGivern exclaimed jubilantly. He pointed at his trembling slave. 'The proof of ultimate servility and a testament to absolute mastery.' As he switched his gaze from Frankie to Simon, he heard number three sob. The sound of her misery was almost lost beneath the reluctant applause that Simon was beginning. McGivern grinned his acceptance of the man's praise then turned to the slaves at the wall. Snapping his fingers he selected a pair and said, 'Take number three to the garderobe.'

They rushed to help the slave, half-carrying, half-leading her as she struggled to escape the banquet hall without embarrassment. It was a graceless gait and he supposed it was a disappointing exeunt for the show's leading lady but neither of the guests seemed to notice. McGivern watched the slave leave, a triumphant grin still revealing his teeth. 'That was the dance of submission,' he told his guests. 'And that's the crux of the challenge that I'm laying down for the three of us.'

'Go on,' Frankie said. She was relighting her cigar, having scratched her match across the polished surface of the oak table. 'You've intrigued me now.' She lazed back in her chair and blew a thoughtful smoke-ring into the air. Her eyes shone with an obvious appreciation for the scene she had just witnessed.

McGivern turned to Simon and waited for his encouragement before speaking.

Simon nodded and, with the silent assent given, McGivern drew a deep breath to lay down the challenge.

15

'We all consider ourselves masters in the art of domination. And we each dismiss the others' abilities as being inferior to our own. My proposal is to put our skills to the ultimate test and see which of us really is the best. We each take an unbroken initiate – a new and untested slave, if you will – and whichever one of us can make our initiate do the dance, wins the castle.'

The banquet hall fell silent. The air between them was so still, McGivern thought he could hear the wails of number three as she finally released the enema in her distant garderobe. He turned to Frankie. 'Earlier, you asked where your money was.' Glancing at Simon, he said, 'I guess you were wondering the same thing. Well, take a look around. Look at the stone walls and the gothic architecture and see what's happened to your money. For the moment, this place is your money.'

Frankie almost choked on her cigar. 'You bastard!' she gasped, struggling not to cough as she made the explosion.

McGivern laughed.

'How the hell did you manage it?' Simon demanded.

McGivern's smile was reassuring and he waved their questions away with a noncommittal hand. 'I won't bore you with all the details. It's sufficient to tell you that the owner upped the price at the last minute. I had the chance to make the purchase but I didn't have the resources. However, I had access to the money that you two had put up and, to cut a dull story short, I bought the castle. We three are now the proud owners of this remarkable building and that leaves us with two choices.'

Frankie's ice blue eyes were glowering passionately. 'You'd better make this good,' she growled between clenched teeth. 'The money I've invested was the full asking price for this castle, a week ago.'

'The same here,' Simon agreed. His tone remained calm, but McGivern could sense Simon was concealing his anger. 'How could the asking price go up threefold? How come we weren't told about this?'

McGivern shrugged. 'What can I say? The owner is greedy and uncommunicative. We all have our faults. Are you both going to shout at me because the owner put the asking price up? Or do I explain the choices available to us?'

'Go on,' Simon said, fingering the azurite stone again.

Frankie glared at McGivern. 'As I said, you'd better make it good.'

McGivern pointed at Jane. 'We have two choices available to us. We can either have this solicitor find some legal loophole, to extricate us all from this purchase, or we can have this bet.'

'It's a hell of a lot of money to stake up as a bet,' Simon told him dourly.

'It's a hell of a prize for the winner,' McGivern countered. With a sly smile, he added, 'Or don't you think you could win?'

Simon lazed back in his chair, not rising to the bait.

'How long do we give it?' Frankie asked.

'Three days. After that, the legal recourse won't be an option. The cheque will have cleared and the purchase will have been made.'

'What if it's a draw?' she persisted.

He shrugged. 'We could either have a tie-breaker or get the solicitor to step in and cut our losses.' He wasn't surprised by her volley of questions. Like him, she was a disciplinarian and used to thinking quickly. He wouldn't have expected anything less from someone with her reputation.

'Where do we find unbroken initiates on this island?' Simon asked. 'It's not exactly Milton Keynes, is it?'

McGivern's grin widened. 'Are you in?' He glanced from Simon to Frankie. 'Are you both in?'

Simon nodded. 'I'm in. If you can show me your source of unbroken initiates, then I'm in.'

'Take a look in the courtyard. There's a party of students doing some archaeological study or something. They arrived this morning, so I've not had the chance to corrupt them yet. Frankie can pick one for you to dominate.'

Simon eased himself from his chair and went to the

17

window, seeming not to mind the condition that had just been imposed on his choice. 'Students,' he laughed. 'This is going to be easier than I could have hoped for. I've yet to meet the student who isn't five pounds and a packet of a fags away from coprophilia.'

'This is preposterous,' Jane whispered. She directed the words into her lap, glaring at her interlaced fingers as though they were the source of her unhappiness. 'Absolutely preposterous.'

McGivern rounded on her with an accusing finger. 'I'd thank you to keep your opinions to yourself. You're here as a solicitor and you'll do well to remember that.' Not waiting for her response, he turned to Frankie and asked, 'Are you in?'

Frankie rested back in her chair and studied the ceiling. She struck another match and brought life back to her cigar before blowing smoke rings toward the roof. There was a faraway expression in her eyes and McGivern wondered if she was considering the bet, or simply trying to look provocative. The tight leather waistcoat pushed her breasts upward and deepened her cleavage. The hem of her mini was barely low enough to cover the top of her legs and, as she rested back in the chair, McGivern felt sure he could see the dark curls of her pubic thatch. He was snatched from his lecherous study by a noise at the banquet hall door. He glanced away from Frankie and saw that number three was returning to the room. The star of his performance was now dressed in the same uniform as her contemporaries and, although she strove to look unaffected after her ordeal, McGivern saw that she was walking on unsteady legs. It was a small distraction and he was barely aware of his own smile as he watched the slave take her position at the wall. Shaking his head to dismiss images of number three's servility, he glared at Frankie and demanded, 'Are you in?'

She lowered her gaze from the ceiling and smiled at him. 'I'm in, on two conditions. Do you want to hear them?'

McGivern nodded. He saw that Simon was glancing from the window, his attention caught by something in

Frankie's tone. McGivern had heard the sound, too, and wondered if his assessment of Frankie was correct. She sounded like a woman striving to conceal an advantage and he wondered how she could believe herself to be in such a position when he was the one controlling this situation.

'First and foremost,' Frankie said pointing, 'I want her as my initiate.'

McGivern followed the direction of her finger and coughed his disbelief. 'You want number three!' he exclaimed. 'You can't be serious. She won't do the dance for anyone other than me.'

Frankie shrugged. 'Then you'll have no problem letting me have her.'

McGivern chewed his lower lip and decided the point wasn't worth arguing. He could have reminded Frankie that the bet was meant to involve unbroken initiates but that would have sounded petty. There was no doubt in his mind that the slave would remain wholly loyal to him. In spite of Frankie's reputation, he felt certain she wouldn't be able to master number three. It was a safe option to allow her to take the slave, but he wondered why Frankie wanted to make the challenge so much more difficult for herself. Not wasting time on the notion, he simply nodded and agreed.

'OK. What's your other condition?'

Frankie's smile was an ugly glower. '*Your* initiate.' She was speaking around wisps of smoke. '*Your* potential prima donna for the dance of submission.' She took the cigar from her lips and pointed towards the end of the table. 'I want you to have her.'

With a wave of unease, McGivern saw who she was pointing at. In an instant, he realised his meticulous planning hadn't allowed for every detail. There was one variable he had overlooked and, with her infuriating command of the situation, Frankie had found his weak spot. He saw now that if he wanted to win the bet, he would have to dominate Jane. With a sick smile, he realised this wasn't going to be the easy victory he had imagined.

19

Two

'No.' Jane tried to say the word decisively but it came out as a whisper. 'No,' she repeated, trying to say it with more force. She saw the three of them were ignoring her again, just as they had done throughout the whole of this awful morning.

Frankie grinned, the smile made more evil by its attractiveness.

Unable to meet the challenge of her gaze, Jane looked away. She had been aware of Frankie's curiosity from the moment the woman entered the banquet hall. Because her own tastes didn't travel down that avenue, Jane had found the woman's interest unsettling. Admittedly, Frankie was sexually appealing in an obvious manner, but Jane didn't want the woman's attention. She had repeatedly assured herself of this fact, for fear that her body might forget.

Glancing up from her lap, Jane saw Frankie flex her smile for a final time before turning to the two men. Her presence was as commanding as either McGivern's or Simon's and Jane felt intimidated being in the banquet hall with the three of them. The near-naked women, adorning the walls like living suits of armour, only added to her unease.

'So now we have to sort out a potential conquest for Simon,' Frankie declared. She pushed herself from her chair and stalked towards his side at the window. As she moved, she smoothed her hands over the uncreased hips of her leather skirt, drawing Jane's attention to the enticing curve of her buttocks.

'I want that one,' Simon said, pointing.

Jane curled her lip, not concealing her distaste.

Simon was a stark contrast to Frankie, as effeminate in appearance as the woman was masculine. His blond hair framed a pretty face made unnaturally attractive with lip-gloss and eyeliner. The frock coat and ruffle-fronted shirt should have made him look foppish, but his tight PVC trousers and thigh-length boots added a menacing sexuality to his appearance. Despite looking outrageously camp, he maintained an air of unquestionable authority.

McGivern joined them at the window.

While Jane couldn't see the courtyard from the seat where she trembled, she knew exactly what they were looking at. She had noticed the bedraggled group of students when she arrived at the castle. They were digging through the dirt in a forgotten corner of the bailey and she remembered there were about half a dozen of them. They had all been clad in jeans and T-shirts with serious frowns on their young, work-soiled faces.

'The one with the shovel?'

'God, no! That one's wearing an anorak.' Simon snorted his disgust at the notion. 'Credit me with some principles. I'm having the one standing behind her. I want him.'

Jane thought there was something incredibly perverse about the way they were picking and choosing their way through the students. They were treating human beings with such casual disregard that she felt sickened. Her revulsion for the masters began to rise until she realised she could direct that feeling towards herself. If McGivern had expressed a desire for one of the students instead of her, Jane knew she would have encouraged him. The knowledge that she had already sunk to their level inspired a wave of self-loathing. Her need to flee the castle turned into an urgent longing and, with her panicked thoughts raging, she tried to formulate a plan of escape. Regardless of what else was happening around her, Jane knew that she had to get away from the castle.

'Him?' McGivern asked. He was peering through the window, staring at the selected student with obvious distaste. 'Why him?'

Simon's confidence shone like a blazing brazier. Jane could see the bulge pushing at the front of his pants as he stared avariciously into the courtyard. 'I could have that one eating out of my hand within twenty minutes.'

McGivern shrugged. 'If that's the one that you want, then . . .'

'No,' Frankie broke in.

McGivern glared at her.

Frankie ignored him. She pointed down into the courtyard, seeming to make the gesture at random. Holding Simon's gaze, she said, 'You can have her.'

'Why not him?' Simon asked. His tone was petulant and he glowered at Frankie as he pointed towards his own selection. 'Why can't I have that one?' As his voice rose, Jane thought he sounded like a spoilt child.

McGivern watched the exchange, looking just as perplexed as Simon. 'Yes. Why can't he have that one?'

Frankie turned on him. 'Simon thinks he can dominate that one within twenty minutes. Given Simon's reputation, I don't doubt he'd be able to and I don't want him to win this bet that easily. Therefore, I'm making the challenge that bit more difficult for him, just like I did for you.' She glanced in Jane's direction and twisted her smile into a wicked sneer.

Jane looked away, hating the insinuation she could see in Frankie's eyes.

'But you were allowed to pick your choice of initiate,' Simon protested.

'More fool you two for allowing me that privilege. You either try and dominate the one I've just pointed at, or we call it off now.' She spoke with such authority that it sounded as though she had made the bet they were negotiating.

Simon shrugged and glanced indolently back into the courtyard. 'Are you pointing at the shrimpy one in the orange top and the snatch-freezer skirt?'

Frankie nodded.

'OK,' Simon agreed. With offhand arrogance, he added, 'But she might take a full half hour before she's ready to dance.'

22

'We have three days,' McGivern told them.

Jane could hear a decisive note in his voice and she realised he was preparing to dismiss his guests. The knowledge that they were about to be left alone chilled her.

'I'll have a formal contract drawn up, outlining the terms and conditions of this arrangement,' McGivern explained. 'And I'll supply you both with your own copies within the hour.'

'Am I being a little dense, here,' Frankie asked, 'or have you given any thought to our accommodation for the next three days?' She stared at McGivern with a challenge lighting her eyes. Casually, she raised the cigar to her lips and sucked on its rounded end. When she exhaled, smoke billowed from her nostrils in twin flares.

'The castle has four keeps,' McGivern replied stiffly. 'This one is the north keep and I'll be residing here. The south is uninhabitable but you should be able to make yourselves comfortable in the east and west keeps. The east has been extensively modernised while the west retains the same authentic charm as this one. Fight between yourselves as to who gets the electric lighting. If there's anything else you need, I don't doubt you'll let me know.'

'You've thought of everything, haven't you?' Frankie purred.

Jane could see that McGivern was stung by her words, but he managed to control his rising antipathy.

Simon dragged himself away from the window and asked, 'Where are the students staying?'

'They're dossing down in the south keep.'

'I thought you said it was uninhabitable.'

McGivern nodded. 'It is. But they're only students.'

They seemed content with his explanation and moved away from the window.

'May I take your slave now?' Frankie asked McGivern.

He glanced at the woman with the number three tattooed on her breast. With a snap of his fingers, he summoned the slave to his side. 'You can take her, Frankie. But she won't do the dance for you.'

Frankie shrugged and drew on her cigar. 'That's what

23

you think.' She placed her arm around the slave's waist and led her away from McGivern. Simon held the door open for the couple and, when he had left, Jane realised she was alone with McGivern and his entourage of slaves. The knowledge engulfed her with a wave of desperation.

'I won't do it,' Jane told him. She made a determined effort to raise her voice, then wished she hadn't. There was a quivering undercurrent to her words and it made her sound weak and vulnerable. Trying to ignore that hateful sound, Jane continued, 'I'm leaving now, and there's not a thing you can say or do that will stop me. Goodbye, Mr McGivern.' She stood up, aware that her hands were shaking.

'Sit down and shut up, you . . .' He stopped himself short of an insult. After taking a deep breath, he shook his head, curled his fingers into a fist and then uncurled them so that the knuckles cracked. 'Please sit down. We have to talk.'

'I won't do it,' Jane insisted. 'I'm telling you now, I won't do it.'

He rolled his eyes and reached for a bottle of wine from the centre of the table. Without asking, he poured two glasses and presented one to her.

'Don't think you can get me drunk so I'll do it,' Jane told him. 'Because I won't.'

'Stay quiet for a moment, and let me quell my urge to slap you.'

Jane took the offered glass and remained silent. She made a show of ignoring the chair he was pointing at, preferring to stand defiantly.

'I suppose Frankie was quite clever, selecting you,' McGivern said thoughtfully. 'It would have been difficult enough to take any unsuspecting initiate and teach her to do the dance of submission. But you've seen the dance, and that's made you determined not to do it, hasn't it?'

Hiding behind her untouched glass of wine, Jane said nothing.

'That was very clever of her,' McGivern conceded. He smiled with grudging admiration then shook his head. 'But it won't matter either way in three days. The bet will be

24

over and I doubt she'll be feeling so clever, then.' Dismissing the serious air that had gathered around them, he laughed and slapped a hand against Jane's backside.

She froze beneath his touch and glared at him.

McGivern ignored her, draining his wine glass in one effortless swallow. Before speaking, he dried his lips on the back of his hand. 'You're here for a professional purpose, Jane, and that's of paramount importance at the moment. Your place in my bet is only secondary. Can you draw up a contract that gives ownership of this place to the winner?'

Jane stared at him incredulously. She wondered how he could talk about legal technicalities in the face of her blatant outrage. 'I can't do any such thing,' she said. 'I won't be able to, because I'm leaving.' Placing her untouched glass of wine on the table, she started towards the door.

'You're not leaving,' he told her. His voice wasn't raised but it was filled with the same ingrained authority with which he made every declaration. 'You're staying in this castle until that contract is finished. Once you've done that, we'll discuss the possibility of your leaving.'

'I'll have the office send a replacement,' she called over her shoulder. 'I'm leaving and there's not a thing you can do or say that will stop me. Goodbye, Mr McGivern. Goodbye'.

He was fast, she had to grant him that much. He was also silent. Walking towards the door, the click of her heels had been little more than a whisper, yet it had been sufficient to mask the sound of his approach.

His fingers encircled her arms and she stiffened. He grabbed her firmly and turned her round so that they faced one another. There was a frightening power in the fingers that held her, made more chilling by the glower that lit his gaze. She caught the threat of malevolence in his eyes, then realised he was pushing her backward. Her spine struck the banquet hall's door, sending pain through her shoulder blades and buttocks. Before she had a chance to stop him, Jane realised that McGivern was pushing himself against her. His command over her body was indisputable.

'Let me go,' she hissed. The words should have been spoken by someone with a braver voice. Her own weak tone made the cry sound forlorn and desperate. 'Please, let me go.'

'I've worked long and hard to prepare this little wager,' McGivern growled. 'I've worked too hard to have a dizzy little bitch like you screw it over before it's begun. Get back to the table and talk me through the contract you're about to draw up.' He released his grip on one arm so he could point at the seat.

'Why should I?' Jane managed the words without tears, but it was a close thing. The hand that remained on her arm was as intimidating as his nearness. His body was dangerously close and she tried not to think about the weight of his hard length against her hip. It was easier to dismiss the pulse of his arousal than she would have believed and Jane felt thankful for that small mercy. His threatening manner filled her with fear, but that meant she didn't have to torture herself with images of his sexual excitement.

McGivern's grin was salacious. 'You should do it for a lot of reasons, not least of which is your career. Did you know the head of your firm is in the same lodge that I frequent? We're not close friends, but we both know the club handshake and everything it implies. I don't think we would have to talk for long before we both agreed that there's no place in the working world for a solicitor who can let clients down.'

Jane glared at him, not doubting a word of his thinly veiled threat. Her employer made no secret about his lodge membership and on more than one occasion he had boasted about how it helped business. She could see her career teetering on the brink of a precipice and Jane realised there was only one way to save it.

McGivern had to have seen some of those thoughts in her defeated expression, she thought dismally. His smile broadened and he released her arm as he took a step backward. 'Now, I would never use an advantage like that to make someone act against their will,' he assured her. 'Nor would I remind them that there's only one boat in the

26

island's port, and that it won't set sail without my express permission.'

Jane closed her eyes and groaned. His every sentence seemed to slam another door in the face of her hopes. Not wanting to hear another word, she stormed miserably back to her chair and threw her briefcase on to the table. Tearing pads and pencils from inside, she fixed him with a defiant glare. 'I'll draw up the contract and then you'll let me leave.' It was meant to be an ultimatum but she could hear her own meek voice deliver the line as a question.

'Draw up the contract,' McGivern said, replenishing his wine glass. 'Then we'll talk.'

She considered arguing again, then saw there was no point. With a heavy sigh, she turned to the documentation she had pulled from her case and started to scribble notes on to one of the pads. The work was a blissful distraction from McGivern's watchful gaze and she found herself more able to contend with it than she had anticipated. Within five minutes, she had scrawled precise notes over three pages and her mind was twisting its way through the nuances of the most unusual contract she had ever written.

'Have you ever been involved in a sub-dom relationship?' McGivern asked coolly.

Jane glanced up, slapped from her concentration by his question. 'I'm here to draw up a contract, Mr McGivern,' she reminded him. 'I'd rather not discuss matters of such a grossly personal nature.' Trying to dismiss him with a haughty sniff, she turned back to the paperwork.

'Do I take that as a yes, a no, or a God but I've always wanted to?'

Jane stiffened, made a mark against the pad, then scrubbed it out. Her cheeks were burning bright red and her stomach was folding in on itself.

'Was it Jane Austen who wrote that one half of the world cannot understand the pleasures of the other?' he asked.

Jane blushed and carried on making notes. 'If Jane Austen did write that, I doubt she was trying to sell someone on the idea of becoming a sexual submissive.'

27

McGivern laughed. 'Don't try and tell me the idea doesn't appeal to you, because I'll know it's not the truth. I saw the way you were watching number three when she danced and I could see you were hot.'

Jane glanced up at him. 'That dance was depraved.'

His smile was infuriatingly agreeable. 'It was, wasn't it? And it was just as depraved for you to enjoy it.'

She turned away, forcing her attention back to the contract. Wasn't it bad enough that she was here against her will, having to endure the perverse atmosphere that filled the castle? Did he have to make it worse by reading her mind and confronting her with private thoughts that she was loath to acknowledge?

'Which part excited you the most?' He seemed content to continue talking without her involvement in the conversation. 'Were you aroused by my control of number three? Or did you find her submission more appealing?'

Jane closed her eyes. She was trying to switch off the sound of his voice but the darkness offered no respite. Instead, she found herself more easily able to remember the slave's dance. Every contour of the woman's body was indelibly imprinted on her mind's eye. With her eyes closed, Jane was able to remember the scene with unsettling clarity. It took no effort at all to see the slave wanking herself with the gnarly head of the mace. Without wanting to endure the image again, Jane found her thoughts returning to the moment when the woman's labia had peeled open for the misshapen implement.

And the worst part of it all was that McGivern was right. She had found the sight exciting. If the tingling between her legs and the stiffness at her breasts was anything to judge by, she still found it exciting. Unhappily, she realised that if her eyes had been open, she would have seen her hands shaking.

'Look at you,' McGivern laughed. 'You're the epitome of every reason why Simon, Frankie and I want to escape to a place like this.'

She opened her eyes and saw him gesture grandly at the surrounding walls of the castle.

'You're a bundle of neurotic needs and desires, wrapped up in a frigid suit of disapproving normality.'

She glared at him. 'And what would you know about normality?'

He laughed again and she saw she had made a mistake. At least with her eyes closed, or her thoughts focused on the contract, she could make a pretence of ignoring him. Now that she had spoken, she was interacting with him, and that boded poorly for her future in the castle.

'I know a lot about normality,' he told her. 'I've been trying to avoid it for the best part of my lifetime. I'm not as strong-willed as you. I can't go around hiding my true desires beneath a cloak of respectability.'

'You make me sound like the worst kind of hypocrite.'

'You're no worse than the rest of the *normal* people out there,' he said, injecting the epithet with a sneer of contempt.

'And you think I should be more like you?' Jane asked. 'You think I should submit myself to every licentious whim, just for the reward of a moment's pleasure?'

'You can't even say it so that it sounds bad. Have you ever caned a bare backside?'

She looked away and willed her concentration back to the notepad.

The click of his fingers echoed from the walls. The sound was commanding and Jane had to make a positive effort not to look up from her work. Determinedly, she kept her gaze fixed on the notepad, reminding herself that she wasn't his slave and never would be.

Footsteps by her side ridiculed Jane's notion of self-possession. She couldn't resist the urge to sneak a glance and see who was approaching. With growing unease, she saw that McGivern had summoned one of his slaves. Curiosity forced Jane to study the woman's indecent attire.

The slave's shoes were built with cripplingly high heels, forcing her gait into a hesitant strut. She also wore fishnet stockings with impossibly straight seams. The gaudy hosiery clung to her legs like a second skin, stopping in a broad, black band at the tops of her thighs. However, compared with the rest of her outfit, Jane thought the stockings looked positively demure.

With a furtive glance, Jane saw the slave wasn't really wearing clothes. Her body was merely bound by lengths of black leather. Crossing twice over her chest, the leather forced her breasts into unnatural ovals before travelling over her shoulders and down her back. The strips reappeared between her legs and, after snatching a daring glimpse at the woman's cleft, Jane saw they had tapered to thin lines of black, running along either side of her sex-lips.

Jane looked away, feeling perverse and voyeuristic for having glimpsed such a sight. With an unconvincing voice, she assured herself that she hadn't found the vision exciting. The slave stood respectfully close to McGivern, waiting for his next command. In one hand, she held a dressage whip and Jane swallowed when she saw it. She was suddenly aware of a thousand unsettling scenarios.

McGivern placed his hand on the slave's bare arse and squeezed one buttock.

Jane glanced into his face and, for an instant, their eyes met. Flustered, she looked away and tried to make sense from what she had written in her notepad.

'You didn't follow my instruction very well, did you?' McGivern growled.

Stiffening in her seat, Jane hoped that his words weren't directed at her. It sounded as though he was talking to the slave, but Jane was already plagued by a paranoia that McGivern's nearness inspired. She dared to glance up and then sighed with relief when she saw he was addressing the submissive. Glancing at the woman's face, Jane recognised her as being one of the two who had performed the enema. The memory of that moment caused a shiver to tickle over her flesh and Jane told herself the sensation was inspired by revulsion.

'I don't understand, sir,' the slave told McGivern hesitantly.

He drew his finger beneath her jaw, tilting her lips up so she was poised in preparation for his kiss. 'You understand

30

perfectly well, you lying little slut. You were fingering number three's arsehole before she received her enema and you were doing it for your own pleasure.'

The finger that had rested beneath her chin became a hand. He held her face still as the slave tried vainly to shake her head.

'That was an act of disobedience,' McGivern growled. 'And you know what happens to slaves who perform acts of disobedience, don't you?'

The slave's eyes widened and she nodded fearfully. 'They're punished, sir.'

He nodded and his cruel smile resurfaced. 'That's right. They're punished.'

Jane watched with a combination of excitement and disgust. When McGivern turned to face her, she looked away. She didn't think there was any sign of arousal flickering in her eyes but, if there was, she didn't want him to see it. Common sense was already telling her that would be the gravest folly.

'I'll ask you again,' McGivern began patiently. 'Have you ever caned a bare backside?'

Jane blushed and said nothing. She tried to write words in the notepad but the shapes seemed as meaningless as hieroglyphics. Her head was bereft of clear thought, save for the echo of McGivern's question.

'Answer me now, and I might let you leave without preparing the contract.'

Jane glanced up, her attention caught by the hint of an escape. 'You'll let me go?'

'Have you ever caned a bare backside?'

She shook her head, her cheeks darkening to crimson as she made the admission. 'Never,' she whispered.

'Why don't you try it?' McGivern suggested. He took the dressage whip from the slave's hand and offered the handle to Jane.

The worn grip hovered enticingly close to her face and she stared at it with fascination. She swallowed and fixed him with a pleading expression. 'I can't do that.' She almost sobbed. 'I just can't'.'

31

He continued to hold the whip out for her. His hand was so steady that the tip didn't even waver as he spoke. 'I'm sure you could do it if you tried,' he insisted. 'And who knows what might happen if you do?' The timbre of his voice was reminiscent of the sales pitch he had used for his guests. 'You could find yourself enjoying it,' he told her. 'Or you could find yourself envying the slave.'

She opened her mouth, determined to refute such an idea, but he didn't allow her to speak.

'Maybe you could prove yourself a lover of domination, and I might decide that you're beyond the talents of my mastery. If that happened, I'd have to give up on my hope of making you do the dance and we'd have to send you off the island and organise a replacement.'

Jane knew it wasn't a promise of release, and she told herself that he was only making the suggestion so she would do his bidding – but the opportunity for escape was already a deep-rooted desire and she couldn't resist the thread of hope he was dangling in front of her.

'If you showed that you have the heart of a dominatrix, then I'd have to give up all hope of dominating you,' McGivern pushed. 'But we won't know any of those things, unless you try it.' His gaze left hers for a moment and he glanced at the worn grip of the dressage whip before meeting her eyes again.

Jane came to a swift decision. She snatched at the handle and leapt from her seat. A part of her wished that she hadn't seen the triumphant smile on McGivern's face but, with the implement in her hand, she knew there was little she could do about that. She marched to his side and tried to make her diminutive posture look as commanding and as authoritative as his. 'What do I have to do?'

With a snap of his fingers, the slave bent over. She rested her chest on the table, displaying the rounded orbs of her arse-cheeks. The leather strips of her outfit were secured with a stainless steel ring that sat over the small of her back. As she bent over, the strips that slid alongside her pussy-lips were pulled taut. Jane could see the excited pout of the woman's labia pressing between the thin lines of black.

Hurriedly, Jane snatched her gaze away from the distraction. 'What do I have to do?' she asked again.

'I don't think anyone's ever written an instruction manual for this situation,' McGivern replied. 'You're standing there with a whip in your hand and a slave's bare arse in front of you. If I really have to tell you what to do, then I don't think I should be trusting something as complex as legal matters in your hands.'

Jane resisted the urge to squirm beneath his sardonic tirade. 'How many times? And where?' she asked stiffly.

'Six of the best, striping her arse.'

The slave drew a shocked breath, as though the words had already scored painfully against her flesh.

Jane glanced at her, hesitating as she grasped the enormity of what she was about to do. For the first time, she noticed the slave's face and realised her features were framed with platinum blonde curls, reminiscent of her own. Her eyes were closed but her lips were a sensuous pout as she anticipated the punishing sting of the whip. Her need was so clear that Jane felt her hesitancy return. Whatever depraved motivations lay at the heart of this woman's need, Jane was certain that she wasn't the person to satisfy them.

'Are you going to do it?' McGivern demanded sharply. 'Or are you going to confirm my suspicions that you're just another unbroken initiate, ripe for my bet?'

His calculated words were the exact impetus she needed. Without giving the matter a second thought, Jane raised the dressage whip high in the air and swept it down towards the slave's backside.

The sound of the whip spat loudly in the hall's tense silence. The slave stiffened and Jane watched as a thin line of red erupted across the woman's exposed cheeks. She could see the end of the whip trembling furiously and, for an instant, Jane was overwhelmed by disbelief. Her breathing had deepened and, as she stared at the punishing stripe on the woman's backside, she wondered if she had really caused it. She almost asked the question aloud, shocked by the immensity of her own actions.

'Five more to go,' McGivern prompted.

Jane raised the whip again and brought it back down in a sweeping arc. This time, the sound didn't spit – it cracked wickedly. A second line appeared on the slave's arse-cheeks, thicker than the first and flaring a painful red. The submissive groaned, a sound that had been born from somewhere between contentment and agony.

Not thinking about it, Jane raised the whip and put more weight into her arm for the third blow. Her fears of the morning began to fade with each strike that she delivered. She didn't know if the experience was cathartic, or if she had tapped some undiscovered fetish that had always lurked beneath the surface of her psyche. Whatever the cause, the effects were indisputable and she began to grin as she delivered a fourth and fifth blow.

The distaste she had suffered during the dance of submission was now little more than a memory. For the first time, Jane felt able to admit that she had found the scene perversely exciting. The admission wasn't an easy one to make, even to herself, but as she raised the whip and brought it down against the slave's backside, Jane felt able to confront the arousal she had enjoyed throughout the dance. It was easier to accept her own excitement as she sliced the whip against the slave's arse. The voyeuristic pleasure of number three's dance was nothing compared to the thrill that Jane was now experiencing. Her heart raced and, as her breathing lowered to a dull pant, she realised the act of caning was having a profound effect on her body.

Her nipples felt infuriatingly compressed in the confines of her bra and, between her legs, she could feel the urgent heat of an awakening desire. She knew that memories of this moment would colour her masturbatory fantasies for the next year or more. The excitement of wielding the whip, the thrill of striping a bare backside and the arousal that came from domination were unimagined stimuli and she could picture herself mentally revisiting this scene again and again.

And there was more than that. While Frankie had been

34

studying her throughout the morning, Jane had repeatedly reminded herself that the woman's attention was unrequited. Over and over again, Jane had assured herself that she wasn't sexually interested in any woman, regardless of how appealing they might really be. Yet, as the slave's backside darkened beneath the whip, Jane realised she hadn't been honest with herself. Her gaze was drawn to the slave's wet slit and, with growing excitement, Jane studied the tell-tale signs of the woman's arousal. The labia parted like a kissing mouth, revealing a dark, inviting channel. The slave's gasps, louder with each slap of the whip, added fuel to the burning frenzy that flamed between Jane's legs. Daringly, she wondered what it would be like to go further. She could imagine herself reaching out and stroking the peach-like mounds of the slave's arse. It took no effort to picture her fingertips tracing the ripple of raised lines she had inflicted; she didn't need to close her eyes to imagine her hand moving nearer to the gaping swell of the woman's sex.

Before raising the whip for the final time, Jane squeezed her thighs together. The sensation caused a debilitating wave of excitement and she laughed giddily as the pleasure shook its way through her body. To vent that sensation, and to try and regain some composure before McGivern noted her unbidden arousal, Jane slashed the whip down for a sixth and final time. She hurled a massive effort into the blow, beyond caring about the slave's feelings as her own need took precedence.

'Well done,' McGivern murmured.

Jane glared at him, still despising the smug grin he graced her with. The thrill of the whipping was forgotten as a rush of embarrassment drained the colour from her cheeks. She tried to remember why she had given in and agreed to use the whip but her mortified thoughts wouldn't allow her to retrace those steps.

'You did that like an expert,' McGivern told her.

There was a genuine note of approval in his voice and Jane found herself despising it. She couldn't think of a reply for him. Realising the whip was still in her trembling fingers, she opened her hand and allowed it to fall. As she watched it clatter against the stone floor, Jane caught sight of the slave's bare backside. Striped with lines of red, the submissive's arse-cheeks were trembling and Jane could see that the slave had derived a good deal of satisfaction from the whipping. Her entire body quivered, as though she was holding herself on the brink of a cataclysmic orgasm. Jane supposed it was comforting to know that her use of the whip hadn't caused any real suffering, although she didn't dwell on this notion for more than a moment.

'It's difficult to say which of you got the most out of that.' McGivern's voice was infuriatingly matter-of-fact. 'I can see you're panting like an asthmatic pit pony, but this one seemed to get a lot out of it, too.' With absolute indifference to the suffering she had just received, he slapped his hand against the slave's raised buttocks.

Jane knew his fingertips had landed where the whip had bitten because the slave stiffened beneath the friendly pat.

'Look at her,' McGivern grinned. 'You've really made her horny with that whipping.' To prove his point, he drew his hand against the cleft between the slave's arse-cheeks.

The sides of his fingers were coated with the submissive's arousal and Jane willed herself not to see the sight. She tried to wrench her gaze away as his casually exploring fingers probed deeper, but it was impossible not to watch.

The slave murmured gratefully beneath his touch.

McGivern raised his hand and sniffed her excitement with the authority of a connoisseur. He grinned broadly and held out the hand for Jane's inspection.

With her self-disgust rising, Jane found it easy to snatch her face away, but she wasn't quick enough. Before she could turn away from him, she had seen the shimmer of pussy-honey on McGivern's hand. Her nostrils caught the musky perfume of arousal and the scent filled her lungs. As she blindly studied the corners of the banquet hall, Jane's temples pounded with the quickening beat of her pulse.

'I'm sorry,' McGivern said quietly. 'You obviously didn't want to know how much you excited her. You can turn back now; I've moved my hand away.'

From the corner of her eye, she saw that his honey-coated fingers were no longer hovering in front of her face. Instead, he had pushed them towards the slave's mouth and the woman was lapping at her own spent arousal. Her tongue slid quickly over the wetness and, when she had licked the last remnant from him, she began to suck greedily on his finger ends.

Jane shivered.

'Should we see how good you are at caning her tits?' McGivern asked.

The slave's guttural moan mirrored Jane's own spiralling dismay. She glared at McGivern and set her jaw determinedly. 'I whipped her backside, just like you insisted: but I'm telling you now, I won't do any more than that.'

His smile broadened and, with a snap of his fingers, the slave turned over. She knelt down between the pair of them, holding her bared breasts on the same level that her buttocks had been.

'Pick up your whip and stripe her tits,' McGivern snapped briskly. 'This one likes that more than having her arse whipped.'

'I won't do it,' Jane insisted. She was already filled with self-loathing for the indecency she had just committed. To inflict more blows on the slave would only compound that crime. 'I won't do it and you can't make me do it.'

There was something in his expression that unsettled her.

'Of course I can't make you do it,' he agreed.

His tone was amicable and so pleasant that Jane felt more intimidated than if he had screamed a demand at her. She could sense the impending delivery of his threat in the same way that the slave had been able to sense the moment before the whip struck her bare arse. Her entire body stiffened and she braced herself for the impact of the deftly delivered blow.

'But you were trying to prove to me that you have the heart of a dominatrix,' he reminded her. 'And this is what a dominatrix would do. If you want to stay here for the next three days, while I try and prepare you for the dance, then you won't do it.'

Jane glared at him and knew there was no other recourse. Glancing down at the floor, she bent to retrieve the whip. It was an awkward posture, made more difficult by the tight skirt that went with her business suit. She knew that the shape of her own backside was displayed to him as she bent but, once she had started to reach for the whip, arrogance forbade her from appearing modest.

He muttered a base appraisal of her figure and Jane blushed. She snatched the whip from the floor and dared to brandish it at him. 'I'll do this, and then I'm leaving.'

'We'll see,' he said glibly. 'You haven't proved you have the heart yet.'

With mounting fury, Jane turned to the slave and studied her expectant body. The slave was burdened with a helpless expression, made more obscene because she seemed to be smiling at the implement of her torture. Jane drew back the whip and brought it smartly across the slave's bared breasts. The leather struck beneath the dark circles of her areolae and they both recoiled from the blow.

When Jane had beaten the submissive's backside, she had been unable to see her face. Now, she wished couldn't. The slave smiled fondly up, her lower lip jutting forward as she relished the exquisite pain that flared through her body.

Jane tried to shut thoughts of arousal from her mind as she studied the woman's elated smile. From the corner of her eye, she saw McGivern absently stroking himself. The sight did little to staunch the lurid images that hurtled through her mind. Jane slapped the whip across the submissive's breasts again and again, delivering each blow with the same punishing force. Her accuracy was better than she had expected and lines appeared above and below the dark tinted flesh of the slave's nipples. With the final blow, Jane aimed the dressage whip across both thrusting nubs.

The slave squealed. She had been trembling beneath each stroke of the whip but she had remained comparatively still. The final blow proved too much. She turned away from the punishing pleasure and almost collapsed on to the stone floor. Her body shook with violent tremors and Jane thought she had gone too far.

When she saw the flushed cheeks and broadening smile on the slave's face, she realised that her fears had been groundless. Rather than writhing in agony, the slave was relishing the thrills of a brutal orgasm.

'Do you know what I do at moments like this?' McGivern asked coolly.

Jane glared at him, not daring to speak. She was overwhelmed by the excitement of the whipping and she didn't trust her voice to retain that secret. Inside her bra, she could feel her nipples bristling against the fabric and each exhalation was threatening to evoke a wave of bliss.

'I get as aroused as you when I've been whipping a slave,' he went on. 'And I get the slave to relieve me.'

Jane curled her lip and met his gaze with a ferocious expression. She didn't bother taking issue with his remark about her arousal, knowing that her high colour and ragged breath would have ridiculed a denial. With deliberate concentration, she willed herself not to think about having the slave give her relief and tried to focus on the more imperative matter of escaping the castle. 'I didn't doubt you would do something so base.' Jane sniffed piously. 'I trust you'll allow me the privilege of not witnessing that.'

His laughter was infuriating. 'Of course I won't subject you to that,' he grinned. 'But I do expect you to examine your charge and see how much you aroused her.'

Jane stared at him, not bothering to hide her revulsion. 'You can't be serious.' She knew he was, even before the last echo of the words had fallen from her lips.

He snapped his fingers and the slave turned over, responding quickly to his unspoken command. She knelt on all fours, holding her backside high in the air.

Jane stared warily at the crease between the woman's legs. She knew that she was required to touch the glistening slit of the slave's sex and the idea was so enticing that she felt repelled by her own base desires. When McGivern had touched the woman, Jane had imagined herself following his lead and teasing an inquisitive finger against the slippery, hot cleft. Now, with the opportunity being presented to her, she didn't know if she dared to perform an act of such lewd intimacy.

Without realising she had been about to do it, Jane saw that her hand was moving closer to the submissive's hole. She watched her manicured fingertips reach out and slide against the slick lips of the slave's sex. The combination of wetness and warmth was something she had encountered during her own exercises in self-exploration but she had never touched another woman so intimately. With a sudden rush of guilt she saw herself and what she was doing. She snatched her hand from the slave's backside and took a step away.

McGivern's triumphant grin was sickening.

Jane sighed as she saw how close she had come to succumbing to his perverse brand of pleasure. Swallowing thickly, she hurled the dressage whip to the floor and turned her attention back to the forgotten papers beside her briefcase. 'There,' she exploded. She spat the word as though it settled everything. 'I've met my side of your challenge and I've proved that I'm capable of domination.' She stared at her briefcase and paperwork as she spoke, not wanting to meet his gaze, for fear that he might see some weakness that he could use to his advantage. Absently, she rubbed the slippery wetness of the slave's pussy-honey between her fingers, then stopped herself when she realised what she was doing. In a flustered voice, she said, 'I'll have your contract drawn up within an hour and then I'd thank you to honour your promise and make arrangements for my transportation away from here.'

He slapped his hand against the slave's backside, dismissing the submissive. 'I can't do that just yet.'

Jane glared at him, shocked from her pretence of control by his cold refusal. 'But you promised. You said that once I'd written the contract I could leave.'

'I said that once you'd fulfilled your obligations, you could leave,' he corrected. 'And part of your obligations include overseeing my wager to its conclusion.' His grin widened and he said, 'I don't know about the others, but I think I'll need a solicitor close to hand when the bet is finally won.'

She glared at him, sickened by the unspoken threat in his words. Whether she liked it or not, Jane knew she was trapped in the castle. And the most frightening part of that realisation was the fear that she might begin to enjoy it.

Three

Sally didn't mind that his arm was around her waist. Since starting at university, she had met plenty of tactile people who casually touched while they spoke. Not giving much thought to it, Sally assumed that Simon was just another of those overly familiar people and she happily allowed his embrace. Besides, although she barely knew the man, she found there was something reassuring in his nearness.

A late morning sun peered over the crenellated embattlements, flooding the bailey with sunlight. As they walked from the courtyard's warmth, Sally took comfort from the weight of his hand on her hip and the pressure of his body at her side.

'And is this your castle?' she asked.

His hand squeezed tight against her and she could hear the smile in his voice. 'I'll soon be on the point of acquiring it,' he replied. 'What can you tell me of its history?'

'What do you want to know?' She was delighted that he had picked her to explain some of the castle's features, and for more than one reason. Being asked to show off her knowledge of medieval history and architecture was a flattering ego-trip but, for Sally, there was something else. There was the chance that Carl might get jealous.

She wondered if Carl was watching as Simon escorted her into the castle's gloom but she resisted the urge to glance back and find out. Instead, she simply crossed her fingers and hoped that he was. Carl hadn't been paying her enough attention lately and she thought Simon's intimacy might spark the seed of possessiveness that their relationship seemed to need. Since they had arrived on the island, Carl had been fawning around the foreign exchange student with the slutty dress sense and Sally had been desperate to find a way of recapturing his affection. She thought that Simon's appearance might be just the thing they needed.

Not that Carl would have any reason to be jealous of someone like Simon, Sally reminded herself. His flamboyant clothes and light make-up declared his sexuality with the subtlety of a neon advertising hoarding. When he had appeared at the dig, Sally had seen Simon's smile as he studied Carl and she could guess where his real interests lay.

'It's built in the traditional Byzantine style but with a handful of features that make it something of an enigma,' she started carefully.

'Really?'

'The rounded walls of the keeps weren't a traditional feature for the period when it was built,' she told him. 'They came about two hundred years later, and the fact that it's a stone building, rather than the typical wooden frame, make it even more of an anachronism.'

'How fascinating.'

Simon sounded anything but fascinated yet Sally continued, eager to show off the fruits of her years at university. 'Most castles have a definite history as to why they were built and who built them but this one is different. There are a couple of others like it – I've heard of one off the coast of Crete that has the same unusual architecture – but I've never had the chance to visit there.'

'What a shame.'

'But it's one hell of a puzzle,' Sally went on. 'That's why we're doing this dig. We're looking for clues to its history and answers to our questions about its inception. There's very little written detail concerning its construction and the fact that it's out here, on an island miles from anywhere, has puzzled historians for years. There are some unfounded rumours that it's often been used as a sort of Byzantine bordello but there's nothing to substantiate that.

43

Who built it? Who was it meant to defend? Who was the builder trying to keep out?'

'Perhaps he was trying to keep people in?' Simon suggested.

They had entered the east keep and stood in a stone walled corridor, broken by broad oak doors. Baffled fluorescent lights and a sumptuous burgundy carpet made the castle habitable without detracting from its charm. Sally admired the decor, surprised that it was so pleasant and tasteful. The south keep, where she and her fellow students resided, was like a dirty and forgotten corner in comparison.

'Was there something specific that you wanted me to explain?'

Simon nodded. 'This place has got a dungeon.' He pointed towards one of the oak doors. 'Do you know anything about dungeons?'

'God, yes!' Sally exclaimed. She didn't bother trying to disguise her excitement, knowing that she wouldn't have been able to. The macabre history of the dungeon was her favourite subject and she was always passionate about it. 'I'm going to do my dissertation on dungeons.' She laughed. 'It's a hobby-horse of mine. What do you want me to tell you?'

He squeezed her again and she shivered beneath his touch. He probably hadn't realised it, she thought, but his hand had slipped from her hip and he was now holding her buttock. When he squeezed, his fingers brushed through the fabric of her short skirt and caught the cleft between her legs. The accidental pressure sparked a delicious thrill that travelled up her inner thighs. A tingle at her chest told Sally that the arousal wasn't isolated to one area and, without looking, she knew that the shape of her hardening nipples would be visible through the fabric of her top. Not that it mattered, she reminded herself. Her thoughts were a whirl of excitement as she looked forward to exploring the dungeon, but she had already decided that there was no need to appear prudish in front of Simon. Ignoring the sparkle of arousal, she asked, 'May we go down there? Can you take me to your dungeon?'

'I was hoping you'd ask that,' he grinned. Still holding her buttock, he guided her towards the oak door and threw it open.

'Wow!' Sally gasped. 'This is beautiful.' She stood at the top of the wooden stairs, admiring the view beneath her. Illumination came from subtle wall lights and their muted glow enhanced the dungeon's medieval atmosphere. Manacles hung from the walls and the occasional chain dangled from the low, grey ceiling. An iron maiden stood in one corner and Sally saw a pair of stocks in another. She noted a scold's bridle, a set of thumb screws and the open kiln that had once been used to warm branding irons. Taking pride of place, in the centre of the dungeon, stood a rack.

The grin on her lips felt wide and inane but she couldn't suppress it. This was the history that she had spent the last three years studying and the castle's artefacts all looked to have been kept in immaculate condition. 'I didn't expect anything like this,' she told him, as they started down the steps.

'I'm quite taken by it myself,' Simon agreed rolling the azurite ring around his finger.

'What did you want to know about it?' Her thoughts were racing as she quelled the urge to run from one fascinating corner to the other. Trying hard to maintain an air of learned authority, she leant against him and asked, 'What was puzzling you?'

'There are quite a few areas,' he allowed. 'These manacles at the wall. Would people have really been chained here?'

She nodded. 'Certainly they would. I don't know about the political doctrines that were employed in this particular castle but, speaking generally, a day wouldn't have gone past when someone wasn't chained to the dungeon's walls. Dissenters, spies and even petty criminals would be hung from the manacles. Often they were just left there but it wasn't uncommon for them to be whipped, flogged or branded as part of their punishment.'

'How barbaric,' Simon whispered.

She was pleased by the shocked tone she had inspired. He sounded almost breathless as he contemplated the torture she had just described.

'It was more than barbaric. Some of the dungeon keepers were positively sadistic.'

He moved his hand from her buttock and took a step away. 'You sound like quite an authority.'

Sally beamed at the praise. 'This is my field,' she told him. 'The dungeons are the most fascinating parts of the history books because that's where they were written. The decisions that were made in places like this are the ones that we've all had to live with. Kings died in dungeons, devout believers were forced to recant and all forms of treachery were allowed to prevail. I'm going to call my dissertation, "dungeons are where the history was written".'

'What's this?' Simon asked. 'It looks like a medieval cycling helmet.'

Laughing, Sally took the contraption from his hands. 'It's a scold's bridle,' she explained. Working the cast iron through her fingers, she silently marvelled over its condition. The criss-cross basket of metal was black with age but untouched by rust or corrosion. If she hadn't known better, she might have thought it was a brand new acquisition, bought from some tacky shop where such items were sold as novelties. Holding it over her face, Sally told him, 'It was meant to be for nagging wives. It fastened and locked at the back. And this part –' she tapped the flat, metal spatula over her mouth '– this kept the wearer's tongue pressed down so they couldn't scold their husbands.'

'I suppose they had some good ideas, back then.'

She made a face at him and handed the scold's bridle back. 'Was that the only thing puzzling you?'

'This is a rack, isn't it?' He had walked to the side of the huge frame and he patted it curiously.

'It's in fantastic condition,' she said, stepping closer to the crude furniture. The size and shape of a double bed, the rack was tilted to a forty-five degree angle facing the dungeon's stairs. Barely aware that she was doing it, Sally ran her fingers over its coarse wooden sides, amazed that it was so well maintained. 'Whoever has been looking after this place has really taken care of these things.'

'I've been told that it still works,' Simon said quietly.

'You're kidding me?'

'That's what I've been told. But I just can't believe that it would be as torturous as people say,' he went on. 'It's not like the iron maiden, or the branding iron, is it? I mean, it's just for stretching people.'

'This was the worst,' Sally said. She licked her lips and continued to stroke her fingers over the rough-hewn wood. 'Victims were held on the rack for hours and hours and the gaolers made their lives a living hell.'

'But it can't have been that bad,' Simon insisted. 'It was just being stretched – and that can't be that torturous, can it?'

'It has to have been the worst,' she said decisively. 'Imagine yourself being stretched out for hour after hour while someone does their best to make you act against your will?'

He shook his head and, although he was trying to smile for her, Sally didn't think he looked convinced.

'Let me show you how bad it was,' she offered. Not giving him the opportunity to stop her, Sally climbed on to the rack and began fastening herself into it. She slipped her feet through the rope loops at the base and reached up for one of the metal cuffs from above her head. She had expected him to be reluctant about helping – the rack had to be at least five hundred years old, possibly a lot older, and she could have understood if he hadn't wanted her to treat it as a plaything – but Simon seemed to have caught some of her excitement and he fastened the second cuff around her remaining wrist.

As he secured it, his grin glinted wickedly and, if it had been anyone else, Sally knew she would have been unnerved. Instead, she took solace from the pout of his painted lips and the reassuring sparkle in his grey eyes. 'That's brilliant, Simon,' Sally told him. 'Now tighten it a little and then you can see how it pulls me.'

Wordlessly, he obliged.

Sally groaned. She couldn't stop the sound from escaping as her entire body was pulled taut from the ankles and wrists. It was impossible not to grimace as Simon turned the rack's wheel through one full circle. She felt as though she were the rope in a tug of war game. Glancing down at herself, she saw that the strained position had pulled her orange T-shirt away from the waistband of her skirt. A glimpse of her pale stomach was now exposed but she brushed away the urge for modesty, reminding herself that she was with Simon.

'Do you see how helpless and vulnerable I am?' she asked him.

He nodded. He was smiling slyly and she tried to read his expression. There was something peculiar about the way he was looking at her and she wondered if she had infected him with her enthusiasm for dungeons.

'And this is just the start of how bad it would have been for one of the rack's victims. A good gaoler would soon start to question me, threaten me and torture me.'

He swallowed. 'Why, that's just terrible.'

'Turn it again,' she told him. 'Another half circle should do. Then you'll see the unnatural position that my arms are forced into.'

He did as she asked and Sally grimaced against another bolt of pain. Her body hadn't been designed to be pulled by all four extremities but she dismissed the health-conscious notion, not wanting to give up on the physical involvement of this history lesson.

'That looks so uncomfortable,' Simon told her. She could hear that he was trying to sound sympathetic but his tone didn't quite manage it.

'It's on the point of being unbearable,' she agreed, giving no thought to his peculiar voice.

'But surely, you could get out of there if you wanted to?'

She shook her head and then stopped herself, surprised by how awkward the movement was. 'No. I'm completely secured.'

'I don't believe that. I'm sure you could get out of there if you really tried.'

'I couldn't,' she insisted. It seemed ridiculous that he couldn't grasp the simple fact that the rack was inescapable. She wondered what else she could do to prove that it was impossible to break free.

'What if I did this?' He reached towards her and his fingers caressed her exposed stomach. His touch was light, almost ticklish, yet he inspired a response that was more disturbing than a mere tickle.

'Simon!' she gasped. She was blushing but there was something innocuous about his touch that made her smile, rather than treat him to an angry outburst. 'I mean it, I'm completely secured here. I'm going to have to ask you to let me free in a moment.'

'And in a moment, I will,' he assured her. 'But first, I want to be certain that you're properly secured.'

His fingertips continued to stroke over her bare stomach and she realised his hand was moving upward. He traced over the ripple of her rib-cage and she felt the gentle scratch of his nails beneath her breast.

'What are you doing, Simon?' she asked. Her voice had deepened to a husky whisper and she wondered why it sounded so right for the circumstances. 'Why are you touching me like that?'

'I'm proving that you're properly secured. We both know that if you had the chance to escape and stop me doing this, you would.'

She tried to nod seriously, as though she understood tests like this, and had expected as much from a fellow enthusiast in medieval history. 'But it's kind of embarrassing,' she began. 'You see, I'm not wearing a bra under this top.'

His fingers traced against the lower swell of her breast and her pulse raced madly in response. The tips of her nipples bristled with an eager need to endure the same caress and she drew a startled breath as she tried to banish the thought from her mind.

'My God!' Simon exclaimed theatrically. 'You aren't wearing a bra, are you? Is it the same on the other side?'

Before she could properly work out what he had said,

49

his fingers had moved to her other breast. This time he trailed the tips higher, stroking the lower arc of her areola. The frisson against her bare skin was searing and Sally felt giddy with desire. The ache in her arms and legs was now little more than a whisper, compared to the other sensations she was enjoying. Earlier, his accidental hand at her backside had sparked an unbidden thrill of arousal, but this was far more intense.

'You shouldn't be touching me like that, Simon,' she told him firmly. 'I have a boyfriend.'

'I understand,' he agreed. 'You have a boyfriend, so the last thing you'd be interested in is sexual excitement.'

'That's not what I meant.'

He grunted. 'I'm almost convinced.'

His hand had moved down to her stomach and a sigh of relief rushed through her. His delicate touch had been fuelling an appetite that she wouldn't have been able to ignore if he had continued. Her heartbeat was already hammering and her sex felt sodden with eagerness. Beneath her T-shirt, her nipples ached with unsatisfied need.

'How secure are these ropes?' Simon asked.

His fingers circled her ankles where the rope loops held her. Again, she was treated to another tremor as he casually caressed her. It occurred to her that Simon had the most sensual hands she had ever encountered and she wondered if he was aware of the arousal he was inspiring.

'Is there really no way out of them?' he asked. As he delivered the question, she felt his hand move against her calf, climbing slowly upward.

'I've told you,' she gasped. 'There's no way to get off the rack, once you're secured to it; now, please, unfasten me.'

He acted as though he hadn't heard. His hand continued to move upward, stroking over her knee to her inner thigh. Glancing down, she saw his fingers disappear beneath the hem of her skirt and she sucked air greedily.

'Please, Simon,' she whispered.

His smile was annoyingly reassuring. He stroked small circles against her inner thigh, creating whirlpools of desire that swept onward through her body. Although she didn't want to think about it, she felt sure his fingertips were edging closer to the cleft between her legs. The delicious tickle against her inner thigh was an intolerable distraction that dragged her thoughts away from the task of stopping him.

'Would someone on the rack have screamed for release?' Simon asked.

His hand was still moving upward and Sally heard the tremor in her voice when she replied, 'Of course they would. But I doubt that would have done them any good.'

'Do you think you might scream for release?'

The tips of his fingers had reached her crotch and she held herself rigid. He stroked the lips of her sex through the gusset of her panties. The dungeon's atmosphere had become thick with anticipation and she studied his face, trying to decide what he was planning. His smile told her that it was something similar to the need he had nurtured in her, but that didn't assuage Sally's fears.

'You shouldn't be touching me like that,' she told him.

'You don't want me to stop, do you?'

She looked away. 'I already have a boyfriend.'

'I wasn't offering myself as a boyfriend,' he replied. 'Just a lover.' He pressed his finger firmly against her sex to punctuate the statement.

She could feel her own heat warming him through the flimsy cotton. A flurry of tingling pleasure rushed through her. She glanced back to face him, thrilled by his touch and the devilish suggestion he was making. 'I could never be unfaithful to Carl.'

'I'm sure you could, if you put your mind to it.' His finger moved up and down, tracing the shape of her pussy-lips through the clinging fabric.

She was acutely aware of every subtle movement and knew that her labia had separated in readiness for him. The longing he inspired was accentuated by the delicate scratching of his nails against the cotton's weave. Her clit throbbed dully, desperately needing to be touched, but so far he had avoided that particular intimacy.

Simon continued to touch her as he spoke. 'In this

position, it's not like you have to try and do anything to be unfaithful. It's simply a matter of not screaming.'

'I could scream.' She licked her lips, realising they had become parched. 'I could scream, and I think I will if you don't set me free.'

He shook his head. 'You won't scream,' he assured her. 'At least, you won't scream for me to let you go. If you were going to scream, you would have done it by now.'

'I will,' she insisted. 'I really will scream.'

He shook his head again, his smile filled with an annoying confidence. 'If you screamed, your student friends might come to rescue you from this indignity. And you wouldn't really want the embarrassment of being found like this, would you?'

'It's not *that* compromising a situation,' she declared loftily. It was becoming difficult to maintain her side of the conversation. Her words were carried by trembling breaths that spoke more honestly than her pious denials. His finger was working a delicious magic against her sex and, despite her arguments and demands for release, she didn't want to make him stop.

'You're right,' he agreed. 'It's not *that* compromising a situation.'

She was mortified as he snatched his hand from beneath the skirt. The sensations he inspired were unwanted but not unpleasant and she could have endured them for a lot longer if Simon had decided she had to. Watching him, she swallowed uneasily as she realised that might still be a prospect.

From her fixed position, Sally saw him tug the button free from her wraparound skirt. He pulled the garment from her body like a magician snatching the cloth from a laid table. Sally gasped, shocked by the sudden feeling of vulnerability that swept through her. His hands went to her T-shirt and she wondered how he was going to drag that off her. Her arms were secured above her head and she knew he wouldn't be able to remove it using the same dramatic sweep with which he had taken the skirt.

The sound of rent fabric filled the dungeon and she saw his nails tear through the orange top. It split down the centre and she watched the T-shirt burst open to reveal her bare breasts. Her gasp of excitement was lost beneath the scream of ripping cotton.

'Now, *that*'s a compromising situation,' Simon declared cheerfully. 'If you want to be released, go ahead and scream now. I'm sure you'll give all your student friends something to talk about if they rush in here to your rescue.'

Sally glared at him, too shocked to think of a response. She knew he was right, and they both knew that she wasn't going to scream for any assistance. Not only would the social stigma of discovery be too unbearable, there was also the thought that a lot more could happen before she became totally unhappy with this position.

She stared down at herself, shocked by the display of her own nudity. Her exposed breasts were trembling and the nipples were as hard as bullets. The deep V of her high-legged panties was the only thing retaining her modesty, but she doubted that was a demure sight. Simon had already sparked a need in her that had soaked the gusset and she didn't think any would-be rescuer would have to look long and hard before noticing her sodden crotch. Turning back to face him, she saw his smile was not an unkind one.

'If you don't want to scream for help,' he began, 'I'm sure I can find something else to take your mind away from the pains of the rack.' Before she could raise a word of protest, he moved his mouth over her nipple.

Sally's response was a shuddering sigh. The warmth of his lips was the balm that her aching nub had needed. An explosion began to tremble through her as he greedily sucked. His tongue traversed the rounded end and his playful nibbles teased her body to new heights of desire.

'I really do have a boyfriend,' she whispered.

Simon nodded and climbed on to the rack. 'How very, very nice for you,' he said glibly. 'I'm sure the pair of you make a wonderful couple.' He positioned himself over her and lowered his head to her other breast. As soon as his lips touched her areola, he treated the nipple to the same titillation he had given the first.

53

In her spread-eagled position, Sally could feel the pressure of his hard length against the flat of her stomach. The realisation of his excitement was a dark spur to her own arousal and she groaned. Her arms and legs still ached as she endured the rack's relentless punishment but, beneath Simon's tongue, it was easy to forget that discomfort.

'I don't think Carl would approve of our doing this,' she gasped. It was an annoying thought: painfully intrusive, given the circumstances. She wanted Simon to continue taking advantage of her defenceless body, but a sense of rightness insisted that she behave honourably towards her boyfriend.

Simon moved his head from her breast and considered her thoughtfully. 'He sounds like a proper gentleman. You'll have to introduce us one day and we can all discuss your passion for dungeons and medieval torture devices.'

'I don't want to hurt him,' she insisted.

Simon laughed. He stroked his fingernails between her breasts, scratching lightly at her pale skin. His hand moved to her stomach and she saw him shift position so he could delve further. 'You don't want to hurt him,' he repeated. 'There's only one person at risk of being hurt around here,' he told her, 'and it's certainly not your boyfriend.'

Staring up at him, Sally tried to make sense of his words. She was dizzied by the thrill of his scratching fingernails and torn between the conflicting voices of her conscience and her desire. 'What are you going to do to me?'

His finger had reached the waistband of her panties and he drew his nail beneath the elastic. 'I'm going to make you the happiest woman who has ever been tied to a rack.' He tugged at the garment roughly, dragging the panties down over her hips. They didn't tear and he made no real attempt to rip them away from her. Instead, she was left with a biting band of elastic that cut into her hips and across the lower curve of her buttocks. Simon combed his fingers through the triangle of dark brown hairs that covered her sex, delving lower.

'I'm not happy with this, Simon.'

'I haven't started, yet,' he replied. 'Once I've started, then you'll be happy.'

She shook her head, infuriated by his facile response. Her mouth opened and she tried to think of words that would make him stop. When his exploring finger touched her sex she closed her mouth, suddenly wondering if he might be right. His hand brushed against the dewy lips of her pussy, chilling and thrilling her in the same moment. She shivered beneath his touch and her unease was swept away by a wave of pleasure. He pushed against her wetness and she felt the delicious intrusion of his finger. Her body seemed unduly responsive to his touch and she could feel every nuance as he probed further along the inner walls of her sex.

Simon lowered his mouth to her breast again and began to suckle against her nipple. The combination of his lips at her breast and his finger inside her was a debilitating blend. Sally could feel herself being propelled towards a furious climax that she hadn't anticipated. No longer trying to resist the urge, she relaxed and allowed him to treat her body as he wanted.

'You're very, very wet down here,' he informed her.

'Are you surprised?' She had already decided that there was no point trying to appear demure. She wasn't just naked and vulnerable beneath him, she was also desperate for him and they were both aware of that fact.

Simon moved his finger from her wetness and brought it to his lips. With an avaricious tongue, he lapped the pussy-honey from his hand then grinned at her. 'Very, very wet, and very, very tasty.'

She closed her eyes and shivered, laying back against the uncomfortable bed of the rack. His finger returned to the lips of her sex and a thrill of delight tingled through her. As he placed soft kisses against her mouth, she could smell her own arousal on his breath. The musky scent was exciting and her racing heartbeat quickened.

'Do you want to taste?' Simon asked.

He had snatched the finger back from her pussy and was brandishing it beneath her nose. Every inhalation was redolent with the sweet scent of her own desire. She glanced into his eyes and saw his earnest need for her to share this experience. Not wanting to spoil the atmosphere, and eager to experience every wicked moment that Simon could treat her to, Sally moved her head forward. His finger was dripping with her wetness and she was treated to the syrupy flavour of her own excitement. The cloying taste filled her mouth and acted like an aphrodisiac on her hyper-responsive body. Her pulse raced faster and her head felt light with the sudden rush of adrenaline. Every inch of her flesh quivered with a growing need for him. Her inner muscles were trembling with longing, while her clitoris and nipples ached as though they had been bitten. She licked greedily on his finger, her appetite for the taste augmenting with each lustful swallow.

'Doesn't that taste good?' he asked.

She nodded, her muffled response made around a mouthful of finger. The taste was phenomenal and the word 'good' wasn't adequate for the flavour that filled her mouth.

'That tastes so good, you make me want to drink it from the source,' Simon declared. He slid the finger from her mouth and drew his tongue over the remnants that still lingered there. Caressing her cheek with the stone in his azurite ring, he asked, 'Would you like me to drink it from the source?'

She couldn't respond fast enough. The heat between her legs was so strong, she felt sure her pussy-lips were about to spontaneously combust. Although she had studied all the torturous ways of the dungeon, she doubted that anyone who had ever been tied to a rack had suffered such a searing heat as the one that now burnt between her legs. The idea of having his tongue against her was almost as orgasmic as she knew the reality would be. 'Yes, Simon. Please, yes. Yes!'

He moved down her body, stroking his fingers over the curves of her naked flesh, before placing his head above her sex. 'Are you sure you want me to do this?'

'Do it, Simon,' she urged him. 'Please, do it.'

He did. His tongue touched the febrile lips of her sex and she shivered. He flicked the tip against the nub of her clit and she quelled the urge to roar in response. His finger had worked magic through the gusset of her panties and, once he had removed those, the pleasure had been immense – but this was divine. The euphoria erupting from her cleft was almost miraculous.

His tongue squirmed wetly against her sex, teasing the clit, then daring to enter her. Her pussy was aflame with need and she twisted against her bindings, unmindful of the pain that jolted from her wrists and ankles. Her body was rushing towards a tremendous climax and no amount of discomfort was going to distract her thoughts from that goal.

'You're really enjoying this, aren't you?'

His face loomed over her and she smiled at him through a hazy mist of pleasure. 'You're a wicked man,' she giggled. 'But I'm learning to live with it.'

He laughed, and kissed the corner of her mouth.

She could taste the flavour of her sex on his lips and she inhaled the scent greedily. Lifting her head closer to him, she kissed his mouth, plunging her tongue between his lips so she could experience the taste he had been enjoying. It was an action made awkward by the restrictions of the rack but the pleasure she received was enough of a reward.

His hand went to her breast and he stroked his thumb over her rigid nipple. The tip bristled beneath his caress and a ripple of delight exploded from her chest. The burgeoning need between her legs was amplified by his careless touch.

'You look as though you could learn to live with a life of submission,' he told her.

She gasped, thrilled by the forbidden suggestion. 'Would it always be like this?'

'Like this, and a whole lot worse,' he grinned. 'I'd have you dressed like a slut and you'd spend your days doing exactly as I said, or suffering the consequences.'

'Consequences,' she repeated, giggling throatily around the word.

His thumb touched her breast again, stroking at the sensitive ring of her areola. Without looking, he was able to catch the hardened nub of her nipple between his thumb and forefinger. The pressure he exerted was harder than she thought necessary but, because it satisfied her mounting need, Sally saw no reason to complain.

'Would you want to become my submissive?'

Even in her state of nearly delirious bliss, Sally could sense the question was an earnest one.

'Would you want to become my submissive, and spend your waking hours tied to a rack, waiting for me to come and torture you with this pleasurable pain?'

'It sounds like a living hell,' she laughed. 'But I think I could cope with it.'

'You'd like to become my submissive?' he pressed.

'You have me tied to a rack, begging for you to tongue my clitty,' she reminded him. 'Could I become much more submissive?'

'We'll have to find out about that,' he said slyly. 'Given the time and the proper encouragement, I think the answer to that one is a big yes, but we'll have to find out together.'

His expression looked triumphant but Sally didn't have time to consider that as he moved his head back between her legs. His mouth kissed the pouting lips of her sex and she felt his tongue touch at her clitoris.

The explosion that had been welling finally burst. Sally closed her eyes and pulled hard against the ropes and manacles. Unable to stop herself, she shivered and groaned as the wave of pleasure hurtled through her body. Every muscle was painfully stiff as she suffered the orgasm, but she barely noticed the discomfort. Her thoughts were lost in the pure joy caused by Simon's darting tongue.

A second orgasm threatened to strike her and Sally stopped struggling against the restraints. She simply opened her eyes to stare happily at the dungeon ceiling. Movement by the door snatched her thoughts from the heaven where Simon had taken her. Without thinking, she released a horrified shriek.

Simon glanced up. He cast a concerned expression over

her face; then, seeing that she was staring towards the dungeon's doorway, he followed the path of her gaze. 'McGivern,' Simon growled, climbing from the rack. 'I should have expected something like this.'

Sally glared at the pair of them, horrified by her own exposed vulnerability. The man he had called McGivern was studying her bound and naked body with an avaricious glint in his eye. The pleasure she had just enjoyed was all but forgotten as she struggled against her bonds. She needed to be released and away from the frightening embarrassment of this situation.

'I'm just bringing you your copy of the contract.' McGivern had a sly smile on his lips as he held up the sheaf of papers. 'I didn't mean to interrupt anything.'

Simon snatched the contract from his hand. 'If that was all, I won't keep you any longer.'

McGivern was either exceedingly stupid, or he had chosen to miss the note of finality in Simon's voice. Sally was comforted to hear that Simon was trying to dismiss the intruder but that didn't ease her fear beneath McGivern's lecherous gaze. She continued struggling against the manacles, chafing her wrists in the process.

'Of course,' McGivern agreed. He started towards the door, paused and then turned back. His gaze was fixed on Sally and she knew he was staring at the wet hole of her sex.

She squirmed helplessly.

'I could stay for a while, if you needed me to,' McGivern told them both.

Sally was sickened by the lewd intimation of his words. Her eyes opened wide and she stared at the man with spiralling horror. She wanted to scream the word 'no' but her throat was held closed with terror.

'You're neither needed nor wanted here,' Simon replied flatly. 'But if you do stay for another minute, I'll tear this contract up and make you eat it.'

McGivern glared at him and Sally saw that Simon had just won some minor battle of wills.

'If that's the way you feel about it,' McGivern began coolly.

'That's exactly the way I feel about it,' Simon agreed.

She watched McGivern frown and then, with a wave of relief, she saw he was storming away, up the wooden stairway and out of the dungeon.

'You have to let me go,' she insisted. 'I have to get back to the dig. I have to get back to Carl.' She could hear that her voice was on the verge of breaking into tears but rising hysteria quelled any concern that she might have had.

'McGivern won't say anything, if that's what's worrying you,' Simon said. He had moved to the side of the rack and his fingers were tracing lightly against her bare flesh. The sensation had been pleasurable before, and she knew that, if he continued, it would return to that stage, but the mood had been broken and she fought against the urge to submit to him again.

'McGivern's a bastard,' Simon told her. 'But he's not that much of a bastard that he'd tell your boyfriend.'

'Please. Let me go.' There was the danger that her wailing tone would spiral into a scream, but she was beyond caring. A million nasty images tormented her and she could already imagine the expression of disgust on Carl's face if he was to discover what she had done. 'I want you to let me off here now.'

Simon reached for the manacles, then stopped. 'I'll let you free on one condition.'

Rather than meeting his eyes, she stared towards the dungeon's door. McGivern had left the door ajar and she could imagine Carl appearing there and seeing her in this invidious position. 'No more conditions,' she begged him. 'No more of this. Just release me, please.'

'I'll let you free if you promise to come and have dinner with me this evening.'

'You can't be serious,' she gasped. She turned to face him and saw that the offer was genuine. 'You're kidding me, right?'

'I want to have dinner with you,' Simon insisted. 'We've had a wonderful morning together and I'd like to share a meal with you.'

'Just release me,' she demanded.

'Promise me we'll have dinner tonight first.'

She looked away from his face. She didn't want to meet his eyes as she agreed to the invitation, in case he saw that it was a hollow promise. 'Dinner tonight.'

He began to unfasten the cuffs, a cheerful smile on his lips. 'I'm looking forward to it already.'

Four

It was called the toy room and, of all the rooms in the entire castle, Jane decided that this one had to be the worst. It occupied the uppermost floor of the north keep, with windows overlooking the courtyard and the endless, inescapable ocean. McGivern had led her there while two of his entourage followed with Jane's bags. He had said this was where she would be allowed to sleep and then demanded she start printing copies of the contract. As soon as the first one was complete, he had snatched it from the printer tray and rushed towards the door.

'Feel free to make use of the room's amenities,' he had grinned. It was a nasty smile, made more malicious because it always seemed to broaden in proportion to her discomfort. 'These two will stay with you,' McGivern said, nodding at the slaves. 'So if you need help understanding how anything works, they'll be only too willing to show you what to do.'

And then he had left her.

She sent a second copy of the contract to the printer and tried to distract herself from the perversity of the surrounding room. The walls were adorned with whips and canes. Two shelves of sex-aids – huge dildos and all manner of plastic phalluses – rested over the bed where she was supposed to sleep. Normally such implements brought a smutty grin to her lips, but in this atmosphere their effect was different. In the castle's oppressive keep the row of dildos looked threatening. To add to her unease, there were stocks and manacles, ropes and chains, and countless other devices that would have been better suited in a medieval torture chamber. The idea of spending a night in this haven of the perverse left Jane feeling nauseous.

'Is there anything you want to play with?'

Jane said nothing. She stared at the flat screen on her laptop, hoping the slaves would take offence at her ignorance and leave. She had no right to expect such good fortune – especially when she considered the way the day was developing – but she clung to the hope as an act of desperation.

With her back to the two women, she studied them through the reflection on the laptop's screen. They were similar enough to be sisters, although one was blonde and the other was a redhead. They were not tattooed, like the woman she had seen in the banquet hall that morning, but each wore a brass badge with a number on it. The redhead's number was eleven and the blonde was seven. It was the bubbly blonde who had spoken.

'There's some really great gear in this toy room,' the blonde went on. 'I think it's almost as good a place as the dungeon.'

Jane muttered a blasphemy. She dropped her head into her hands and tried not to sob. It was unsettling to discover that the castle had a dungeon as well. The slave's appreciation of both rooms was equally disquieting and threatened to send Jane's thoughts on a further downward spiral. Steeling herself to appear calm and composed, Jane turned away from her laptop and tested an uneasy smile.

'You don't have to stand guard over me,' she began.

It was difficult to maintain a calm tone of voice as she looked at the two women. They were McGivern's slaves and both were dressed for that vocation. Their bodies were adorned with the ridiculous uniform of black leather strips that offered neither warmth nor modesty. The secrets of their intimate flesh were an obvious display and she couldn't stop herself from glancing at their bodies as she talked to them. They stood expectantly before her, their arms casually draped around each other's waists. It was such a familiar posture that Jane could picture the two

63

women being far more intimate together. Her mind was filled with images of the blonde and the redhead naked and caressing each other as their fingers and tongues explored.

Jane shook the notion from her head and drew a heavy breath. 'I've already been told that there's no escape, so I won't be foolish enough to try and run away.'

The blonde laughed. 'We're not here to guard you. We're here to show you how these things work.' She stepped from her friend's embrace and rushed towards a trestle beneath a pair of manacles. 'Take a look at this wooden horse,' she gushed. 'Isn't it just marvellous?'

'I really don't want to see any of this,' Jane told her.

The redhead held out a hand, encouraging Jane to join them. 'You have to see the wooden horse,' she agreed. 'It's wicked.'

Jane sighed and decided that the best course of action would probably be to go along with the two slaves for the moment. She could look at whatever it was they wanted to show her, then ask them to leave her alone. Deliberately ignoring the redhead's offered hand, she walked to where the blonde was standing.

'It's just the most marvellous contraption ever,' the redhead declared. 'I was on it for a full day when we moved here last year. I couldn't walk for a week afterwards.' She giggled at the memory, then seemed surprised when Jane didn't join her mirth.

Jane frowned at the trestle, still trying to work out what it was supposed to do. When she first noticed it, she thought a careless builder had left it there by mistake. With that first glance, she had simply dismissed it as being unnecessary paraphernalia. Now, watching the redhead giggle and enthuse, she felt a macabre corner of her curiosity being piqued. 'What does it do?'

'Watch,' the blonde slave told her. She cast one leg over the trestle and straddled it, as though she were riding a horse. The centre bar was high and, although the blonde stood on tiptoe, it still touched the crease of her sex.

Jane blushed when she realised she was studying the woman's exposed labia. If her curiosity hadn't been so great, she knew that she would have looked away. Instead, her vision focused on the blonde's cleft as her pussy-lips splayed against the wooden beam.

The blonde threw her arms above her head and reached for the manacles. 'You have your hands locked in these,' she explained. 'Then you're forced to dangle over the horse.'

'Don't fasten them,' the redhead warned. 'The master wouldn't like it if you did that without his permission.'

The blonde giggled at her friend's concern. 'I won't fasten them. The master would have a fit if I did.' Her delicate laughter deepened to a throaty chuckle as she rode her sex lips against the wooden horse.

To Jane, the posture looked exceptionally uncomfortable and she wondered how the blonde could enjoy herself in such a stance. The woman was shivering as though her body were being treated to unimaginable pleasures and Jane found herself simultaneously fascinated and appalled. As the slave rocked back and forth along the top of the trestle, her pussy lips left a dewy reminder of where they had been touching. Her nipples stiffened to a dark hue and her cheeks blushed with arousal.

Daringly, the redhead reached out and caressed the blonde's breast.

Jane tried to drag her gaze away but the scene was captivating.

The blonde sighed, smiling at her friend. She turned the grin on Jane and said, 'You're absolutely helpless on the wooden horse. If someone wants to do things to you, you can't stop them. All you can do is hang above it, put up with your punishment, and rub yourself against this.' To demonstrate, she ground her sex-lips hard against the unyielding length of wood. The redhead chose that moment to caress her other nipple and the blonde's throaty chuckles deepened.

'Do you want to try and do something to me, while I'm dangling here?'

Jane shivered, repulsed by the suggestion but unable to find the words to express that emotion. Neither the blonde nor the redhead seemed to notice her distaste.

'Go on,' the redhead encouraged. 'You won't hurt her.' To prove her point, she teased the blonde with brutal fingernails. Her talons found spaces between the strips of leather and she scratched hard at the blonde's exposed flesh. With a wicked grin, the redhead stepped back and studied her handiwork. She seemed pleased by the raised lines that were left in the wake of her caress.

The blonde gasped and began to ride herself more furiously against the wooden horse.

'I think that you'd better leave me alone now,' Jane whispered.

The redhead continued to stroke at her friend's breast and the blonde's cries became darker and more guttural. They both ignored Jane, indulging themselves in the excitement of each other. The redhead pressed her mouth over the blonde's nipple and was rewarded by a throaty groan.

'I asked you to leave,' Jane repeated.

'But you don't really want us to,' the redhead observed.

'Go on,' the blonde pleaded. 'You know you want to touch me while I'm hanging here, all helpless and vulnerable.' She giggled again, as though this was an enviable position rather than an invidious one.

'Leave now, or I'll tell McGivern that you were insolent to me.'

The threat had them both staring at her as though she had slapped their faces. They studied Jane with cold dismay and looked as if they were trying to gauge her sincerity. Jane stood resolute beneath their hurt expressions, pointing towards the door.

The blonde slowly lowered her hands from the manacles and, after linking her arm with the redhead's, she dismounted from the wooden horse. Rather than leaving the room, the two women marched over to Jane and stopped when they were only inches away from her.

Jane swallowed, wishing she didn't feel quite so intimidated by their nearness.

The blonde glared at her, snaking her fingers into her friend's hair as she held Jane's gaze. With a harsh tug, she pulled the redhead's face towards her own and they kissed with a lurid blatancy. Her tongue was pushed out and she thrust it into the redhead's mouth. All the time, her eyes were fixed on Jane's. Their locked gaze was only briefly broken as the blonde's eyelids fluttered with obvious pleasure. Her free hand caressed her lover's nubile curves and the redhead grunted passionately. When the two women parted, their shining eyes and blushing cheeks were the only reminder of the intimacy they had just enjoyed.

Jane suppressed a shiver, struggling to appear strong beneath the blonde's defiant glare.

'Don't get too high and mighty,' the blonde warned Jane. She circled her arm around the redhead's waist and pressed her body closer. Her expression was ominously threatening. 'The master may be favouring you with kindness now, but you'll be one of us before long.'

'Leave,' Jane insisted. 'Leave now, I don't want you here any more. I want you to go.' She was panting the words to their backs as they moved towards the door. When they finally left the room, she released a pent-up sigh. Her thoughts were racing as ideas and images assailed her from a thousand different directions.

She turned to the laptop and checked its display for the printer's progress. The contract was only half printed and she cursed its slowness. When she turned her back on it, she glared at the closed door, wishing she could think of a way to escape the castle. She knew that her thoughts would have been helped if the place wasn't an endless well of stimulation. The dance of submission had been an obscene performance but Jane couldn't deny that it had stirred her arousal. Afterwards, being forced to whip the slave in the banquet hall had inspired a greater excitement. Even the sight of blonde slave straddling the wooden horse, then kissing her redheaded lover, had warmed the wetness between Jane's legs. There was so much erotic stimulation in the castle that Jane couldn't stop her thoughts from returning to those darkly exciting moments. She knew that none of those memories would help her attain the clarity of thought that her escape plans needed, but she couldn't stop herself from revisiting every torrid event.

When the idea came to her, Jane acted quickly. She marched swiftly to the door, checked the empty corridor outside, then slammed it closed. She turned the cast iron key in its hole, then pocketed it. If she wanted to assess the situation with a clear head, she knew that there was something she had to do first. Her mind was ablaze with exotic images and they continually intruded on her plans for escape. She knew that if she didn't act quickly, she would be trapped between her own indecision and McGivern's manipulative plans. Hurrying over to the bed, Jane lay down and pulled up the hem of her skirt.

She wasn't indulging the carnal need that motivated the rest of the castle's occupants, Jane told herself. She was simply going to give her body the release it craved. Her mind insisted that there was nothing wrong or perverted in what she was doing, but its high-pitched tone left her doubting. She wanted to believe that she was taking the first step on a pathway out of the castle. Once she had orgasmed, she knew that she would be able to concentrate without the interruption of her lurid imagination.

Silently, she prayed that was how it would happen.

With the first caress of her fingertips, she was rushing towards a climax.

The urgency of her need had dictated that she shouldn't undress. She lay on the bed, with her skirt pulled up and her fingers forcing the gusset of her panties to one side. Her reflection smiled down from a mirror above the bed and her excitement intensified. The thatch of her pubic curls was visible in the reflection and Jane found the sight exhilarating. It warmed her to think she could look as sexy and exciting as the slaves who filled the castle, and she cherished that thought without acknowledging its sinister implications. The haste and depth of her arousal was clear in the image of the woman who beamed down at her. She was too eager for satisfaction to undress and too desperate to let it bother her.

She plunged an index finger into her hole and groaned. The moment of climax was threatening to come in a hectic, inescapable rush. While Jane craved the release of an orgasm, she didn't want it to be over with so quickly. But, as much as she wanted to delay her explosion, it was impossible not to be driven closer to the peak. With her eyes squeezed tightly shut, Jane knew she could revisit every episode that the morning had treated her to. The dance of submission was replayed again and again in the view of Jane's inner eye. The naked, tattooed slave was spinning and dancing, then wanking herself to a furious climax.

And then it was the whipping.

Jane had known the image would intrude on moment's like this but she hadn't expected that truth to be proved so soon. As she rubbed against her exposed clitoris, Jane returned to the instant when she had beaten the slave's backside. Remembering the raised lines and the slave's discomfort, Jane shrieked as the first waves of orgasm tumbled through her. She writhed on the bed, her entire frame racked with pleasure. When she opened her eyes, she met the breathless smile of her own reflection and was aware of an overwhelming truth.

That single orgasm hadn't been enough.

Her body still burnt with a furious need and, although the satisfaction had been a bitter-sweet pleasure, she still needed something more. Rather than releasing her mind from the torrid images, her solitary passion had stirred a greater appetite.

Jane tested a fingertip against the pulsing nub but then withdrew it, aware that the sensation had now become uncomfortable. All too often in the past, she had found herself plagued by a similar problem. She could frig herself to a climax and then, when she needed the pleasure of a second explosion, her body flinched from the pressure of her fingertips. But this time Jane was determined.

She glanced at the shelves of dildos, then tried to shut that thought from her mind. Her resolve barely lasted long enough for her to blink. Her craving for a second release gnawed at her and, without considering all the reasons why she shouldn't do it, Jane reached up and snatched a phallus from the collection.

The plastic cock was short and thick, fashioned to look like an erection and coloured with the hue of prosthetic flesh. Jane ignored all of this, needing the implement for one thing and one thing only. There were other dildos she could have selected if she had given herself time. The shelves were laden with all different sizes, shapes, colours and variations. There were long, smooth dildos that could have treated the urgent itch at the neck of her womb and fatter ones with knobbed shafts that would have satisfied the lips of her sex.

Jane had simply grabbed the first one that her fingers fell on, needing nothing more than penetration. Before placing the plastic cock against herself, she twisted its base and started it buzzing. She hadn't expected it to be working but she wasn't overly surprised at the discovery. Everything about McGivern alluded to a passion for some sort of sexual pleasure and she supposed it was only fitting that such a man would keep his stock of dildos operational. Not wasting precious moments contemplating the thought, Jane pushed the tingling tip against her pussy.

Her entire body was touched by echoes of the vibrator's buzzing. She could feel the tremors hardening the tips of her nipples and the dildo's deafening roar sang in her ears. But it was against her sex where she could feel its greatest effects. The plastic slid inside her, pressing its throbbing body against her clenching inner walls.

The threat of another orgasm was immediately upon her and Jane knew that this one would be more fulfilling than the last. She urged the shaft into herself, allowing it to tingle just beneath the aching bud of her clitoris. The sensation was so exquisite it was almost unbearable and she began to slide the phallus out. She was sodden with excitement and the dildo slipped effortlessly from her hole. Its head rested against the crease of her sex. In a heady rush, Jane pushed the dildo back inside.

She was already on the brink of a second climax but determined not to rush this one as she had the last. With her calm returning, she forced her mind to ignore the images that had previously taunted her and concentrated on the pleasure of the plastic cock between her legs. Her breath became laboured and she studied her reflection for a moment before deciding to ignore it. There was something darkly secretive about this act and she didn't need her own image showing her how wrong it all was. Using one of McGivern's vibrators, lying on the comfort of one of his beds, and then wanking herself senseless, seemed like the embodiment of foolishness. She didn't need to see her own reflection to be reminded of that. She simply wanted another orgasm.

With her eyes closed, the vibrations seemed far more intense. She was able to enjoy each tremor of the shaft as she pushed it in and out of her wetness. If she had dared to caress her own breasts, she knew that the climax would have been inevitable. It would only take three rapid thrusts and Jane felt certain she would be doubled-over with a gratifying explosion of delight.

She resisted the temptation, desperate to prolong her pleasure for as long as she could. She teased the length against her sex lips, relishing every tremor as it rode back and forth. Her pace became slower and less forceful as she deliberately avoided the pleasure of release. Even then, it seemed as though she had reached the moment all too quickly. She could feel a gargantuan eruption welling inside her and knew that one more insertion would plunge her into ecstasy.

'That looks like a lot of fun,' McGivern told her. 'Can I ask? Is this you enjoying yourself? Or are you still working as my solicitor?'

Jane's eyes flew open and she glared at him with mortified horror. She snatched the vibrator away from her sex and quickly tried to straighten her skirt.

'Don't stop on my account,' McGivern implored her. 'I was enjoying the show.'

'How long have you been standing there?'

He laughed. 'Longer than you would have wanted but not long enough for my own satisfaction.'

She shivered, repulsed by his lecherous smile. She had heard people saying that they almost died from embarrassment but this was the first time she had appreciated that phrase in its fullest context. Her cheeks were crimson with a shame so intense it clouded every thought. She wondered how she could have been so stupid as to get caught in such a way, then remembered that she had taken the precaution of locking the door. She glared at him, despising his lecherous grin and the sparkle in his eyes. 'How the hell did you get in here?' she demanded, starting to climb from the bed.

By way of explanation, McGivern held up a chatelaine with a dozen or more keys dangling from it. He fastened it to his belt, continuing to appraise her with his smile. 'You didn't look as though you'd quite managed to bring yourself off,' he told her. 'Do you have any appetites that I could satisfy before we get back to business?'

'You're disgusting,' Jane told him.

'I'm only driven by the same need that you were just enjoying,' he reminded her. 'Does that make you as disgusting as me? Or does it just mean that we have a lot in common?'

'We have nothing in common,' she said passionately. 'I doubt we're even the same species.'

He started to laugh at her outburst, but she saw a menacing sparkle in his eyes. 'Don't think you can insult me like that,' he warned her. 'I've just taken an unnecessary amount of shit from that pious faggot, Simon. I'm not prepared to take it from you as well.'

'Then why don't you let me leave?' Jane pressed. 'If you don't want insults and rudeness, why don't you let me leave? If I'm not on this island, I can't insult you, can I?' With growing dismay, she saw that it had been the wrong thing to say.

He stepped closer, his eyes shining with the same authority that he used over his slaves. 'Perhaps there's another way for me to be assured of your obedience,' he began. He reached out to stroke the loose platinum tresses from her shoulder and Jane flinched as though he were striking out. She raised a hand, attempting to slap his fingers away. Before she could touch him, he had grabbed

72

her wrist. His grip was as unrelenting as a manacle and her skin was pinched by his forceful fingers.

'That hurts,' she gasped.

'You'd rather I gave you pleasure than pain? Very well.'

It hadn't been what she meant and they both knew that, but McGivern acted as though she were encouraging him. He pushed her wrist down and pressed his mouth over hers.

Jane kept her lips pressed tight together, determined to prevent the intrusion of his tongue. She tried to struggle from his embrace, hissing spiteful words at him as he attempted to make the kiss. 'Stop it, you bastard! Stop it!'

'I would if you really wanted me to,' he assured her. His hand went to her leg and his fingers quickly climbed to the top of her thigh. 'But you don't want me to stop, do you?' As he asked the question, he traced her pussy-lips through the sodden fabric of her panties.

The touch inspired a moan and Jane felt herself weaken in his embrace.

'That's what you want, isn't it?'

Dizzy with need, Jane nodded. Despite her arguments, regardless of her protestations and ignoring the rational voice which shrieked that this was an insane course of action, she said, 'Yes.' She still had no intention of being his submissive and she was determined not to be the plaything for his challenge, but her body now ached with the need for an orgasm and she knew he would be able to satiate that appetite.

She allowed his kiss, welcoming the intrusion of his tongue. His lips were cool against hers but they inspired a heat that matched the burning between her legs. Without considering the mistake she might be making, Jane pushed her tongue into his mouth.

The embrace was over all too quickly. His fingers still rubbed at her wetness, but she sensed that he was caught by a need that equalled her own. He released his grip on her wrist, pushing her forcefully to the bed.

Jane gasped as she landed, staring wantonly up at him as he began to undress. She still didn't like him and she felt

73

certain that she never could, but that didn't quell her need for him. It was easy to rationalise that dichotomy, remembering that she had enjoyed lovers in the past whom she had despised on waking. At least with McGivern she could expect that emotion and not find that it filled her with disappointment.

He tugged the shirt from his body and loosened his belt. The strip of leather hung between his fingers as a thoughtful expression crossed his brow. He grinned down at her and, after winding the belt around one fist, he tested it between both hands.

Jane saw his intention and recoiled from the idea. 'Don't even think of trying to use that on me,' she warned him. She raised a defensive finger that pointed somewhere between his face and the belt. 'I won't tolerate that.'

He studied her with a superior expression. 'I always whip my slaves before I pleasure them. It's one of the castle's rules.'

'I'm not your slave,' she reminded him.

'But you want to be, don't you?'

McGivern didn't allow her to deny the accusation. He held up a steadying hand, still holding the leather belt in the other. 'Forget your bullshit ethics,' he told her. 'And forget all this talk about slaves, masters and the dance of submission. We both know you're desperate to find out what this feels like. Let me stripe your arse three times so you can finally experience it.'

She wished she knew how he was reading her thoughts. She wondered if he was a skilled observer of human nature or if she was more transparent than she had ever believed. However he had managed it, he had seen the need in her eyes and he was responding to it the way her libido would have wanted. The pulse between her legs quickened as she imagined herself succumbing to the threat of his belt. There was still a voice in her mind that insisted she should flee but arousal quashed her ability to hear it.

'Not three,' she told him. 'Just one.'

He tested the belt again and this time she heard it crack loudly. The sound stirred an uneasy growl in the pit of her stomach.

'Are we haggling?' McGivern asked. 'Do I badger you to accept two now?'

'Just one,' she whispered.

'I doubt one will excite me enough,' he told her. 'Two, or I'll forget my offer to pleasure you.'

Jane glared at him with renewed venom. She wanted to refuse and say that was fine with her. She knew that such a response would be the most sensible one she could give, but her body insisted that she relent. Despite her shame and embarrassment her arousal hadn't abated. Every pore in her body ached with the need for release.

'Two,' she agreed meekly.

She saw his grin broaden and knew she had said the wrong thing. He didn't give her a moment to retract her decision. Before she could stop him, he had reached down to the bed and turned her over. The air was knocked from her lungs and Jane found herself facing the sheet.

'You aren't going to hurt me, are you?'

'No more than necessary.'

His hands stroked up her thighs and pushed her skirt away from her backside. He grabbed roughly at her panties and then dragged them away from her. It was a demeaning position and she knew she should have been struggling to escape. Common sense told her that she shouldn't be allowing him to use her like this but her need for satisfaction dictated otherwise and its voice was more strident than that of her rational mind.

McGivern caressed the cheeks of her arse and Jane bristled with unexpected excitement. His fingertips were daringly close to the crease of her sex and she suddenly saw that she had made the right choice. Perhaps he was a despicable bastard and perhaps there would be inevitable repercussions from this moment, but she didn't doubt he would give her satisfaction.

'Two,' McGivern growled. 'You needn't bother counting them.'

He moved his hand from her arse cheeks and Jane braced herself for the inevitable crack of the belt. A lifetime-long moment passed as she squeezed her eyes closed and held her buttocks rigid in anticipation.

It landed like a knife against her right cheek. She heard the short whistle of its descent, then felt a stripe of pain flare against her backside. A blazing agony shrieked through her body with an alacrity that left her breathless. She had expected the blow to be purely unpleasurable and had half-hoped it would quell her desire. As the heat spread out from her backside, she saw that had been a foolish dream. The warmth in her pussy-lips burnt with renewed passion and her nipples ached ever more urgently. Her need for him now was greater than she could have believed possible.

The belt whistled again but Jane didn't have the time to brace herself for this blow. It caught her unaware, landing painfully on her other buttock.

It was impossible to decide if she was screaming with agony or delight. The roar rushed from her lips and she rolled on the bed lost in an undiscovered world of pain-tinged joy. She felt a brief moment's regret that she hadn't allowed him to deliver three blows, then an after-wave of the pain rushed through her and she screamed again.

McGivern's hand reached for her arse-cheeks and Jane flinched as he caressed the stripes he had made. 'That wasn't all bad, was it?' he murmured.

It was one hell of an understatement. She tried to agree with him but her throat was still locked around a sigh of elation. He seemed to take her silence as acquiescence and she felt him move between her legs.

He had been standing over her, wielding the belt and she doubted he had been given the time to undress before approaching her. Nevertheless, she felt his naked legs touch her inner thighs as he moved himself closer.

The head of his shaft poked at her sex and Jane groaned again. The explosion of her orgasm was inevitable now, spurred on by the aftermath of her beating and the threatening intrusion of his cock. He was spreading her arse cheeks to facilitate his entry and his fingers pressed against the painful lines he had branded her with. Each renewed flare of discomfort was only an echo of the shock the belt had caused but it was still sufficient to leave her giddy.

McGivern pushed himself into her with an effortless lunge. His shaft was thick, spreading her wide as it filled her. Jane guessed he was roughly the same build as the dildo she had been using, but his cock was infinitely more satisfying. The pulse in his length inspired a greater response than the vibrator had managed.

Her orgasm was incredibly close and Jane clawed her fingers into the sheet as she readied herself for the moment.

McGivern moved his hands from the bruised cheeks of her arse, holding her hips in a firm, inescapable grip. His thrusts were slow but powerful, each one pushing her closer to the point of euphoria. As his grip tightened, she felt herself being pulled on to him and knew that she was in the control of a formidable lover. It was a torrid exchange and she doubted she could stave off the orgasm for a moment longer. She was struggling to avoid it, sure the pleasure would be that much more intense if she resisted its release as long as possible.

And then she felt his climax.

His cock began to pulse with a force that shook her frame. She could feel the explosion of his seed burning at the neck of her womb. His forceful thrusts stopped with one final, determined lunge.

Her responding orgasm was no less than she had been expecting. A massive ripple of joy swept over her, made more intense as McGivern stroked her burning arse-cheeks again. Pleasure erupted through her body and Jane screamed. The sound of her elation echoed from the toy room's stone walls.

When McGivern eased himself from her, he was laughing softly. 'Now,' he said, 'I want you to lick me clean.'

Jane rolled over and glared at him. Her body was still shivering with the tremors of her release but, now that the orgasm had passed, she felt a return of her distaste for him. There was nothing inherently wrong with what he was suggesting. The idea of gratefully running her tongue over

77

his flaccid length, and enjoying the taste of their shared passion, would have seemed like the ideal way of concluding their lovemaking. But Jane could see a triumphant gleam in his eyes and she didn't want him to think that she was already his submissive.

'I'm not doing that,' she told him.

He frowned. 'Each of my slaves knows that it's expected.'

'I'm not one of your slaves.'

'Not yet.'

'Not ever.'

'I could force you.'

Jane shut that image from her mind before it could start to work adversely against her. Too late, she caught a mental picture of McGivern holding her head against his spent shaft. She could see him threatening her until she had lapped up the final remnants of their mingled juices. It was an intoxicating scenario and she was relieved when his words brushed the thought away.

'Perhaps that's a pleasure we can look forward to next time,' he said.

'There won't be a next time,' she returned defiantly.

He laughed and shook his head, stepping back into his clothes. 'You told me there wouldn't be a first time, this morning,' he reminded her. 'So I'll treat your denial with the same pinch of salt.'

Jane closed her eyes, wishing he hadn't pointed that out. The orgasm had cleared her thoughts, exactly as she had hoped it would. However, McGivern's after-play, and his promise of future encounters, now added more inspiration to her lecherous imagination.

'Is this finished?'

When she opened her eyes, she saw that he was pointing at the printer tray. Unable to find any enthusiasm for the drudgery of the paperwork, she simply nodded.

'I'm taking this to the bull dyke,' McGivern said, snatching the second copy of the contract from the printer. 'I'd like you to print a final copy for me before you put this contraption away.'

Jane nodded, then frowned. 'The bull dyke?'

'Frankie,' McGivern told her. 'Didn't you know? Did you think she was just admiring your blouse this morning in the banquet hall?'

Jane flushed and tore her gaze from his. Today had been a revelation in a world that she had never wanted to know and, although she had already begun to enjoy some parts of it, there were many aspects that she was loath to explore. Frankie's interest in her had to be counted as one of those areas and Jane suppressed a shiver as she remembered the woman's blatant appraisal.

McGivern was oblivious to the train of her thoughts. He paused by the door and smiled at her. 'I'll be having you for dinner tonight, won't I?'

She didn't like the way he said it, but she nodded anyway. She didn't want to have dinner with him but she knew there was nothing else to do in an empty castle on its own deserted island. 'There won't be any of your slaves in attendance, will there?'

'Not if you don't want.'

'I don't want,' Jane told him. She was thinking about the blonde slave who had ridden the wooden horse. Her parting phrase had been unnerving and Jane didn't want to revisit that experience over dinner. Before she could brush the blonde from her mind, Jane remembered something the woman had said before mounting the wooden horse. She had barely acknowledged the remark at the time but it now seemed incongruous with the other things she had been told about the castle. The blonde had said she had ridden the wooden horse last year but McGivern had suggested that he and his entourage were as new to the castle as Frankie and Simon.

Jane was about to ask him to clarify the slave's comment, wondering if McGivern had lied. She already suspected that was the case, but she could see no reason why he should fabricate such a thing. Before she could give voice to her question, McGivern had gone.

Jane sighed with exasperation.

The need to know what was happening nagged at her

like toothache. Her body was still warmed by the glow of their lovemaking and she had already resigned herself to further indignities before McGivern allowed her to leave. But, whatever else happened, she was determined not to be a party to deceit. With that resolution at the forefront of her mind, she racked her brains for a possible reason behind his deception. With a frown creasing her forehead, she wondered why he was lying, and how she could find out more.

Five

The echo of number three's stiletto boots rang from the stone walls, snapping Frankie out of her contemplative reverie. Normally she would have refused permission for a submissive to visit the garderobe at such an early stage. Toilet training was a particularly effective tool for controlling slaves and she had seen it break the hardest of spirits. However, after watching her suffer the enema, Frankie had felt obliged to let number three go there again. The minutes had dragged by as she waited for the slave's return and her mood had grown more menacing as she realised the time for this challenge was slowly ebbing away. When she saw the submissive hurrying to rejoin her, Frankie toyed with the idea of punishing number three for taking so long.

She waited until the slave had reached her side and then stood up to glare menacingly into her face. 'We could sort this out right here,' Frankie growled. 'I want you to do the dance, and you're determined not to. I'm more determined than you are, so why don't you make things easy on yourself and give in now?'

They stood in one of the north keep's stone walled corridors, caught in the dusty slats of light. The midday sun brought out the lustre of number three's unruly dark hair and Frankie could feel herself warming to the slave.

Number three held her gaze. In a steady voice, she said, 'My master has told me not to do the dance for you.'

Frankie chewed on her lower lip. 'Forget your master,' she said tersely. 'He's not here, is he? He's not the one who'll be making your life a living hell for the next three days. That's what I'll be doing, unless you agree to dance for me.'

Number three blinked and shook her head. 'My master has told me not to do the dance for you,' she repeated.

Frankie glared. She threw her cigar to the floor and ground it into the stone with the heel of her boot. Being honest with herself, she had expected this much but it would never do to let the submissive know such a thing. Years of successful experience had taught her that slave-breaking was little more than a matter of patience and discretion. She had no intention of forgetting those disciplines when the challenge was as important as this one.

There were some people who said that being a professional slave-breaker was its own reward. Having recently completed her tax returns for the year, Frankie knew there was some truth in the adage. The few benefits that her occupation did give her were certainly not financial. She knew it wasn't the same for Simon and McGivern. They both acted as though they owned the world's riches. Even if their wealth wasn't quite that great, Frankie knew they were better placed for this bet than she was. Investing in the castle had taken the last of her spare capital.

Gambling that money now felt like the stupidest folly she had ever committed but she was determined not to let those doubts trouble her. Negative thinking like that wasn't an indulgence she could afford at this point in the challenge.

'I'm giving you a last chance to take the easy option,' Frankie explained. 'This is your last chance to escape all the horrible little devices I intend to use on you.'

Number three shivered but she remained silent.

'I'll cane you,' Frankie continued. 'I'll beat you. I'll humiliate you so bad, your shame will sting worse than the welts I leave on your backside.' She licked her lips, her mouth dry with excitement as she delivered the threats. She was tempted to reach out and stroke one of the slave's bared breasts but she overcame the impulse, sure that such an action would undermine her authority. It was difficult to quell the urge – her fingers longed to caress the number three that had been tattooed into the slave's flesh – but Frankie managed to resist with a huge exertion of willpower. Glaring into the slave's eyes, she said, 'You can avoid all that torment if you just say that you'll do the dance for me.'

'My master has told me that I should submit myself to anything you say,' number three replied. 'But he's forbidden me from doing the dance. I can't do it.'

As the slave spoke, her chest heaved lightly up and down and Frankie's gaze was caught by a twinkling of light. A sliver of sunlight danced against one of the rings penetrating the slave's breasts. Once her attention was drawn, Frankie found it difficult to look away. The pierced nipples were a distraction and Frankie was torn between the choice of focusing on them, or the conversation. She sighed and snatched her gaze away from the enticing view. 'Take me to the west keep,' she growled. 'I'll make you change your mind there.'

Number three nodded and turned. 'It's this way.'

Frankie grabbed her briefcase from the floor and followed along the stone corridor. She had selected this slave as her challenge for two reasons and now they both seemed equally important. Initially, as she sat at McGivern's banquet table and mulled over his proposal, she had seen the slave as the easiest option. The woman was already pliant enough to do the dance of submission and skilled enough to do it well. Frankie had reasoned that if she had to make someone do the dance, it would be easiest to use someone who already knew the steps.

But now, climbing a spiral staircase lit by burning torches, she realised there had been another motivation behind her choice. Number three was exceptionally pretty and, regardless of whether the woman intended submitting, Frankie wanted to enjoy her. Wearing the uniform of her slave status, she was displayed more obviously than if she had been naked and Frankie couldn't deny it was an arousing sight. Her slender back narrowed to a tiny waist, then blossomed to her hips and long, fishnet-clad legs. The black leather strips of her uniform contrasted with her pallid flesh but that only drew Frankie's attention more.

With each step up the staircase, her buttocks rose into Frankie's view before parting slightly. The glimmer of steel that pierced the slave's sex was constantly visible and the sight fuelled Frankie's growing desire. The twinkle of cruel metal against the dark secret of her sex was a reminder of the slave's servility.

Although she was determined to win the challenge, Frankie hoped that number three didn't make it too easy for her. She was looking forward to having some fun before she finally took possession of her prize.

'How long have you known McGivern?' Frankie asked.

'Almost a year now.'

'And how did you meet?'

'I used to work in a fairground,' number three replied. 'There was a change in ownership that I didn't really enjoy, and that was when I met my master. He took me away from all that and he's been taking care of me ever since.'

Frankie nodded. She wasn't particularly interested in the slave's answers but the conversation was a distraction from her lecherous thoughts and the magnificent splendour of the castle.

They had reached the top of the staircase and stood on the keep's northern embattlements. A cool breeze swept at them from the endless blue ocean. Frankie felt her hair being teased by the wind's playful fingers. She inhaled the briny air and blinked her eyes until they were accustomed to the overhead sun. It was a glorious building, made more spectacular by the tranquillity of the surrounding emptiness. She knew that if she had squinted in the right direction she would have been able to catch a faraway glimpse of Land's End, but Frankie didn't know which way to look and had no interest in seeing any corner of her homeland. From this vantage point, she could see the tip of the castle's island as an oasis of green foliage in the azure waters. McGivern hadn't been exaggerating when he described the place as a paradise for sexual mastery. To be able to live somewhere as isolated and beautiful as this was the dream of every dominatrix that Frankie knew.

She shook her head and dismissed the castle's perfection from her mind. There would be plenty of time to concentrate on the surrounding splendour when she had won the challenge. For now, it was important to invest her efforts in forcing her will on to the slave.

Frankie continued to follow her along the high stone wall, startled by the growing need of her arousal. Against the backdrop of the endless blue sky, the slave looked like a vision of beauty. The combination of leather and naked flesh was dizzying. Coupled with the straight seams of her fishnet stockings, she looked like a portrait of servility. Frankie could picture the woman submitting beneath her and the cleft between her legs began to throb. With imagination goading her libido, she could see the slave kneeling on the floor as she reluctantly prepared to do Frankie's bidding. The image was exhilarating and Frankie relished it as they strolled along the embattlements.

'Do you have a name?' Frankie asked. 'Or are you just a number?'

A blush touched the slave's ears. She didn't stop, or turn to reply. She simply called the response over her shoulder. 'My master has said that I'm not allowed a name. I'm only known as number three.' There was no hint of upset in her tone when she delivered this news. If Frankie had been asked to guess, she would have said that the slave was elated by her nameless status.

'Did you have a name before you met McGivern?'

'Not one that I use any more.'

Frankie chewed her lower lip and grinned ruefully. Getting straight answers from the submissive was proving to be as pain free and effortless as pulling teeth. For the first time, she saw that she was competing against equals and the thought added an exciting hue to her arousal. Previous experience had taught her that Simon was a gifted master and, if she hadn't been able to control so many of the bet's conditions, she wouldn't have wanted to test her skills against his.

But now she could see that McGivern was just as talented.

He had taken control of this woman, robbed her of an identity and filled her with an all-encompassing devotion. The woman was a testament to his prowess in the art of domination and Frankie grudgingly amended her low opinion of him. Having seen the other slaves that attended at the banquet hall, Frankie wondered if they were all as submissive. It was a disconcerting thought and she decided that, if he was that good, then she had many reasons to be nervous about this challenge.

They had reached the turrets of the west keep and, before she stepped inside, Frankie took a final glance around. The view was tremendous enough to take her breath away but, instead of glancing out towards the ocean, she looked down into the courtyard.

The overhead sunlight bleached the grey stone walls to a dirty shade of white, illuminating every corner of the bailey. The students were still working at their dig but Frankie could no longer see the distinctive orange T-shirt that had marked the girl she had chosen for Simon. It wasn't surprising, she thought. Simon was a fast worker and Frankie guessed that he was already employing his inescapable charm on the poor bitch. The thought reminded her that she had no time to waste.

'Is there a particular form of punishment you'd like me to avoid?' Frankie asked as they stepped back into the castle's gloom.

'I . . .' The slave stopped herself and risked a sly smile over her shoulder. 'With all due respect, do you really think I'd be dumb enough to tell you if there was?'

Frankie grinned, aware that the slave had come close to doing just that. 'That sort of response could be viewed as insolence,' she said. 'I've had slaves before and they've all known better than to risk insolence. But I'll forgive you, on this occasion.'

Number three frowned, then turned her head away so Frankie couldn't see her worried expression.

'I'll forgive you,' Frankie explained, 'because I know I

can get all the answers I want once we begin your training.'
It pleased her to see number three's back stiffen and she
chuckled quietly when she realised the slave wasn't as
sanguine as she was trying to appear. She didn't doubt that
the rest of her composure would be just as easy to destroy
and the thought cheered Frankie's spirits.

They began to descend into the west keep and number
three explained the building's layout. 'The keep is built on
three floors. The top floor has been made up as a
recreational room. Below that is your bedroom, and then
a banquet hall.'

'Is there a dungeon?'

'Each of the keeps has a dungeon beneath it,' number
three said quietly.

Frankie grinned, already guessing why the slave hadn't
bothered to explain that particular feature. 'Is it a fully
equipped dungeon?' she asked. 'With whips and chains and
all manner of punishment devices?'

With an unhappy nod, the slave said it was. In a hurried
voice, she added, 'There's also a fully modernised
garderobe on each floor.'

Frankie grunted acknowledgement of that fact, trying to
decide if she should exploit the slave's reluctance for the
dungeon, or let her think that she had been given a
reprieve. The decision wasn't a difficult one. 'Take me to
my bedroom. We have business to discuss.'

With another unhappy nod, the slave led her to a
doorway and pushed it open.

Frankie didn't waste time admiring the room. There was
an ornate four poster bed, draped with a heavy velvet
canopy. The windows were glazed and leaded and the
stone floor was almost hidden beneath a huge, careworn
rug. By normal standards, it was still less than basic, but
Frankie already felt comfortable. She supposed that Simon
was enjoying more luxuriant comfort in the modernised
east keep, but the west keep's medieval charm was enough
to warm her. Not that Frankie thought there would be
much time to admire those charms as she tried to dominate
the slave. She had already guessed that number three was

going to fight hard not to succumb to her mastery and she expected the battle of wills to be a ferocious one.

Frankie stepped towards the bed and peered beneath the burgundy drapes. 'This will do,' she whispered. Before the slave could question her remark, Frankie turned on her with an austere frown. 'I'm going to take a traditional approach to breaking you. That doesn't worry you, does it?'

Number three shook her head and swallowed. 'Of course not.'

'Good,' Frankie beamed. 'You will call me mistress, and you'll be punished when you forget. You will do everything I tell you, and if it's not done properly, I'll punish you. You will speak only when spoken to, with one exception.'

The slave remained silent but she studied Frankie expectantly. Her acceptance of the rules and her immediate understanding of them filled Frankie with an annoying respect for the slave's servility.

'You may speak without permission if you decide you're going to do the dance of submission for me. Other than that, I want you to remain silent.'

Number three nodded.

'Punishment comes in three forms. Caning, humiliation and torment. I shall combine and vary the three of them so you won't know which to expect. I shall punish you again and again until you relent and say you'll do the dance. Do you understand all of this?'

'Yes, mistress,' number three said quickly.

Frankie smiled, simultaneously annoyed and delighted that the slave was such a quick learner. 'Will you do the dance for me?' Frankie asked.

Number three shook her head. 'I can't, mistress.'

'Then you've just earnt your first punishment. Take that ridiculous costume off, and lay down on the bed.'

Number three frowned. She was clearly reluctant but she began to unfasten the strips of leather and remove them from her body.

Frankie had already enjoyed the sight of the slave's nudity but that didn't hamper her mounting arousal as she watched the woman disrobe. When number three had done the dance of submission, Frankie had been taken by her naked charms. Her servility had been enthralling and her tattooed and pierced body had filled Frankie with an urge to possess. Now, at such close proximity, she felt the moment of that particular triumph was nearing.

Number three dropped the strips of leather to the floor, then knelt down to unfasten her shoes.

Looking down on her, Frankie felt the tingle of arousal sweep up from the lips of her sex. Her clitoris was already pulsing with an urgent need and her entire body was quickly filling with a deepening desire.

After removing both shoes, the slave reached for the top of one stocking and began to unroll the fishnet fabric down her muscular thigh.

Frankie watched, relishing her awakening appetite and toying with the various opportunities that were now available to her. 'Does McGivern whip you?'

'Yes, mistress.'

'What with? A whip? A cane? A slipper? His bare hand?'

'Yes, mistress. All of those, and more.'

Frankie chewed her lower lip. She reached for a cigar from her jacket pocket and lit the end as she studied the slave's naked body. Her mind was racing in a desperate search for inspiration. 'How long have you had those piercings?'

'A year. The master wanted me to have them.'

'Are they fully healed?'

Number three nodded. 'Yes, mistress.'

'And does McGivern use them to punish you?'

'Occasionally, mistress,' she mumbled. Her cheeks were darkening and, although she was answering properly, she was staring at the floor and studying Frankie's feet as she spoke.

'Back in the banquet hall,' Frankie snapped. 'Was that the first time you'd had an enema?'

'No, mistress.'

Frankie sighed, unable to conceal her mounting exasperation. 'Has he ever used a candle on you?'

Number three looked puzzled. 'How do you mean?'

Frankie drew on her cigar. 'Has he ever dripped hot wax on to your intimate flesh? Your nipples? Your pussy-lips? Your arsehole?'

The slave nodded. 'Yes, mistress. Frequently.' Her answer was tinged with a soft smile, as though this inspired a fond memory.

'Has he fucked you with one?'

'Yes, mistress.'

'Watersports?'

'Yes, mistress. But not while using a lit candle.'

Frankie scowled. She had wanted to introduce the slave to a new form of punishment: something different from the way McGivern treated her. Such a chastisement would remind the slave that she was being dealt with by a different authority figure and it could make her more willing to do the dance. Yet it seemed as though McGivern had treated the submissive to every degrading act imaginable. It was an invidious position to be starting from and Frankie chewed unhappily on her cigar as she tried to think of a new way to humiliate the slave.

A knock on the door disturbed her thoughts and she glanced up to see McGivern walking into the room. In one hand he held a sheaf of papers with the word "contract" written on the cover page. His grin widened when he caught sight of his naked submissive. He turned the smile so that it incorporated Frankie.

'You seem to be progressing very well,' he noted dryly. 'You've already undressed her. What's the next stage? Does she make cups of tea? Or are you playing a game of statues?'

'You have a lot to learn about discretion,' Frankie told him.

McGivern shrugged indifferently. 'Perhaps you're right. What a shame there's no one here to teach me some manners.'

Frankie scowled and opened her mouth to shout abuse at him. She stopped herself, suddenly taken by a brilliant idea. Turning to the slave, she said, 'Tell McGivern to fuck off.'

Number three blinked and her mouth closed abruptly. She glanced nervously from Frankie to McGivern and, for the first time, Frankie saw that the slave was genuinely unsettled. It was an invigorating sight and Frankie realised she had finally found that "something different" she had been racking her brains for.

'You're under orders to do everything I say, with that one debatable exception,' Frankie reminded her. 'Tell McGivern to fuck off. Tell him now.'

Blushing, number three stared down at her feet. Her cheeks were painfully red and her body was trembling. 'Fuck off.' She mumbled the words in a whisper so quiet it was barely audible.

'Say it louder,' Frankie encouraged. She could see that McGivern was glaring at her but his antipathy meant nothing. The important thing now was forcing her will on to the slave. 'Say, "Fuck off McGivern," in a really loud voice, and then call him a twat.'

The slave groaned. Her gaze was fixed on the floor and her mild tremors had turned into miserable shivers. 'Fuh . . .' she began.

'Look at him while you say it,' Frankie barked. 'And don't worry about repercussions. He's the one who told you to do everything I say. Just do as I say.'

'Fuck off, Mr McGivern,' number three whispered.

'Louder,' Frankie cheered gleefully.

'There's no need for this,' McGivern warned Frankie. He looked as uncomfortable as his slave and Frankie took a great deal of pleasure from that sight. His cheeks were burning pink and his eyes were as black as coals as he glared at her.

Frankie ignored him, her spirits soaring. 'You forgot to call him a twat,' she told number three. It was difficult to keep the wicked laughter from her voice, but she managed it with an effort. 'Tell him to fuck off again; and, this time, call him a twat.'

Number three sighed heavily. The weary sound was torn from her body. She glared desperately from McGivern to Frankie, her eyes wide with distress.

Frankie simply grinned at her, enjoying the slave's dilemma. 'Do it now,' she pressed. 'McGivern's on the verge of forfeiting his bet because of your insolence.'

'Fuck off, McGivern,' number three snapped sharply. As an afterthought, she glanced at Frankie and added, 'Twat.'

Unable to hold it any longer, Frankie began to laugh. Her chuckles deepened when she saw McGivern's dour frown. The knowledge that she had deeply offended him only added to her hilarity.

'It's an impressive display,' McGivern told her tersely. 'Will you be teaching her the other six words from your vocabulary? Or are you going to concentrate on the bet now?'

Frankie's laughter began to subside but not because of McGivern's sarcasm or his irate frown. The fun and games were over and it was time for her to get on with the bet. 'Get out of here,' she told him good-naturedly. 'Get out of here and, the next time you want to see me, I'd like it if you didn't just barge in.'

He was still scowling. 'I'll try to bear that in mind.' He dropped the sheaf of papers on a set of drawers beside the bed and said, 'I was simply bringing your contract. I trust you'll be reading through it to check that everything is in order.'

'I'd better read it quickly,' Frankie told him. 'I don't think there's a lot of time left before I win this bet.'

McGivern turned his back on her and stormed out of the room. He slammed the door closed behind him, its heavy echo shaking from the walls.

'My God, that was fun,' Frankie said, turning to the slave. 'Now lie down on the bed and prepare to have your arse properly beaten.'

The slave moved obediently, turning her face so that Frankie couldn't see the streams of unhappy tears that wetted her cheeks. As the slave climbed through the layers of velvet and on to the bed, Frankie began to pull the drapes aside.

She had noticed the cord-like sashes before and she was determined to use them. The bed was made from wrought iron and fashioned with a cold simplicity that suited the medieval surroundings. The head, pressed against the wall, was invisible beneath half a dozen well-fluffed pillows. Rows of iron bars, like the windows of a prison cell, ran down from the foot.

'Push your tits through there,' Frankie barked. She pointed at the foot of the bed for clarity, winding a length of sash through her hands as she spoke.

Sniffing back a tear, number three moved reluctantly forward and did as she had been told.

It looked like an uncomfortable position but Frankie wasted little time with that thought. She was still trying to dismiss her growing arousal as she watched the slave do everything she was told. Seeing her push her pale orbs through the spaces between the bars brought an exhilaration that demanded satisfaction. Determined not to succumb to that need just yet, Frankie began to bind the slave's breasts. She wrapped the cord tightly around one orb, squeezing its shape so that the protruding flesh was oval and melon-like. The steel rings in number three's nipples glimmered dully and Frankie deliberately ignored the excitement that the sight generated. With half of the rope still left, Frankie began to bind the other breast. She worked quickly, pulling the cord hard and ignoring number three's groans of discomfort.

When she was finished, she didn't waste time admiring her handiwork. Instead, she reached for her briefcase and popped the catches open. From inside, she removed a short riding crop and tested it through the air.

The crop whistled.

The slave stiffened on the bed and Frankie smiled. She walked quickly around her, tapping the riding crop lightly against number three's legs and sides and barking instructions for her to attempt to kneel. The hand she used was light, and she doubted the crop could have hurt more than a gently prodding finger, yet the slave recoiled from each blow as though it had broken flesh. When Frankie was satisfied with the slave's posture, she took a final draw on her cigar and stamped it into the floor.

Number three was trembling. She knelt on the bed with her head forced down because of her bound breasts. Her hands clutched the top bar of the bed's foot, where her clavicle pressed uncomfortably. As she tried to glare up at Frankie, her features were transformed into a thunderous scowl.

'Are you still unwilling to dance?' Frankie asked. As she spoke, she teased the riding crop against one of the slave's nipples. Because of its piercing, the nub was in a permanent state of arousal but it seemed to grow harder beneath the crop's crude caress. The areola darkened to a chocolate colour and Frankie saw the other nipple responding sympathetically. She teased the spatula-like end of the crop more forcibly against the slave, trying to push the broad leather tip through the tiny circle of steel. She had bound others in this position before and she had always taken a lot of pleasure from titillating their nipples. In this position, a slave's breasts seemed more acutely sensitive and Frankie had yet to meet one who didn't respond meekly to the threat of the riding crop. When she had employed this technique in the past, she invariably received the slave's promise of eternal devotion. All it ever took was one well-aimed blow.

It was tempting to try and break number three with such an effortless display but Frankie doubted it would be successful. She had already noticed that there was a streak of iron in the woman and she suspected it was as unyielding as the bedstead she was bound to. 'I'm placing the choice in your hands,' Frankie told her. 'You could spend the next three days suffering like this, or you could relent and enjoy your freedom.'

'I can't, mistress.'

Frankie bit her lower lip and snatched the crop away from the woman's breasts. She raised it high in the air then brought it down against the slave's bare arse.

Number three stiffened. Her hands gripped the top bar tighter and her eyes squeezed shut. There was a grimace on her lips as she grunted her wordless response.

Frankie smiled and raised the crop again. 'I'm a difficult

mistress to please,' she said, bringing the crop down. This time it scored the other cheek and she was gratified to see twin lines of red marking the slave's backside. 'You might find the next three days pass a lot more slowly than you're anticipating.'

Number three remained silent and Frankie glowered. She raised the crop again and this time brought it down along the top of the slave's legs, just beneath her buttocks. It was a sensitive area to aim for and she was rewarded by an indignant squeal. Staring down at the reddening cheeks of number three's backside, Frankie cast her eye towards the crevice of the slave's sex. Her shaved labia had peeled open and the lips of her pussy glistened with arousal.

Frankie's grin widened and she struck the cheeks with another blow. It occurred to Frankie that there was another form of punishment that McGivern would have been unable to administer, and she took the two steps to the front of the bed, determined to exploit the idea.

Number three glared up at her, her eyes filled with muted loathing.

Frankie stepped closer, so that the front panel of her skirt brushed against the woman's nose. 'I could see my punishment was exciting you,' she explained. 'It's exciting me, too. I want you to lick me.'

The slave shook her head, a defiant flicker appearing in the corner of her eye. 'That was one of the reasons I left the fairground. Mr McGivern has never made me . . .' Her voice trailed off and she stopped shaking her head. Staring awkwardly up at Frankie, she said, 'I mean, I don't . . .'

'You've just earnt yourself six strokes of the cane for talking out of place and another six for forgetting to call me "mistress",' Frankie broke in. 'Another word, and you'll have earnt six more. Stay silent and lick me.' Without allowing the slave to consider her options, Frankie raised the hem of her skirt.

Since becoming a dominatrix, she had stopped troubling herself with things as restrictive as underwear. As she lifted the leather miniskirt, she knew that the dark curls of her pubic mound were being revealed to the slave. From her standing position she couldn't see herself, but she didn't doubt that the lips of her sex were already slick with arousal.

Number three remained still on the bed, making no attempt to nudge her tongue forward and tease the folds of Frankie's pussy. Her face was close. Frankie knew that much when she felt her thighs being tickled by the warm breath of the slave's exhalations. The tresses of her unruly dark hair brushed at the tops of Frankie's legs, inspiring a shiver of anticipation. Yet number three refused to push her tongue forward. Although she was bound, and unable to move properly, Frankie knew that the slave was trying to act defiantly.

'Lick me, or I'll make you suffer,' Frankie growled. She teased a finger against the pulsing nub of her clitoris, surprised by the thrill that her own caress inspired.

Number three did nothing. She remained rigid, her face hidden by the veil of her hair. Her backside was trembling and Frankie could see that the reddened lines on her arse-cheeks were already beginning to fade.

'Lick me, or I'll cane you again,' Frankie told her.

The threat brought no response. Frankie teased another finger against her clit and shivered with more forceful ecstasy. She contemplated raising the riding crop and trying to mark the slave's backside from this position, but it would have been a weak blow and she doubted it would have moved number three to do as she was told. She discounted the idea when a more subtle threat occurred to her.

'Lick me, or I'll take you from here and make you swear at McGivern again.'

The words worked like a switch. Number three pushed her head forward and began to trace her tongue against the burning lips of Frankie's sex.

It was an enthralling sensation. The slave's nose pushed into her pubic mound with a force that was almost uncomfortable. Her tongue slipped forward and Frankie could feel the end gently flicking at her pussy. The pleasure that her own finger had inspired was feeble compared to the joy that now rushed through her. She bucked her hips forward, making the length of her sex-lips more easily attainable. Using outstretched fingers, she teased her labia wide open so that the slave's tongue could reach her most intimate folds.

Number three sensed where her mouth was needed without needing to be told. Despite her initial reluctance, Frankie noted that she licked pussy with a skill that had to be born from some practice. Her tongue flitted purposefully against the exposed flesh, evoking shivers that left Frankie weak-kneed and breathless. The slave used her mouth to place subtle kisses against Frankie's clitoris, constantly working her tongue against the dewy lips.

Unable to stop herself, Frankie began to laugh. She was delighted by the pleasure that swept over her. She moved away, unsure that she should be indulging herself so fully at this early stage in the proceedings.

The slave's back trembled whilst sobs racked her body. She stared down at the floor and, because of her unruly hair, Frankie was unable to see the woman's face. She could see a dark pink cheek blushing through the veil of the slave's fringe but, other than that, number three was now avoiding her gaze. 'Don't worry,' Frankie told her kindly. 'I'll let you do some more of that before we're finished.'

The slave groaned unhappily, attempting to stifle the sound but managing it poorly.

'If you wanted, we could call a halt to this punishment right now,' Frankie said. She felt a little giddy with the pleasure that the slave's tongue had inspired but she managed to keep her tone even and unaffected. 'We could stop your torment right now, if you just promise to do the dance for me.'

'I can't, mistress.' It was a miserable admission.

Frankie shook her head. If the slave had been staring through her fringe, she would have seen the gesture, along with Frankie's expression of sympathy. 'That's not such a shame, though, is it?' Frankie spoke in a consoling voice. 'It means that you get a lot more discomfort until you learn the right way of doing things, but it means I get a great deal of pleasure.'

Still staring down, number three quivered.

Frankie tested the tip of her riding crop against one bound breast. It was the breast labelled with the number three tattoo and Frankie found her gaze lingering over the beauty of the cruel branding. The tattoo suggested a servility that went beyond the norm and Frankie longed to use that submissiveness for her own ends. The slave was exciting her far more than she had allowed for when she accepted this challenge. With a wilful effort, Frankie forced her thoughts back to the task in hand. Rather than caressing the pierced nipple, she pressed the crop hard against the slave's erect flesh. With her target identified, she drew the whip back, then returned it with a sharp smack.

This would be the turning point, she told herself. This was the punishing delivery that had broken so many slaves in the past and, although this submissive was more determined than most, Frankie saw no reason why it shouldn't work. She relaxed her blow a little, unwilling to cause too much suffering on an area that was pierced, but even with that little leeway, she knew the pain would be intolerable.

Number three winced as a red line overstruck the tattoo on her breast. Her hands clutched tightly at the top bar of the bed's foot and her entire body stiffened. Frankie caught a glimpse of the woman's cheeks and saw her face was a dark, orgasmic purple.

Annoyed that the woman was gleaning so much pleasure from this punishment, Frankie raised the crop again and slapped it hard against the other breast. No longer trying to appear thoughtful, she delivered the blow as forcefully as she could. The crop screamed through the air and landed with a slap. Staring down, Frankie saw that this time she hadn't scored the nipple. Her aim had been less sure and she had branded a blazing line of red along the slave's areola.

Number three remained completely silent. She drew a

startled breath, her rigid back expanding as she consoled herself with lungfuls of air. Her knuckles were a bloodless white as her fists gripped the iron ever tighter. Every muscle in her body was held so taut, she looked to have been carved from marble.

But she remained wordless.

'Are you ready to dance for me?' Frankie asked.

'I can't. The master would never forgive me.'

'And you may never forgive me if you don't.'

The slave said nothing. She drew noisy breaths, coughing back her arousal with hitching rasps.

With her mood darkening, Frankie stormed to the side of the bed and admired the slave's arse. The stripes she had administered were already fading to a warm pink glow and she raised her crop swiftly. 'I owe you twelve from before, and six for just now when you forgot to call me mistress.'

Number three couldn't spit the words out fast enough. 'I'm sorry, mistress.'

Frankie was barely listening. She brought the crop down and delivered a stinging succession of blows to the exposed backside. Frankie kept the count in her own mind, delivering nine to one cheek before marching around to the other side of the bed. The echo of the crop slapping flesh rang in her ears. She struck the final nine with short sharp blows that were designed for maximum discomfort. The exertion left her arm aching and fuelled a furious heat between her legs.

'Now, tell me you're ready to dance,' Frankie panted.

'I'm . . .' The slave hesitated, her faltering voice breaking into muffled tears. 'I can't, mistress.'

A broad smile split Frankie's lips. She had heard the first word and knew that the slave had been about to submit. The knowledge that she was so close to triumph left her dizzy. For a moment, she revelled in a wave of self-congratulation as she contemplated her own skill. Admittedly, the slave hadn't said she would dance, and perhaps that moment was still a long way off, but Frankie could see that the time would arrive and, when it did, she was going to take her place as the castle's owner.

Positioning herself in front of the slave, she said, 'Lick me some more, and try to decide if you should be rethinking your answer.'

The slave's groan smacked of reluctance but she obeyed Frankie's command. As soon as the skirt was raised high enough, she began to nuzzle her tongue against the sodden lips of Frankie's sex. Her tongue pushed furiously against the glistening folds. She lapped at the clitoris, then delved into the dark wetness.

Frankie trembled. She was already heady from her brush with success and now she was reeling with the pleasure that the slave's tongue evoked. Pulling the top of her waistcoat open, she released one breast and began to tease the nipple between her fingers. A thrill trembled from the orb and she felt herself moving closer to a climax. Dropping the riding crop to the floor, she pushed her other hand into the slave's hair to hold the bound woman steady. With a roll of her pelvis, Frankie began to rock herself backward and forward on to the slave's burrowing tongue.

Number three made a few murmurs that could have been caused by discomfort, or her own submissive pleasure. Frankie was aware that the beating she had administered had been enjoyed from two sides. Although she was building to a quickening climax, she forced part of her concentration to remain focused on the slave's mumbling. If number three suddenly decided to relent, Frankie didn't want to miss the moment.

It was a difficult task to manage. Her pussy lips were tingling and the slave had a gift for cunnilingus that went beyond anything Frankie had previously experienced. If she hadn't chosen to bind the slave – if she had allowed the submissive free access to her body – Frankie knew she would have already been taken by the throes of ecstasy. This position allowed the slave little purchase to use her tongue properly but the small amount she could manage was worth enduring.

Number three used her tongue to part the folds of flesh, licking up and down the labia before occasionally kissing the clitoris. She lapped at the skin, playfully nibbling the lips between gentle teeth. In spite of her reluctance to perform this act, Frankie could hear the slave's groans and she knew the sounds weren't drawn entirely from unhappiness.

When the orgasm hit her, Frankie screamed. She pushed her pelvis forward and felt the rush of a climax. She tugged the slave's hair harder, determined to squeeze every last droplet of delight from the submissive's tongue. Frankie tweaked her own nipple for a final time before she released her punishing grip. Shrill shards of joy prickled at her intimate flesh as the climax swept through her. The intensity was surprising but no less pleasurable because of that. Grinning broadly, Frankie released her hold on the slave's hair and staggered back on unsteady legs. She took a moment to catch her breath, staring at the slave with renewed respect.

Number three was studying the floor, her shoulders undulating slightly.

'Are you going to do the dance for me?' Frankie asked. Her body was tingling with pleasure but she had started to grow tired of repeatedly asking the question. She had pleasured herself, and she had made some headway with breaking number three, but now it was the time to show that she really meant business. She made her tone forceful so that this mood change would be conveyed to the humiliated slave.

'This is the last time I'm going to ask you today, then I'm going to bind your mouth so you can't speak. That doesn't mean I'm going to stop punishing you. But it means you won't have a chance to stop things when I take them too far.'

The slave's eyes were wide with a growing dread. She shook her head and opened her mouth preparing to say something.

Frankie held her breath and waited expectantly.

Tears welled in the slave's eyes and her lower lip trembled. It was an expression that Frankie had seen countless times on the faces of broken submissives. It was the same tear-stained beseeching that they all invariably turned on her when they were ready to relent.

'Well?' Frankie asked. She was eager to know if she had already won the bet. 'Are you ready to dance?'

Number three stared meekly up, her lower jaw dripping with the remnants of Frankie's pussy-honey. She opened her mouth and prepared to reply.

Six

Jane hesitated before leaving the toy room, not sure if she was doing the right thing. She wanted to make her journey without being seen and she listened intently before daring to open the door. Once she was happy that the corridor was silent, she crept out of the room and bumped into Simon.

Jane almost shrieked with surprise. She placed a hand over the hammering heartbeat in her chest and stared at him with a startled expression. Her cheeks were burning with a guilty flush, even though she had yet to do something wrong.

'Is McGivern in there?' Simon demanded.

He was pointing at the toy room door behind her and Jane could see that he was harbouring an anger that verged on the homicidal. She shook her head and pushed the door open revealing the empty room for him. 'He's not there. Take a look if you like. He left here about half an hour ago.'

'Bastard,' Simon cursed. 'Do you know where he is?'

Jane shook her head. 'Did you need him for something urgent?'

'Only to ram a fist down his throat, but I'm sure that can wait.' He punched the door with a force that made the wood tremble.

Jane flinched from the blow as though it had been aimed at her. She glanced at the point where his hand had struck and saw that Simon's azurite ring had left an imprint in the wood. 'Has he upset you?'

'Doesn't he upset everyone?'

He tested a likeable grin on her and Jane felt her unease toward him vanish. This morning she had thought Simon was a frightening figure but now, looking a little fraught and a lot less self-assured, he seemed approachable. He was still dressed in his frock coat, PVC trousers and thigh-length boots, but the image was no longer intimidating. If she was being honest in her appraisal, Jane would have described his outfit as debonair and not at all out of place for a man wandering around a castle as depraved as this one. The knowledge that McGivern had caused Simon's bad mood made Jane realise that they were united by a common bond.

'I can't even tell you where he is,' Jane explained. 'Because I don't know myself. He did say he was taking a copy of the contract to the bull ... to Frankie, but he should have finished doing that ages ago.'

Simon was nodding as though he had expected this much. 'For a man with so many servants, he seems to be making a special point of delivering those contracts personally.'

Jane frowned, not sure what he was insinuating and unwilling to try and find out more. There were lots of things that she needed to know about McGivern – she had been on the point of going to his room to see if some of her answers lay there – but she felt certain that her own enquiries had nothing to do with what Simon was implying. She racked her brains for something polite to say and, while she had no interest in the subject, politeness insisted that she ask, 'How's your challenge going?'

His frown was immediately suspicious. 'Are you asking as McGivern's spy?'

She laughed, more entertained than offended by the suggestion. 'No. I'm not McGivern's spy. I'm nothing more than McGivern's solicitor and that's as far as our relationship will progress, if I have my way. I'm asking out of morbid curiosity.'

Simon's smile was contrite and he placed a hand on her arm as he made his apologies. 'That was unforgivable of me,' he said. 'I'm in a foul mood and I shouldn't be taking it out on you. My part of the challenge is going well but it would be going a lot better if McGivern hadn't intruded at exactly the wrong moment.'

Jane bit her lower lip, emphasising her sympathetic frown. 'Do you think he did it deliberately?'

'No. I know he did it deliberately.' He shook the austere expression from his face, shaking his blond hair in a silky cascade at the same time. 'But that's not your fault and I have no intention of taking it out on you.' With a brightening mood, he said, 'I read the contract that you put together. It's quite an efficient document, especially considering the circumstances you've had to work in.'

Jane glowed beneath the praise, warming to Simon more and more. 'It was nothing really,' she began modestly.

Simon wouldn't let her downplay the achievement. 'Nonsense,' he said. 'It shows that you work well under pressure and that's an enviable ability. Considering everything that you saw this morning, it's a wonder you could think clearly enough to spell any of it properly.'

Jane beamed, grateful that her efforts had been appreciated by someone. This was the first time she had ever been complimented on the layout of a contract and the experience was so unfamiliar, it was delightful.

'Are you tied to a particular solicitor's, or do you work freelance?'

Jane frowned, wishing he hadn't asked the question. Remembering her faraway office, and the normality she had left behind, evoked a dizzying wave of homesickness. It also reminded her that McGivern had used his friendship with her employer to force her to stay in the castle. 'I don't have enough clients to attempt striking out on my own,' she replied bitterly. The realisation that this was now what she wanted had only just struck. As the idea began to blossom, she saw it was going to be the best path forward for her future career. Forgetting her aspirations for a partnership, Jane decided it would be best if she parted company with her employer as soon as she was free from the castle.

'This is my number,' Simon said, passing her a stiff, white business card. 'If you decide you're going to go freelance, give me a call and you can handle my portfolio.'

Jane gaped at the card, unable to believe she was being given such an offer. For a moment the stifling confines of her imprisonment were forgotten and she found her thoughts had escaped to a world where she was the captain of her own destiny. It was a liberating image. 'Are you serious?'

Simon nodded. 'Never more serious. And you never know – your first freelance case could be handling my acquisition of this castle.'

Considering the idea left her feeling light-headed. 'I don't know what to say.'

He shrugged. 'Say nothing for now and think it over. I won't try and sway your opinion any. I'll just say that, if you helped me with this challenge, I would give you an appropriate bonus to begin our working relationship.'

Jane's excitement was rising and she tried to shake the giddy smile from her lips. The offer was too good to be true and it was that realisation that made her consider the suggestion with a healthy measure of scepticism. She frowned at him and said, 'This wouldn't be a bribe that you're offering me, would it?'

Simon's smile was unoffended. 'A bribe? Why would I want to bribe you?'

She sniffed, trying to mask the disappointment that was threatening to course through her. 'Perhaps you might want to bribe me so I'd screw up McGivern's challenge?'

Simon had the good grace to cast his gaze downward.

'Or perhaps you were expecting me to impart some embarrassing information about McGivern? Something that you could use to your own advantage.'

'Pretty, capable and shrewd. I'd love to read your CV. I bet it makes you sound like Joan of Arc.'

Jane ignored his attempt at humour. In a lofty voice, she said, 'I would never do anything that went against my ethics as a solicitor.'

'Ethics and solicitor,' Simon mused. 'Those are two

words I didn't think I'd hear in the same sentence.' He laughed to show her he was joking and, leaning closer, he squeezed her arm apologetically.

Jane wished he hadn't started to touch her. The castle was redolent with an air of sexual excitement and the weight of his hand on her arm was enough to awaken her carnal appetite. It didn't help that Simon was annoyingly good-looking, or that his effeminate style of dress had piqued her interest.

Simon seemed oblivious to the arousal he was inspiring. 'I'm just teasing you about your ethics and, in answer to your question, no, I'm not trying to bribe you. I'm simply asking you to consider working for me after this debacle is over and done with.'

She studied him warily, not sure if she could trust any of those who were involved with the bet. It was difficult to think rationally as she tried to contend with the tingling pulse at her cleft, but she forced her mind to concentrate on the conversation.

Seemingly ignorant of her response to him, Simon continued, 'It's not as though you have any intention of doing that dance for McGivern, do you?'

'Of course not,' she replied quickly.

'Then maybe my offer will help. Whatever else he threatens you with, you can feel secure in the knowledge that penury won't be a problem.' He blinked and in an instant his face changed. His light-hearted mood evaporated and he coughed into his fist as he graced her with a hard, business-like expression. 'It's a genuine offer, not a bribe. The fact that you've just turned down my offer of a bonus makes me sure that you'd be the right person for the job, but there's more than that. You're very capable and that's a quality I always look for in those people I employ. Whether it's a slave or a solicitor, I always make sure the person is capable.'

Jane decided he was telling the truth and her hopes blossomed again. The future that waited for her after the castle no longer seemed so bleak and the flourishing optimism gave a free flow to her arousal. When he bent to

107

kiss her cheek, Jane turned so that their mouths met. His lips brushed against hers and she trembled.

'Think it over,' Simon suggested, brushing a fond hand against her cheek. The cool stone of his azurite ring chilled the side of her face. 'If the idea appeals to you, you can find me in the east keep.'

She parted her lips slightly and moved her face closer so that he could kiss her again. 'It's a tempting proposition,' Jane told him.

He smiled and shook his head. 'You're a tempting proposition, but I don't want you to think I'm trying to sway you.'

Jane moved her face away, trying to disguise her disappointment.

'I have to make plans for this evening,' Simon said. 'And I need to find McGivern before that.' With a broad grin, he added, 'His teeth aren't going to push themselves down his own throat.'

Jane nodded, unhappy that he wasn't going to take their shared excitement any further, but understanding his reasons. She had prepared the contracts herself and knew that there was an awful lot at stake with the bet. She moved her mouth forward and gave him an impetuous kiss on the cheek.

'The east keep,' he reminded her, taking a reluctant step backwards.

She nodded and, with a fond smile, she watched his effeminate figure disappear down the corridor. It was almost impossible to think of Simon as threatening or menacing now and she wondered how she could have misjudged him so badly in the banquet hall that morning.

A noise at the opposite end of the corridor reminded Jane that she had left the toy room for a reason. She told herself that the sound was nothing more than a hinged door being teased by one of the castle's many draughts, but nervousness made her doubtful. Dismissing the thrill caused by Simon's offer, she hurried towards the spiral staircase and started down to McGivern's bedroom.

Burning torches illuminated her route but did little to

pacify her growing worries about this endeavour. The flickering flames caused shadows to scurry in the corner of her vision and she tried to quell a rising paranoia, sure that each movement was made by McGivern following her. It came as something of a relief to step out of the staircase and into the corridor for McGivern's bedroom.

'And what do you want?'

It was a harsh question, delivered more forcefully than Jane would have expected from one of the slaves. She stared at the blonde guard beside McGivern's bedroom door and wished it wasn't the one who wore the number seven badge. Her knowing smile was an unwelcome reminder of all the new experiences the day had brought. Jane swallowed her nervousness and berated herself for not preparing for something like this. McGivern wasn't just a ruthless master. He was also a secretive bastard and she should have expected him to have placed a guard outside his bedroom. She tried to think of a credible explanation that would get her past the slave but rising panic sapped her imagination.

'What do you want?' the slave barked again. 'If you don't hurry up and answer, I'll tell the master that you were prowling outside his bedroom.'

'McGivern sent me,' Jane snapped quickly. She didn't look at the slave, fearful the submissive would see it was a deception if their eyes met. 'He keeps documentation in his bedroom and I need it for my work.' She wished she had been able to say the words with more authority or conviction. It sounded like a lie to her own ears and she felt sure that the slave was unconvinced.

'Perhaps I should get the master and see if that's true?'

Jane drew on all the resources of her acting abilities and tried to look imposing. She felt sure she missed the mark by a long way but she had no other defence against the slave's threat to involve McGivern. 'Perhaps you should get your master,' she agreed boldly. 'Then, when he sees that you're too stupid to guard a door properly, maybe he and I can punish you together.' She felt sure the threat was too much and too over the top. She could picture the blonde hurrying down the corridor in search of McGivern and, with her deception uncovered, Jane could imagine all types of retribution being visited upon her. The fear left a dryness in the back of her throat.

'The master really sent you?'

Jane resisted the urge to sigh with relief. Maintaining her charade of confidence, she said, 'Has it finally sunk in?'

'I'm sorry, mistress. I didn't realise that . . .' The slave was babbling, embarrassment and unease tripping her words. She began to fumble with the chatelaine at her belt and Jane could see that she had fooled the woman into opening the door.

The sense of accomplishment sent her spirits soaring. She was also aware of a surprising thrill when the blonde called her "mistress". It was an unexpected title and Jane knew that the slave had only used it because she was panicked and nervous. Yet still, she couldn't deny there was an appeal to being addressed with such reverence.

A silence had fallen between them and Jane didn't want it to continue, scared that the slave might have doubts about opening the door. After clearing her throat, she said, 'I don't think McGivern will be happy that you've delayed me.'

The slave glanced over her shoulder and regarded Jane with unhappy eyes. 'You don't have to tell him,' she began weakly. 'I was only doing my job. You wouldn't have him punish me for that, would you?'

Jane found it easy to slip into the role of being a ruthless bitch. She had witnessed so many examples of the part this morning, she already felt like an aficionado. The doubts and fears she had felt on seeing the slave were now gone and she felt a resurgence of her confidence. 'I could tell your master an awful lot of things about you. I don't think he'd be very happy to know that you were trying to intimidate me in the toy room.'

The slave's eyes opened fearfully wide. For the first time, Jane noticed that they were a dazzling cerulean colour. Her eyelashes were long and dark, seeming to emphasise her nervousness. 'I was only . . .'

Jane didn't allow her to continue. 'And I don't think he'd be happy to know that you and your friend were making free use of his wooden horse.'

'But I was just . . .'

Again, Jane broke in. She had seen McGivern use the trick to intimidate his subordinates and she was surprised by how effectively it was working. As soon as the submissive started speaking, Jane interrupted her. 'Mr McGivern strikes me as the sort of man who needs to be kept happy. Wouldn't you agree?'

'Yes, mistress.'

When the slave used the word again, Jane suddenly realised what she wanted. It was a crazy idea but that didn't trouble her. The castle was brimming with craziness and her own lapse into insanity would doubtless go unnoticed. She needed to dominate the slave and no amount of rational thought was going to sway her from that goal now that the idea had germinated.

'Do you think I should ask McGivern to punish you?' Jane whispered.

She stepped closer to the slave, using her nearness to daunt. It was a daring gambit, particularly when the woman towered over her by a good six inches. Jane guessed that, without the high heels, she and the slave would be a similar height, so she didn't let that thought trouble her. She pushed her face close the slave's and said, 'I believe that Mr McGivern can be quite cruel with some of his chastisements.'

'He can, mistress,' the slave agreed. Her words were carried by a timid tremor.

Jane felt the rush of excitement coursing through her. She pressed her body against the slave's, feeling sure that this would inspire even more unease. She continued to glare at her, delighted that the submissive was no longer daring to meet her eyes. 'I don't think you'd want to subject yourself to his anger unnecessarily, would you?'

'No, mistress.'

Jane drew a deep breath. 'Then you'll submit to my punishment and we'll say no more about it.'

'Yes, mistress.'

It was the woman's submission that made her act. She had intended doing nothing more than forcing the slave to open the door. It was all that she wanted from the submissive and she repeatedly told herself that she wasn't driven by the same urges that motivated McGivern and his colleagues. But when she heard the slave quietly surrender, Jane was taken by an irresistible urge to exploit. She remembered the woman's smile in the toy room and knew that, if she had given her a chance, then the slave would have subjected her to this sort of humiliation. While that was no real defence, it helped Jane assuage any guilt that could have coloured her mood.

'Bend over and let me slap your arse,' Jane whispered.

The slave did as she was asked. She turned her back on Jane and, without bending her knees, she reached down to touch her toes. Her hands stopped short of the floor and she circled her wrists around the fishnet-covered ankles.

Jane couldn't believe the submissive was acting on her instructions. In the toy room, the blonde had shown a confidence that Jane had found threatening. Now, the slave was responding to her commands as though this was the natural order of things. Her gaze was drawn to the blonde's backside and Jane marvelled at the sight. She had never looked at women in a sexual way before arriving at the castle, but the day had been a revelation in several uncharted pleasures and this was proving to be one of them. The slave's arse was a perfect moon. The cheeks were beautifully rounded, making Jane want to reach out and touch her. Her cleft was smooth and hairless, the lips of her sex seeming moist beneath the shade of her arse-cheeks.

Jane raised her hand over the slave's backside, opening her palm and preparing to slap. As she flexed her fingers, she could feel a delicious tingle warming her. The knowledge that she was dominating the slave – in the same way that Simon, McGivern and Frankie so effortlessly dominated their charges – brought a cruel smile to her lips. Comparing herself to the sexual predators who had intimidated her this morning left Jane feeling dizzy and excited at her own accomplishment.

She brought her hand down hard against the slave's backside. The slap echoed along the corridor like a pistol retort, far louder than the slave's responding groan. Jane felt the palm of her hand sting but knew that the discomfort would be far more intense on the blonde's backside. She raised her hand again and prepared to deliver a second blow. Staring down, she saw that the perfect impression of her hand was emblazoned in red across the blonde's right buttock. The mark looked as though it were stinging furiously and Jane wondered if the slave was enjoying the sensation of the red glow as much as she was enjoying the sight of it.

'What the hell is going on here?'

It was McGivern's voice and Jane turned to face him with a frightened expression. She still held her hand in the air and considered snatching it down in an attempt to conceal her actions. The blazing handprint she had left on the slave's arse would have been a more difficult matter to conceal and she discounted the idea of deceit before it had properly formed.

'Not that I need much of an explanation,' McGivern added amicably. He tested an easy smile on Jane and said, 'You really are developing quite a penchant for domination, aren't you? Would you mind if I gave you a few hints on how to perfect your technique?'

She swallowed and said a thankful prayer that he hadn't asked why she was outside his bedroom. 'Hints?'

He nodded, stepping past them both and unlocking the door to his bedroom. 'Hints,' he repeated, gesturing for them to enter. 'Tips, pointers, useful suggestions. Hints.'

Jane's thoughts were reeling. She hadn't wanted to encounter McGivern as she tried to find out more about him. As soon as she had heard his voice, she had prepared herself for his wrath. But, rather than appearing outraged or upset, he was being unnervingly genial.

He stood in the doorway, his easy smile appraising her as he held a welcoming arm into the room. Unable to refuse the offer without arousing his suspicion, Jane nodded and stepped inside. The slave followed.

McGivern's bedroom was the same vast size as the toy room, seeming more spacious because it wasn't cluttered with lewd paraphernalia and fiendish contraptions. The four-poster looked a lot larger than the one she had been given and Jane tried not to think why McGivern would need such a big bed.

'I showed you the best way to beat a slave this morning,' he began. 'But I don't think you were paying full attention.'

Jane blushed and said nothing.

McGivern told the blonde slave to kneel beside the bed as he began to unfasten his belt. Speaking to Jane, he said, 'I think you forgot an important lesson.'

She swallowed. Her unease was threatening to return and she prayed that it wasn't showing in her face. He had yet to ask her why she was chastising the slave, or what she had been doing outside his bedroom. If he received an honest answer to either of those questions, she doubted it would be the slave who received the sharp end of his wrath. 'What important lesson did I forget?'

'Punishment isn't just about slapping her backside. You've got to keep the slave excited. You have to remind her that's she's inferior. You have to remind her that she's there for your entertainment and nothing more. That's what keeps the slave excited and I've always found that an excited slave is a loyal slave.'

Jane blinked, surprised that he had developed his twisted philosophy into something that sounded almost charitable. She remained silent, knowing that her saying nothing would be sufficient encouragement for him to continue.

He slipped the belt from his waist and began to wind the buckled end around his fist. He stopped when there was an eighteen-inch length of leather dangling from his hand. Staring down at the hand print on the slave's arse, he grinned. 'You'd made a good start. That one's probably warming her quite well.'

Jane smiled, pleased by his flattering words.

'Did it hurt your hand?'

She flexed her fingers and nodded. 'A little.'

He was smiling and shaking his head at the same time. 'That's why I prefer to use this,' he said, holding up the end of his belt. Without a word of warning, he swept his hand back and slapped the end of the leather across the slave's bare arse.

Jane flinched from the sound.

The slave stiffened and groaned.

When Jane stared into McGivern's face, she saw that his smile was tinged with a lecherous glint. 'That punishes her,' he explained. 'But it doesn't hurt my hand. Why were you punishing her?'

Jane didn't dare to hesitate in replying. 'She wouldn't let me in here.' It wasn't enough of an answer and she could imagine him asking a dozen or more questions that would expose her surreptitious plans. 'I needed to find some of your paperwork to tie up a couple of loose ends for your file,' she added hastily. 'But she wouldn't let me into your room to get the documentation.' For a spur-of-the-moment lie, it sounded impressive to her own ears, but she knew that its true test would be McGivern's response.

He raised his belt again and hurled it sharply down.

Jane stiffened, fearful that the blow could be aimed at her.

The crack sounded harder than before and this time the slave released a dry shriek. Jane glanced at the woman's arse and saw the cheeks were sporting twin lines of burning crimson.

'You'll do as my solicitor says in future,' McGivern growled. 'Do you understand me?'

'Yes, master,' the slave whispered.

Jane knew she should have felt guilty – the slave had only been doing her job, and now she was being punished for it – yet Jane couldn't find the emotion in her body. Instead, she felt a warming heat between her legs as she enjoyed the slave's plight.

'But it's not just about punishment, is it?' McGivern had moved closer to Jane and his arm slid casually around her waist.

115

Jane tried not to stiffen in his embrace. 'How do you mean?'

'It's the excitement that motivates us all. Look at her and see just how excited she is.'

Jane didn't need to step closer to see what he meant. The lips of the slave's sex were sodden with arousal. Her shaved labia glistened wetly and her body trembled with anticipation.

'Touch her,' McGivern encouraged.

Jane tried not to think how exciting the suggestion was.

'You know you want to. You got off on it this morning, although I'd doubt you'd ever admit it. Go on and touch her.'

Jane blushed when he reminded her of the caning she had delivered in the banquet hall. It wasn't that she felt ashamed by the way she had behaved; she was simply unused to casually discussing intimate acts. The concept of talking freely about her gratuitous display in the hall left her feeling sick with embarrassment. If a burgeoning arousal hadn't been weighing on her thoughts she would have tried to change the subject. Stepping out of his embrace, she reached down and stroked her hand over the slave's pert buttocks. Her fingertips traced the raised stripes where the belt had sliced and the woman beneath her quivered.

'You could bring her off like *that*,' McGivern said, snapping his fingers for illustration. 'And that's the secret of being a good master. Always make sure your slave knows that you're in charge, and never let them know whether you're going to give them pain or pleasure.'

Jane's fingers continued to tease the red lines, unmindful of the slave's muttered protests. Each welt was a blazing exclamation on the peach-like skin of the submissive's backside. 'Why are you telling me all this?' Jane asked.

He shrugged, his eyes not meeting hers. 'Put a finger inside her, see how close she is to coming.'

Jane had wanted to do that anyway. She drew her hand over the buttocks, reaching towards the heat of the blonde's sex. The slippery wetness coated her finger as she started pushing inside the woman's warmth. With her face buried against the side of the bed, the slave's responding gasp was muffled but the sound was loud enough for Jane to hear. Her guttural tone and the clenching of her inner muscles told Jane that the slave was close to the point of orgasm.

'You didn't answer my question,' Jane reminded him. 'Why are you giving me a master class on domination?'

This time he did meet her eyes. 'You want an answer? You want the truth? OK. I'll tell you the truth. I didn't expect to be landed with you as a challenge this morning but, since that was one of Frankie's conditions, I had to concede. This is my way of breaking your indomitable spirit.'

Jane considered him doubtfully. 'What are you saying here? Do you think that I'm going to see how much the slaves are enjoying themselves and decide I want to try it for myself?'

He shrugged again. 'That idea had occurred to me, but I thought it was a little far-fetched. I'm trying to gain your confidence now.'

She studied him silently, surprised by how easy it was to treat him as an equal now that he was being honest with her.

'I can see you're getting into the role of being a dominatrix,' he explained. 'I figured that if I helped you to enjoy it more, you might be willing to help me in return.'

Jane frowned, beginning to grow confused. 'You think I'm going to do the dance of submission, just because you've shown me the proper way to leather this slave's backside?'

'Not just for that,' McGivern assured her.

'Then what else are you proposing?'

Now his eyes were set firmly on hers. 'I'm proposing a permanent arrangement. A permanent relationship that will benefit the pair of us.'

'You want me to be your permanent slave?' It was difficult to contain her outrage at the suggestion. 'You have to be kidding.'

He sighed, clearly exasperated. 'No, you dizzy bitch. I'm proposing that you enjoy yourself alongside me – as a fellow dominatrix.'

Stunned, Jane stared at him.

'You're new to sadomasochism but I can see that you're excited by it. I'm offering you the chance to explore all these new pleasures.'

It was a tempting proposition and Jane could feel herself drawn to accept it with a resounding yes. Her finger remained inside the blonde's pussy and she slid it in and out with an absent hand. Her concentration was fixed on McGivern while she contemplated his offer. The slave's grateful sighs went unheard as she tried to decide what to do. 'You want me to live here with you?'

'Live here if you like, or treat the place as a holiday home. The castle is more than large enough to cope with two dominatrices – this bet has proved it can accommodate three. All these pleasure could be yours, for you to enjoy whenever you want. All I'm asking is one small favour.'

The slave's sighs turned into a groan. Unconsciously, Jane worked her finger faster against the submissive's sex. She slipped her index and middle fingers together so she could penetrate the girl with a wider girth. The pressure of the quivering inner walls tightened around Jane's hand and the slave began to shiver.

McGivern's gaze was locked on hers. 'All I'm asking is that you do the dance for me.'

Jane stared at him, wishing she could decide how to respond. It was a very tempting offer and, for the first time since she had learnt of the dance, she realised she wasn't repulsed by the chance to participate. It was already beginning to look like a small price to pay for all the pleasures that McGivern could introduce her to.

'You still have to finish punishing that one,' McGivern reminded her. 'Maybe that will help you to make your decision.'

Jane glanced down and saw she had been frigging the blonde as they spoke. The fact that she had been performing such an intimate act and calmly holding her own in the conversation was already threatening to sway her response. Her thoughts were tumbling madly as she tried to decide if this was what she really wanted, and if the price was worth paying.

'Lick this clean,' she said. She had tugged her hand from the blonde's sex and pushed it towards her mouth.

The blonde rubbed a greedy tongue against her fingers. She lapped her own juice from Jane's hand, clearly relishing the flavour as she removed every last droplet.

'She'll do anything you ask of her,' McGivern said confidently. 'You could slap her arse for a count of one hundred and she'd happily accept it. You could ask her to suck me off, or go down on you, and she'd do whatever you said.'

Jane drew an excited breath, finding all of his ideas appealing. She had never felt a woman's tongue against her pussy but now that the suggestion was voiced, she had a maddening urge to experience it. 'And I could enjoy this every day, if I simply do the dance for you?'

He nodded. 'You could enjoy it whenever you wanted, from whichever side of the coin you decided to land on. You seemed to get some pleasure when I brought the belt across your arse this morning.'

Jane blushed but she didn't lower her gaze from his.

'And you look to be getting a lot of pleasure from doing that,' he observed. 'Whichever aspect appeals to you, you can enjoy it here at the castle, whenever the mood takes you.'

Jane didn't bother giving the suggestion any more thought. She began to shrug the jacket from her shoulders, preparing to make herself comfortable so she could properly dominate the slave. He was offering her an irresistible opportunity and she knew that it would be madness to spend another moment trying to find a reason to say no. She considered telling McGivern her answer straight away, then decided it would be more fitting for a dominatrix to stretch the moment out. He could sweat for a while as he waited for her answer and, at the same time, she could enjoy the slave's submission.

She was unfastening her blouse as the jacket fell to the floor and she was only distantly aware that something had fallen from one of the pockets. It seemed unimportant and she made a mental note to retrieve whatever it was later on. Her attention was focused on the slave's bare arse and the myriad different ways she could deliver punishment.

McGivern picked up the card from the floor and studied it thoughtfully. His frown darkened as he read the text. When he raised his eyes to meet hers, he was glaring angrily. 'This is the faggot's card. It just fell out of your pocket. Would you mind telling me what the hell it was doing there?' His genial tone had evaporated. Now he was speaking to her in the same brusque manner that he reserved for unruly slaves.

Jane stared at him, lost for words. She thought of giving him an honest answer, and then realised that would only worsen his blackening mood. If she told him what Simon had suggested, it would sound as though she was already in his employ and she doubted McGivern would respond well to that.

'I want an answer, Jane, and I'm losing my patience. Why have you got the faggot's business card in your pocket?' He took a step towards Jane's side and glared at her menacingly.

It was unsettling to see the transformation of his features. When he had been offering her a place as his equal, he had seemed approachable and pleasantly exciting. Now he looked like a man who was struggling to control the most violent of urges.

Jane shook her head, her throat closing wordlessly as she searched for some words that might appease him. Her mouth was open but nothing came out as she stared into his ominous scowl.

He grabbed hold of her hair and pulled her face close to his. 'I'm beginning to have my doubts about you,' he hissed. 'First I catch you abusing one of my slaves. Then you give me some cock and bull story about coming down here to tidy up my affairs. And now I find this in your pocket.'

He held the card in front of her eyes, then flicked it away. It spun like a frisbee, disappearing into a shadowy corner of the room. As she watched it fall into the gloom, Jane could see her hopes vanishing with it.

'I think you and I need to have a little honesty,' he growled. With one hand, he reached out for the blonde slave and pushed her away. She took heed of his wordless instruction and moved quietly from the side of the bed. Her eyes were wide and shining with anticipation as she stared at them and, in that expression, Jane could see the fate that awaited her.

'No,' Jane whispered. It was the first word she had managed to mutter since his mood had changed and her throat was so dry it hurt to speak.

Not listening, he pushed her on to the bed and slashed his belt through the air. Its shriek was harsh before it bit the mattress beside her leg. Wishing the idea hadn't entered her head, Jane wondered how loud her own shriek would have been if the tip had landed two inches to the left. The image was so unsettling she felt exhilarated. Her breath came in stammering gasps.

'We need to have a little honesty,' McGivern told her. 'And I know just the way to get it from you.'

Jane swallowed the nervous lump in her throat. 'What are you going to do?'

'I'm going to beat you until you tell me why you had Simon's card,' he explained simply.

'No. I . . .'

He didn't let her finish. 'It's what you've been needing since I brought you in here. And you can forget my offer of a permanent relationship. I don't think you'll be bothered about that little incentive, once I've finished.' He paused and released a bark of chilling laughter. 'I think that, by the end of the day, you'll look on the dance of submission as a reward.'

Seven

The three of them sat around the east keep's banquet table, drinking wine and finishing the last of their broccoli and brie en croute. The windows were blackened by the night outside and Sally could see their reflections caught in the opaque pane. Their meal was illuminated by a combination of candlelight on the table and the burning torches on the walls. There were light switches by the doors, as well as fixtures and fittings overhead, but Simon had elected to use the more traditional torches. Sally wondered if he was trying to recreate the erotic gloom of the dungeon, then discounted that as being too fanciful. Surely, she told herself, not even Simon could be that manipulative.

The dancing flames brightened the room and Sally hoped the constant flicker would be enough to mask the livid frowns she was turning on both of the men. She glared at Simon, angry that he had sought her out and repeated his invitation for dinner in front of her boyfriend. Then she glared at Carl, annoyed that he had accepted for them both without consulting her.

'You two make a lovely couple.' Simon grinned.

Sally blushed and wafted his compliment away with an uncomfortable hand. It had to have been the hundredth time this evening that Simon had said something similar and she was beginning to grow weary of it. Carl's cheeks had turned crimson and he studied his half-eaten meal rather than responding.

'You really do,' Simon insisted. He spoke as though

their silence had been a denial. 'You look like you were made for one another.'

'Please,' Sally told him. 'You're embarrassing us. Let's talk about something else.'

'Such as?'

She shrugged. He had already discounted most of the topics that she had suggested.

Carl glanced up from his plate, beaming as though he had been struck by a bright idea. 'There was a rumour that this place previously belonged to some sort of sexual sadist,' he told them both. 'Elle says she read a history that mentioned this place and apparently it was built by a dominatrix.'

'You've been talking with the slutty foreign exchange student again?' Sally studied him quietly as she asked the question, barely containing her jealousy.

Carl shrugged. 'Elle was only saying that this place has seen some times.'

'You shouldn't even be talking to her,' Sally warned him. 'She has claws.'

'How charming,' Simon murmured. 'The pair of you can argue as well. That is so matrimonial.'

Carl and Sally glared at him.

'Can we talk about something other than the boring history of this place?' Simon asked, shaking his wine glass at the surrounding banquet hall.

Carl glanced at him and said, 'Do you want us to tell you about the discoveries we've made on the dig?'

'The sand pit that you're playing with in the corner of the courtyard?' Simon snorted and made a disgusted face. 'I'd rather not talk about that. It looks so fucking boring, you'll probably send me to sleep. How long have you known one another?'

Sally groaned and looked away.

'We've been together a couple of years,' Carl told him. 'We met on our first day at uni.'

'And you're still very much in love, aren't you?

'Very much,' Sally said stiffly. 'Although we don't like to talk about it.' If he was trying to provoke a response from

123

her, she thought, he was going the right way about it. The idea that he might tell Carl what had happened in the dungeon weighed heavily on her mind. Throughout the meal, his hints about their morning had been growing broader and she dreaded the repercussions if Simon went too far and said something indelicate. Carl was a typical man with all the inherent double-standards of his sex. In his mind, she knew it was acceptable for him to go chasing after Elle, the slutty foreign exchange student, but he would never tolerate his girlfriend's brush with infidelity.

'Do you know how you can tell when a couple are very much in love?' Simon asked.

'You ask them again and again and again and again?' Sally replied bluntly.

Simon shook his head. 'You find out if they know one another.'

Sally frowned, sure he was trying to lead the conversation somewhere and growing increasingly uncomfortable with the direction.

'Can I give you two an example? Are you up for a little party game?'

Sally wanted to say no but Carl had replied before she could manage the word.

'Sure,' Carl grinned. 'What the hell?'

Sally glared at him.

'Great stuff,' Simon said, winking cheerfully. He climbed out of his chair and clapped his hands, encouraging them to stand up.

Carl stepped quickly from his seat, dropping his cutlery to the plate with an embarrassing clatter. The noise made Sally flinch as she slowly dragged herself out of her chair. If she had not felt so light-headed, she might have thought he acted like a man who was anxious to participate in Simon's game. However, she had gone through more wine than she intended and Carl's eagerness for after-dinner entertainment was the least of her worries. She was suddenly nervous that she had drunk too much and that thought unsettled her as she considered Simon's playfulness and Carl's peculiar mood.

Before the evening had begun, she had expected Carl to be scornful of Simon. At the university, she had heard him say the most callous things about a fellow student, just because the guy had been wearing a pink shirt. Carl made homophobic remarks about anyone who didn't watch or play rugby, and he had a vocabulary of three words for men who dressed and spoke like Simon. Usually, the only way to shut him up was to remind him that the most vehement homophobes were trying to conceal the true nature of their own sexuality.

But Carl seemed to be enjoying Simon's genial company and he hadn't made any of the crass comments that Sally had expected of him. Thinking about it through a haze of Chardonnay, Sally knew that she was the only one threatening to spoil the mood of the evening.

'Stand there,' Simon said, pointing. 'Back to back, with your shoulder-blades and buttocks touching.' He walked around them as he gave the instructions, winking at Sally and heightening her unease. 'Don't be uncomfortable. It's not a new sexual position, or an excuse for me to steal your wine.'

Reluctantly, Sally stood as he had told her, pressing herself against the comforting weight of Carl's back. That afternoon, she and Carl had made love and, if she concentrated, she knew she could revisit the moment, but she didn't dare to. She still felt guilty about it. The moment had started off as a passionless affair and, although she hadn't thought about it too deeply, Sally felt sure she had been submitting to make up for her sins in the dungeon.

Carl had made a handful of lewd suggestions to her, a matter of course for him as the day progressed. He had been holding her intimately and she had suggested they go back to their camp beds in the south keep. It wasn't that she particularly wanted to make love to Carl at that moment, and she told herself that it wasn't because Simon's teasing had left her with an unsated need – although, because of McGivern's untimely interruption, it had. She and Carl had crept off to the sleeping quarters and Sally had allowed him to take her.

She was still regretting every second of it. Carl was a tremendous lover with a thick cock and an ability to please that was a fortuitous by-product of his own greedy appetite. But, this afternoon, it had been different.

When Carl began to caress her, Sally found her mind was back in the dungeon. When she closed her eyes, her lover was Simon, not Carl: and it hadn't helped that Carl was trying to excite her by whispering her fantasies.

In a passionate growl, he told her he could picture her being fucked by two men. The concept and the foul language normally fired Sally's darker passions and hurled her towards the brink of climax. It was her favourite erotic scenario and, whenever they had shared the idea previously, her orgasms had followed swiftly. But today she was left remembering how close she had come to fulfilling that goal, without Carl being there. That thought left her feeling cold and unhappy beneath his lovemaking and on other occasions she would have asked him to stop. If she hadn't felt the need to make up for her sins in the dungeon, she would have eased herself from beneath him and apologised for her sudden disinterest.

Instead, and she still hated herself for it, Sally closed her eyes and used him.

After Carl had taken her to orgasm she concentrated hard, so as not to call him Simon when she smothered him with her grateful embrace. It was a difficult trick to manage and, on a couple of occasions, she had stammered back a sibilant as she stared lovingly into his eyes.

'Marvellous,' Simon enthused.

His words snatched Sally away from her memories and back to the room.

'Now, this is a simple test: and with you two being so much in love, I'm sure that you'll pass it with flying colours. You can't see one another, can you?'

'No,' they told him in unison.

'Good. And there's no turning your heads,' Simon went on. 'It's the only rule to this game, so I don't expect either of you to disobey it.' Simon was out of her vision now. She guessed he was standing in front of Carl but, with her eyes fixed forward, she couldn't be certain.

'Which part of Carl's body am I touching?' Simon asked.

Sally could hear the dull pulse in her temples. She was thankful Carl couldn't see her face, because she knew he would sense something was wrong from the depth of her blush. She swallowed and wondered if she should ask Simon to repeat what he had just said, sure that she couldn't have heard him correctly. If this was the type of game he had been planning, she didn't want to participate. Throughout the evening, she had been deliberately avoiding physical contact with Simon. The morning had escalated quickly from a platonic hug to bondage and cunnilingus. While it hadn't been unpleasurable, Sally didn't think that Carl would want to watch her endure a repeat performance.

'It's a little test that I've seen work quite well in the past,' Simon explained. 'When a couple are really close, they can sense things about one another. If you know Carl as well as you think you do, you'll be able to tell me which part of his body is being touched. Come on, Sally. Tell me which part of his body I'm touching?'

Sally drew a weary breath. 'You're touching his arm,' she replied. 'But I didn't sense that. I can feel the lacy cuff of your shirt brushing against my sleeve.'

'What a sensitive woman you are!' Simon exclaimed.

The atmosphere between the three of them was growing steadily intense and Sally found it impossible to stop her thoughts from following crude tangents. In her mind's eye, she could picture Simon and Carl touching one another far more intimately: and, even though the image was ludicrous, it fixed itself firmly in her thoughts. Trying to shake the idea from her mind, she said, 'Can we sit down now? This is beginning to bore me.'

'No you can't sit down,' Simon told her. 'And you're not allowed to be bored. This game is far too exciting for anyone to be bored while playing it.' He came into her vision, his eyes shining as he stepped closer. 'Tell me, Carl.' He was staring at Sally as he spoke. 'Which part of your girlfriend am I touching?'

Sally saw his fingers snake out in the direction of her breast. She tried to draw away from him and then realised she couldn't move without calling Carl's attention to her reaction. She held her breath and fixed Simon with a threatening frown.

Simon continued to grin. Instead of touching her chest, his hand hovered over one orb, then moved down and went to her hip. With his other hand, he held a silencing finger against his lips. Their gazes were locked and his eyes shone with a wicked sparkle. Slowly, he moved his silencing finger towards her mouth and passed a discreet kiss to her lips.

Sally held her breath, glaring at him.

Simon moved his finger away and squeezed her hip. 'Well, Carl?' he asked. 'Which part of her body am I touching?'

'You're touching her hip,' he said. Sally could feel the vibration of his words through their touching backs. 'But, like Sal, I didn't know that from sensing it. Those fancy shirt cuffs of yours gave the game away.'

'Damn my marvellous wardrobe,' Simon said, with mock dismay. 'For the sakes of integrity in this game, I shall make a great sacrifice and remove my shirt.'

'You don't have to do that,' Sally said quickly. She was already feeling giddy with the threat of unwanted arousal and she knew that the sight of Simon without his shirt would only add to those feelings.

Simon's smile was reassuring. 'I have faith in the pair of you. I'm sure you'll both be able to contain yourselves when my magnificent torso is revealed.'

Sally could feel Carl's laughter through the muscles of his back and she suppressed the urge to give his calf a sobering kick. Simon was making her distinctly uncomfortable and Carl seemed oblivious to this.

Simon slid the shirt over his head and hurled it on to the banquet table. He threw his shoulders back and pushed his chest forward, preening in front of her. It was an annoyingly impressive sight, she conceded. His body wasn't overly muscular but his chest and arms had the athletic appearance of a man who regularly worked out. Like his chest, his flat stomach was hairless and Sally thought his skin had the pampered sheen that came from cosmetic waxing. He certainly seemed vain enough and she doubted that he would be troubled by the stigma of effeminacy that was attached to such beauty treatments.

'There,' Simon said, stroking his hand against his own chest. 'My faith in you two was well placed. I knew you'd be able to contain yourselves.'

'I'm really getting bored with this,' Sally told him, wishing that was true. The sight of his bared chest had ignited a flame between her legs and she was wilfully trying to ignore it. 'Why don't you let Carl and I finish our wine? Then we can go back to the south keep.'

'You're not getting bored with it,' Simon countered. 'You're just impatient to hold your boyfriend and embrace him, the way lovers do.' He winked and said, 'Don't worry. There'll be plenty of time for that sort of game later on.'

He stepped out of her vision and she was left to stare at the walls and windows as she contemplated the remark.

'Where am I touching now?' Simon asked.

His words sounded slightly muffled and Sally frowned. She tried to throw herself into the spirit of the game, but it was a foolish exercise. There was really no way she could know where he was touching her boyfriend. Her concentration on the game only emphasised her feelings of stupidity for participating.

'Come on, Sally,' Simon encouraged.

Simon's voice was still muffled and she studied the empty surroundings in search of inspiration. She glanced into the opaque surface of the window and stifled a gasp of surprise. It had to be a trick of the flickering lights, she told herself. The dancing flames, stirred by some unseen breeze, were playing games with the reflections in the night blackened pane. For one crazy instant it had looked as though Simon was leaning forward and kissing Carl on the lips.

'Where am I touching him?' Simon pressed.

She blinked and glanced back at the reflective glass

129

realising it had been an optical illusion. Simon was standing close to Carl, but she could see that their faces weren't touching. The image had just been another symptom of the unease she had suffered all evening. 'I don't know,' she exploded. Trying to shock him with the most outrageous thing she could think of, Sally said, 'You're touching his cock.'

'How very perceptive,' Simon replied. He returned to her field of vision and said, 'I told you that you were good at this game.'

Sally studied him, her cheeks flushing hotly as she tried to see if there was any grain of truth in his words. Of course, she knew that Carl wouldn't allow himself to be touched like that and, while it had looked like the pair were kissing, she doubted the reflection had been a true one. She resisted the urge to hurl suspicious questions at the two men, sure that would cause the damaging revelation she had been dreading throughout the evening.

'Do you think Carl will be able to guess where I'm touching you?'

Sally continued to glare at him. 'Do you think I care?'

He was unaffected by her hostility. He stood so close, she could smell the subtle fragrance of his warm body. He wasn't wearing any perfume or cologne and she was treated to the scent of his clean, fresh sweat. His fingers reached out to tease a mousy brown curl away from her cheek and then his hand moved lower.

Sally expected him to tease a hand over her breast, threatening to touch her as he had before. She watched his hand hover above the swell of her orb and she tried not to let her nervousness show. She knew Simon was using the game to make her feel uncomfortable and his threat to touch her breast was a hollow one. In this situation, with her rugby-playing boyfriend only inches away, Sally knew he wouldn't have the nerve to caress her properly. Defiantly, she held Simon's gaze, waiting for an asexual caress on her leg, arm or side.

He placed his fingers around her breast and squeezed.

Sally drew a shocked breath.

Simon worked his fingers against her, massaging the orb through the fabric of her top and teasing the stiffening nipple beneath. 'Where am I touching her, Carl?'

Sally could feel her cheeks colouring. Her body was responding to his fingers, as though this was what she had been wanting all evening. Vainly, she tried to assure herself that it wasn't.

'I can't tell,' Carl said. 'Is it her side?'

Sally closed her eyes and tried to wish herself away from the situation. To be fondled by another man while she was so close to Carl would have seemed like a dream come true, in different circumstances. The scenario had all the elements of the fantasy she had entertained for a long time, but this was all wrong. If Carl found out what Simon was doing . . .

Sally shivered, not allowing her mind to conclude the thought.

'You're getting warm,' Simon grinned. 'Think about it and guess again. Perhaps it will help if we all concentrate really hard.'

Sally tried to draw herself away but Simon wasn't allowing her to move and Carl's back was as resolute as a brick wall. It wasn't that his touch was unpleasant. Being honest with herself, she thought he had perfected his technique of breast massage since he had teased her on the rack that morning – and he had been bloody good then. Her nipple was tingling as though it was receiving a delightful electric shock and the sensation inspired other needs in more sensitive parts of her body.

It was just that his timing was absurdly wrong. If Carl discovered what Simon was doing, Sally knew there would be repercussions and she felt sure they would be unpleasant. She raised a hand, to try and move Simon's fingers away but his grip was unyielding.

'Give me your answer, Carl,' Simon said, 'or you lose the first point.'

'Her stomach,' Carl said quickly. 'You're touching her stomach.'

Simon made a surprised sound. 'You two are very good

131

at this game,' he exclaimed. 'I've never known two players who are so in tune with one another.'

Sally's thoughts were reeling. She wondered if Simon was saying this for her benefit, his own or Carl's. He hadn't been touching her stomach. His fingers had been teasing the hardening nub of her nipple and they still lingered there as proof. His fingertips seemed to emit electric pulses and her breasts responded to each subtle tremor of pleasure.

Ignoring the build-up of arousal, she wondered if Simon had been lying when he said he was touching Carl's cock. Seeing Simon's deception now confirmed that her suspicions had been correct, but she still couldn't understand why he was lying. If her thoughts hadn't been so wine-fogged, Sally felt sure she would have had a better understanding of what was happening. Instead, the not knowing seemed as difficult to comprehend as a mensa challenge written in a foreign language.

Simon snatched his hand from her breast and disappeared again. 'I'll have to change the rules a little, now. You're both too good for playing it that way.'

Sally wanted to say no. Whatever else Simon was planning, she didn't want to be a part of it. She stopped herself from voicing the word, sure that arousal would be audible in her tone.

'I'm going to place your hand against a part of my body and the other will have to say which part of me is being touched.'

Carl was chuckling. The vibrations echoed through her body and Sally wondered if she should relent and try to enjoy the stupidity of this game. If it hadn't been for the fear of Carl learning about her morning in the dungeon, she felt sure she would already be laughing and joking along with the two men.

'Where is Carl touching me, Sally?'

'Your head,' she said with a shrug.

'How do you two manage this?' Simon asked.

He appeared in front of her again and took hold of her arm. Holding her fingers firmly, he guided her hand between his legs.

Sally tried to ignore the heat of his erection in her palm. She wanted to move her fingers away from him but she knew that such a reaction would make trouble and that was the last thing she wanted.

'You're holding his cock?' Carl guessed. He chuckled again, as if to show them both how preposterous this idea was.

Sally glared at Simon, willing him not to incite a scene by responding truthfully.

By way of reply, Simon rubbed her palm firmly against his stiff bulge.

She didn't know if it was her own eagerness, or the way his hand held her fingers, but she could feel every nuance of his rigid flesh. The PVC trousers allowed her to touch him as though he was wearing nothing more concealing than a condom.

'Am I right?' Carl asked. 'Is that where she's touching?'

'Of course you're right,' Simon said. 'I wasn't ignoring you. I was just waiting for her to finish me off.'

Sally tried to snatch her hand away. Carl's back moved from hers and she knew he was going to catch her in the act of touching another man. She struggled to release her fingers from Simon's grip but he held her firmly against himself.

'My God!' Carl exclaimed. 'It's true! You are holding his cock.'

'You've had your turn,' Simon snapped. 'Don't make the poor girl feel guilty for doing what you've just done.'

Simon released his grip on her hand and Sally pulled her fingers away. She stared from Carl to Simon, trying to work out what was happening. She had expected Carl to be livid but, aside from his theatrical outburst, he seemed in a surprisingly good mood. Simon's words were also unsettling because they were delivered with such a ring of truth. She glanced from one to the other, more puzzled than she wanted to admit.

Carl couldn't keep up the pretence any longer. He began to laugh, then threw a comforting arm around her shoulder. 'Relax, Sal. Simon and I have just been teasing you a little.'

'The same way I teased you in the dungeon this morning,' Simon explained.

She tried to silence him with a glare but his words were already spoken. She glanced at Carl, still fearful of the anger he would display.

'Don't worry,' Simon told her. 'I teased Carl exactly the same way, an hour after that. He seemed to get an awful lot out of it.'

She couldn't decide whether to be angry or amused. 'You two?'

'I thought you weren't going to tell her about that.' Carl sounded put out by the revelation.

Simon sniffed, as though he was offended by the idea of such a deception. 'I don't mind encouraging you two to be unfaithful to one another, but I won't condone lying.'

'Why didn't you tell me?' Sally demanded.

Carl shrugged. 'We thought you might get more of a kick out of this.'

'You bastard.'

'Careful,' Carl warned her. His grin was threatening to evaporate. 'If you're rude, Simon and I might forget the rest of the evening we have planned for you.'

She was untroubled by the discovery that Simon and Carl had become intimate. It would have upset her more if her boyfriend had been with the slutty foreign exchange student. The thought of Simon and Carl being together seemed less like an act of infidelity and more like an incident of laddishness. She studied Carl quizzically. 'The rest of what evening? What have you two been planning?'

'Carl was telling me about one of your fantasies, Sally.' Simon reached for her left breast and cupped it casually. Carl reached for her right orb and the two men held her simultaneously. They were both smiling as their fingertips kneaded her flesh. 'Carl says that you've always fancied trying to accommodate two lovers. Is that true?'

Blushing furiously, Sally nodded. There was little point in appearing prudish with the pair. Carl already knew her most intimate secrets and Simon had come close to discovering some of them, that morning. Switching her

134

gaze from one to the other, she sensed that she was close to the achievement of that secret goal and she found the idea exhilarating. Her unease began to dissipate as she realised the three of them were intent on the same course.

'If that's really your fantasy, then Carl and I have planned an unforgettable night for you,' Simon explained. 'It's time for you to relax and start enjoying it.'

As each of the men rubbed their thumbs over her stiff buds, Sally's reluctance disappeared. She knew that there were two choices available to her. She could either protest about the indecent suggestion and leave, or submit herself to whatever the pair had been plotting. She knew that if she went with the first option, she would spend a lonely night in the south keep whiling away the sleepless hours with torturous thoughts about what might have been. At least if she stayed, she could discover if the reality measured up to her dreams. With that decadent thought colouring her mood, she allowed the pleasure to start coursing through her body and prepared herself for the further joys that the night would reveal.

Simon took the lead, helping her out of her top. He slipped it over her head, hurling it on to the banquet table as he lowered his mouth to her left breast. Carl pushed his mouth over her right and she was treated to the thrill of having both men tease her nipples with their tongues. While Carl held her bare back to steady himself, Simon was exploring her body with more inquisitive caresses. His fingers reached down to her thighs and he began to stroke his hands upward.

'What made you plan something like this?' she asked, her voice made husky with excitement.

'You shouldn't ask questions like that,' Simon told her. 'Isn't it enough that we all want to drink our pleasure from the same source, this evening? Isn't it enough that we're all desperate for one another and headed for satisfaction?'

Sally shivered, unsure if it was the words or the caresses that left her trembling.

'Besides,' Carl broke in, 'it was mainly Simon's idea.'

Simon moved his mouth from her breast and grinned

sheepishly at her. 'I thought that if I did you a favour, perhaps you could do one for me.' His hand had reached the top of her legs and he teased the gusset of her panties with his fingertip.

Another delightful tremor tickled through her body. 'What sort of favour?'

'We can talk about that later on,' Simon said, moving his mouth over hers.

Their kiss was an intimate exchange, made more satisfying because it was so yearned for. Since her first day at uni, when she and Carl had become lovers, Sally had found herself fantasising about a moment like this. Her boyfriend had his head lowered to her breast and he was teasing the nipple with his teeth and lips. At the same moment, she was kissing a virtual stranger, allowing him to explore her mouth with his tongue and preparing to give herself to him as fully as any woman could give herself to a man.

'Are you always this excited?' Simon asked. He was toying with the wetness between her legs and she could feel his fingers were already soaked with her need.

'Under these circumstances, I suppose I could be,' Sally replied.

He began to kiss her again.

Carl was using his hands where Simon had left off. He caressed her inner thighs, teasing at the gusset of her panties and tickling the sensitive crease of skin beside her sex. Simon's fingers were kneading her free breast and Sally gave herself over to the moment.

'I can make this a lot more fun for the pair of you if you follow my instructions,' Simon decided. 'Are you both game?'

'We are,' Carl told him.

Once again, Sally knew that Carl was responding without consulting her, but this time it didn't matter. She was happy to go along with Carl's decision on this occasion, sure that Simon would know exactly how to please her. He had a way about him that left her in no doubt he would be a capable lover. Although he hadn't said as much, she suspected that he had been in liaisons like this before and she was happy to draw on his experience. She pushed her face towards his again, eager to feel the excitement that was generated by his lips against hers.

Simon stepped out of her arms, distancing himself from the pair. 'Sally, I want you to undress Carl.'

She nodded and began to snatch at the buttons on Carl's shirt.

'Slowly,' Simon instructed. 'There's no sense in rushing it, is there?'

She forced herself to show some restraint. Her libido was insisting that she act quickly, but she was determined to do as Simon asked. An evening of unparalleled bliss lay ahead and she knew that obeying Simon's instruction was going to be the first step towards that pleasure. She helped Carl out of his shirt and started to unfasten the belt from his jeans.

'Suck his nipple first.'

Sally inhaled, excited by the way he was barking commands. She moved her mouth over Carl's chest and teased the tiny nub between her lips. Carl stiffened against her and she heard Simon's appreciative groan. There was something in the timbre of his sigh that sounded as though he was experiencing the pleasure, rather than just watching it.

'Now the other one.'

Simon tapped the cheek of her backside as he gave the command and Sally felt her excitement intensify. She began to suck the other nipple as echoes of arousal scorched through her body.

'Take his trousers off,' Simon encouraged. His mouth had moved close to her ear and she prepared herself for his kiss against her neck. Instead, he moved his fingers to her bared breasts and began to fondle them as he stood behind her. She reached forward to take Carl's trousers off, and pressed her buttocks back against Simon's erection. He was still wearing his PVC trousers but his hardness was unmistakeable against the cleft of her arse. He rocked his pelvis to and fro, thrusting his restrained length against her concealed pussy-lips. At the same time, he rolled her nipples between his fingers and thumbs.

Her hands were fumbling to manage Carl's belt and she knew that the task was only made difficult because Simon was exciting her so much. His embrace was the perfect charade for a doggy-style knee-trembler. With the added stimulation of Carl's encouraging smile, Sally felt incapable of the simple task of undressing her boyfriend. She struggled on with her attempt, wishing it wasn't so challenging. Simon's rigid shaft was sparking a delicious friction against the lips of her sex. Even though they were still hidden beneath her skirt and panties, she could feel her labia burning with a desperate need for him.

'There,' Simon exclaimed as she pulled Carl's jeans down to his ankles. 'You managed it. Don't you think you deserve a reward?'

She turned in his embrace, pushing her mouth towards his. 'What are you planning, Simon?' Her breathless tone belied her eagerness. 'What have you got in store for me?'

'I've told you. I'm planning to make this night memorable for you.'

She smothered his face with kisses, arousal hastening her need. 'And what will you want in return? What's the favour you mentioned?'

'All in good time,' he told her. 'Let's deal with your needs first. Carl's cock looks in need of a good sucking. Do you think you can manage that?'

She turned and knelt in the same motion, eager to do exactly as Simon asked. Her mouth encircled Carl's erection and she began to slide her lips up and down.

'Push your arse up in the air while you do that,' Simon told her. 'I want to play with it.'

The instruction was a potent aphrodisiac, sending a quiver through the lips of her sex. She shifted awkwardly on the floor, not daring to move her mouth from Carl's cock as she adopted the position that Simon had said. As she pushed her backside high for him, she raised and lowered her head on to Carl's erection. He was leaking

138

pre-come and she could taste the salty flavour coating her tongue. She greedily swallowed his excitement, wondering how Simon's seed would taste when she got the chance to experience it.

'What a lovely arse,' Simon told her. He was stroking his fingers over her skirt, tracing the outline of her buttocks with the tips of his fingernails. There was a cool draught, and then his finger was touching the bare flesh at the top of her legs. Knowing that he was looking at the sodden gusset of her panties added another spur to Sally's arousal. She sucked harder on Carl's length, massaging his balls with one hand as she rolled his foreskin up and down with the other.

Simon traced his finger along the elasticated band of her panties, gently tugging the garment away from her. There was the warmth of his breath against her lower back, and then he was kissing the line of flesh where her panties had been. His kisses went lower as he tugged the pants away and Sally stifled the urge to cry out as his tongue neared her anus.

'Perfect, Sal.'

She glanced up at Carl, pleased and encouraged by his praise. The excitement was a phenomenal experience and she cursed the inhibitions that had stopped her from trying this before. Her entire body was rippling with waves of pleasure. If she had suspected the reality could be a tenth as satisfying as this evening promised to be, Sally knew she would have tried it on her second day at uni.

The panties were tugged from her buttocks and she felt Simon place a kiss against the centre of her sex. His cool lips touched her febrile flesh and she bristled.

'You are desperate, aren't you?' he observed. He was testing her wetness and she arched her back as she felt the intrusion. His finger slid easily inside, tickling her inner muscles until she felt giddy. The slippery friction was delicious against her heat. Caught up in the heady eroticism of the moment, Sally wondered if sex had ever felt so incredible before.

Carl groaned and she felt his cock stiffen in her mouth.

Using a practised hand, she circled her fingers around the base of his shaft, delaying his orgasm until she was ready for it. She knew that prolonging the moment for all of them would make their pleasure more intense.

'My finger isn't good enough for this task,' Simon decided, drawing his hand away from her sex-lips. 'I'm going to have to use something else on you, Sally.'

Sucking harder on Carl's shaft, she stifled her responding cry and braced her buttocks in anticipation. Her hand squeezed tighter around Carl's girth and she savoured the flavour of his arousal.

'How long have you dreamt of this moment, Sally?'

'A long time,' she conceded. She moved her mouth away from Carl's erection to speak and saw that his length was silver with a mix of saliva and pre-come. The lips of her labia were being teased by the dome-like end of Simon's shaft and Sally sensed that his penetration was only a whisper away. The moment was so long-awaited that she felt sure it would prove to be an anticlimax and she tried preparing herself for the inevitable disappointment. In a terse whisper, she told him, 'I've waited a long time.'

'Then wait no longer,' Simon declared. 'Your dream is about to come true.' He held her hips and pushed himself into her. His cock slid along her sodden hole, stretching and filling her as he thrust deep inside.

It wasn't the anticlimax she had been dreading. If anything, the sensations he inspired were more ferocious than she had dared hope. His shaft was incredibly broad, stretching her more than Carl was able to. She could have given herself over to the thrill of the orgasm in that instant, and she knew it would have been overwhelming. Instead, she steeled herself against it, determined to suck the orgasm out of Carl and squeeze it out of Simon in the same moment.

'You feel divine,' Simon told her.

'Yeah,' Carl agreed, his words carried by a breathless grunt. 'Better than that, even. Perfect.'

She felt giddy, her pleasure enhanced by their flattering words. Simon rode into her at an unhurried pace, his fingers stroking lovingly against her hips and sides. He teased his hand over the mound of her arse and his fingertip touched against her arsehole. The sensation was so intimate, she felt herself being forced closer to the inevitable release.

'Change positions, Sally,' Simon instructed. 'I don't think we've quite fulfilled your fantasy yet, have we?'

She moved her mouth away from Carl's shaft and glanced over her shoulder to study Simon. 'Which part of my fantasy were you thinking of fulfilling?'

His smile was salacious. 'We were thinking of fulfilling every part.'

She snatched the lips of her sex away from him and turned between her two lovers. Thrusting her backside out for Carl's attention, Sally fell hungrily on to Simon's cock. Her mouth worked its way up and down and she savoured the flavour of pussy-juice that still lingered on him.

Carl worked quickly behind her, positioning his cock between her legs and preparing to push himself forward. The head of his shaft nuzzled her pussy lips, and then he raised it higher. The bulbous dome pressed at her anus and she readied herself for his entry. If Carl was going to help totally fulfil her fantasy, Sally knew that he had to slide himself up her arse.

She worked her mouth faster on Simon's length, sucking hard, and wetting him with her tongue. Her excitement was quickly mounting and she didn't want either of the two men to think that she was neglecting them when she became lost in the realms of bliss.

Carl pushed his cock forward and the rim of her anus was stretched as he began to make his forbidden penetration. Her pulse raced faster and harder with every nudge of the shaft at her sphincter. Her pussy-lips still tingled from the pleasure of having had Simon's cock and the rest of her body trembled with mounting elation. Each time one of them stroked a loving hand against her naked body, Sally was treated to a tickle of muted euphoria.

'You have a beautiful fantasy, Sally.' Simon was

caressing her cheek lovingly as she sucked on him. Close to her eye, a sliver of light danced against the blue and green stone of his azurite ring. 'I'm grateful that you've allowed me to participate.'

She barely heard his words, holding her jaw rigid as Carl plunged into her backside. Her sphincter struggled to accommodate his cock's head. And then it was gripping his entire shaft as he pushed himself inside.

Sally knew she was close to coming and tears of delight began to pour down her cheeks. She allowed Simon to slide his cock from her mouth, and place his body beneath her. He moved his mouth to her face and kissed her lips. She responded by exploring him with her tongue and trying to show her gratitude with her avaricious need.

'Your kiss tastes of the best cock in the world,' Simon grinned. 'I could relish that taste all evening, could you?'

She nodded. Wondering if this was his subtle way of asking her to do that again, she tried to move her mouth back to his erection.

'Maybe later,' he said, kissing her again. His cock rested against her sex and she could feel him preparing to press inside her. 'Isn't this the moment you've been waiting for?'

She nodded, too lost in passion to articulate a response. Her pussy felt impossibly tight as he tried to penetrate her and she knew that was because Carl's cock was filling her rectum. With a gargantuan effort, she attempted to relax her muscles, willing Simon to enter her.

Simon caressed her breast with his thumb and pushed his length forward.

Eddies of elation swept through her as the shaft began to enter. Once the head had probed past her lips there was no stopping him. She felt the enormous thrill of having two cocks in her warm confines – her pussy-lips and anus were stretched to a point that was almost painful. It was only a small discomfort, barely noticeable beneath her body's shriek of euphoria, and it was a pain that she was more than happy to suffer. As Simon held himself still, Carl rode back and forth. He pushed his cock deep into her forbidden canal, then pulled back until she could feel her sphincter threatening to expel him. He timed each thrust so that it pushed inside with the explosive joy of his first anal entry.

Sally could hear herself gasping, her voice rising to a faltering shriek. When Simon moved his mouth close to hers, she kissed him greedily.

'You're close to coming, aren't you?' Simon observed.

Sally nodded, not wasting breath on the answer.

'Another couple of thrusts and you won't be able to fight it any longer, will you?'

As if to illustrate what he meant, Simon nudged his cock deeper inside.

Sally felt the threat of bliss preparing to erupt and she wilfully resisted the urge to succumb. Her entire body was aflame with the need for release and she knew that the moment was almost upon her. 'Please,' she begged. 'Harder, faster, deeper, please.'

'Do you remember that favour I was going to ask?'

Simon sounded absurdly calm and she wondered how he could remain so controlled. The world was a firework display of passion and she couldn't comprehend the measured tone of his voice.

'Yes,' she gasped. 'I remember.'

'Do you want me to tell you what that favour was? Or are you simply going to agree to help me now?'

He started to draw his cock out of her and she wondered if this was a threat. If he was going to take his length away from her, she knew she would miss the divine moment she had dreamt of for so long. She guessed that he was trying to pressure her into a decision but that thought didn't trouble her. Every excited tingle in her body was there because Simon had instigated it and Sally had always prided herself on properly showing her gratitude. 'I'll do whatever you want,' she told him earnestly.

'Anything?'

He sounded cautious, but she didn't worry about that. Whatever he wanted her to do, she knew it could never be enough to repay him.

'It might be depraved,' he warned her.

She shivered, excited by the thought. 'I don't mind.'

'It might be humiliating and degrading.'

'I'd still do it.' It was impossible to concentrate on the words and express the honesty of her response. The two men were pushing her towards a climax that threatened to eclipse all conscious thought. In return for the tremendous pleasure she was now enjoying, Sally would have promised Simon her soul. 'Whatever it is you want me to do, I'll do it. I'll do anything.'

He began to ease his cock forward and asked again, 'Anything?'

'Yes,' she screamed, not sure if the word was an agreement, or an exclamation of her impending climax. 'Yes, yes, YES!'

Simon pushed himself fully inside.

Eight

'Please stop this,' Jane moaned.

They were back in the toy room but now it felt like a gaol. McGivern had secured her above the wooden horse. Her naked body dangled over the crude back of the trestle and her pussy-lips pressed hard against it.

'I was just beginning to trust you,' he said. There was genuine disappointment in his tone. He stood by the toy room's open door, his face half-illuminated by the blazing torch beside him. The dancing flames mutated his frown into a menacing scowl. His eyes were black coals that smouldered with fury. 'I was just beginning to trust you, and now I discover you've been bought by Simon.'

'It's not like that,' Jane wailed. 'It's not like that at all. I only had his business card because he said he might need my services in the future. I wasn't trying to deceive you.'

She could see that McGivern wasn't listening. He nodded at the blonde by Jane's side. A shard of orange light glinted against her brass badge and Jane was momentarily blinded by the hateful number seven. Responding to her master's command, the slave snatched a gag from the shelves above the bed. The contraption was fashioned from black rubber with a large ball set centrally between the securing straps.

Jane's eyes opened wide. She shook her head and tried beseeching McGivern with her panicked expression, wondering if she should beg him to show some compassion. It was bad enough having to suffer this degrading punishment. She didn't want to be gagged as well. 'Please. No,' she whispered. 'Not that.'

His responding sneer left her cold. 'I might as well gag you,' he explained. 'I'm tired of listening to your pathetic lies and unacceptable excuses.'

'But I . . .'

Jane got no further. The hard rubber ball was pressed against her teeth and, although she struggled not to take it into her mouth, she was left with no other option. Her jaw was forced wide open and the straps were fastened at the back of her head. The slave stepped back, admiring her handiwork in the medieval torchlight.

'Simon's sent word that he wants to see me,' McGivern told Jane. 'If this is more bad news, I won't just hold you responsible – I'll make you suffer for it.'

If the gag hadn't been staunching her words, Jane would have told him that he was already making her suffer. She supposed it was just as well that he had silenced her. The other things she wanted to say would have sounded challenging and she doubted they would have hastened her release.

'Number seven will keep you company until I return,' McGivern said. 'Make sure you don't give her any trouble.' He slammed the door loudly, leaving Jane alone with the slave.

'You've really upset him,' the blonde said. Her voice was lowered, as though she thought McGivern might be standing on the other side of the door listening. 'I've never seen him this livid before.'

Jane swallowed, surprised by how difficult it was to do something so simple around the gag. She was still contemplating the slave with wide-eyed fear and now her hopes for a painless release were failing.

'Mind you,' the slave went on, 'the master isn't the only one that's angry. I wasn't very pleased with the way you spanked me outside his bedroom.'

Jane closed her eyes and shook her head. She wanted to believe this was all a perverse nightmare that wasn't really happening to her. It was a cruel hope that she didn't dare to entertain for more than a moment. She knew that dismissing this torture as a dream was only going to crush her when she didn't wake from it.

'And you encouraged the master to punish me, even though I hadn't done anything wrong,' the slave continued. 'I was just obeying my orders, guarding the door and doing as the master had said. You made me believe that you had a legitimate reason for going into his room. That was really bad of you. You allowed the master to use his belt on me and that was even worse. My arse-cheeks are still burning from the way he leathered me.'

Jane wished she could make a desperate plea for forgiveness but, even if the gag hadn't been stopping her words, she doubted the slave would have listened. There was a glint in the woman's eyes that threatened revenge and, from her helpless position, Jane saw that blonde wouldn't be swayed from that goal.

The slave stepped closer, her wicked smile shining. Her fingers reached out for Jane's breast and she caressed the orb.

Jane held herself still, glaring venomously, and knowing that she was powerless to resist this indignity.

'I wonder how long the master will be gone?' The slave's fingertips were tracing circles against Jane's left areola. She teased one treacherous nipple to a stiff bud. 'I wonder how long we have together?'

Jane could do nothing but stare. She knew the slave was going to exact revenge, and her conscience was telling her that she deserved as much, but that didn't help quash her fear of what was to come. Above her head, her arms ached in the restricting manacles. The wooden horse was pressing painfully against her labia and each subtle movement of her body reminded Jane of its presence. Her pussy-lips already felt bruised with the constant pressure but discomfort was only a small part of the sensation. In the castle's omnipresent atmosphere of sexuality, it was impossible not to consider the pleasurable aspect of any experience – even one as degrading as this. The sensitivity of her sex was heightened with each exhalation. Jane knew that if she had to spend any length of time on the horse, her body would become a mass of lecherous demands. The slave's circling finger exploited those sensations and Jane tried to ignore her own response.

'There are so many toys in here.' The slave was studying the gloomy stone walls as she spoke. 'Would you like to play with something while we wait for the master's return?' She giggled and said, 'Perhaps it will take that worried expression off your face.'

Jane shook her head but the slave wasn't looking. Her gaze had turned to the shelves and her smile was widening. 'Of course you want to play with something,' she said, moving out of Jane's vision. 'And, since I'm here to keep you company, and you're in no position to decide for yourself, I'll make the choice for you.'

There was little purchase for movement in her position on the horse. Jane managed to twist sideways but she barely got a proper look at what the slave was doing. The pressure of her body's weight rubbed against the horse's back and pleasure rippled from her pussy-lips. She bucked her hips forward, intending to relieve the unwanted delight by resting on a different part of herself. Instead, her clitoris was pinched hard between the wood and her pubic bone. The position augmented the arousal sweeping through her.

'Nipple clamps,' the slave exclaimed jubilantly.

Jane barely heard her over the pounding pulse in her temples. She glanced up and saw that the slave was holding a silver device that looked like a pair of ineffectual nutcrackers. As Jane watched, the slave flexed them open and shut. 'Have you ever used nipple clamps?'

'Ungh!' Jane managed to make a sound. It was muted by the ball-gag, and her panic made it inarticulate but nevertheless, Jane knew that the slave had to have heard it. There was so much emotion in the noise, Jane didn't doubt that it sounded like a plea for release. She stared at the slave with mute hope, willing the woman to understand what she meant.

The slave smiled as though she was being encouraged. 'You like the look of them, don't you? They're really good, too.' To show Jane how good they were, the slave pressed her fingers around her own breast, enticing the nipple to stiffen. After flexing one clamp wide open, she placed its jaws on either side of her flesh, then slowly closed it. The

148

spring action held the device in place and the slave drew her hand away. She smiled at Jane. 'These are so good,' she whispered. Her words were thickened with the husky tone of arousal. 'And I know I should be punishing you, rather than treating you to pleasure like this but . . .' Her voice trailed off and she trembled happily.

Not knowing whether to be intrigued or appalled, Jane could only watch. She had thought that her day at the castle had left her inured to surprises like this, but that notion already seemed naively optimistic. The slave who had performed the dance of submission had been a chilling sight but Jane had rationalised that woman's plight with a fear of retribution. Her master and his influential guests were in attendance and, having learnt how things worked in the castle, Jane guessed that the slave was only dancing because she was scared not to. But this woman was deliberately torturing herself for no reason other than her own pleasure. It was an unsettling revelation and if the image hadn't been so exciting, Jane knew she would have been terrified.

'Should I put the second one on you, or do I take it myself?' the slave wondered aloud.

Jane wished she could voice her own suggestion but the gag was unyielding. She didn't want the nipple clamps anywhere near her body and she struggled to find a way of communicating this to her tormentor.

'I think I'll take it myself,' the slave decided.

Jane heaved a sigh of relief.

'There's another set of clamps on the shelves. I'll get them for you once I've done this.' Ignoring Jane's wild-eyed stare, the slave caressed her other nipple hard, then held the flesh steady to secure the second clamp. Her pleasure was obvious, from the straightening of her back to the broad grin on her lips. She exhaled gratefully and her shining eyes met Jane's. 'You'll thank me for this afterwards.' Her words were laboured with excitement. 'I know you will.'

Jane doubted that, but she was unable to respond around the gag. Shaking her head was only shifting the weight of her body and that movement excited the pulse of her clitoris. It occurred to her that the wooden horse had to be the most unrelenting form of torture imaginable. The constant pressure against her sex was inescapable. When McGivern had fastened her over the device, Jane had thought it was slightly worse than uncomfortable, but the last few minutes had taught her differently. The lessons that waited for her in the hours ahead didn't bear contemplating.

If her mounting fear hadn't been so great, Jane would have laughed at the memory of her own naïveté. She had struggled to stop McGivern from fastening her above the horse but, at the time, her concerns had been with the embarrassment of being treated so rudely. She knew that she shouldn't have had any shame with McGivern. They had already become lovers, and he had introduced her to aspects of sexuality that she had never contemplated before: but being subjected to his rough man-handling had still been a humiliating experience.

That had happened less than five minutes earlier, yet the indignity was already a faded memory. Now, the pressure of the horse against her labia was beginning to grow more noticeable, banishing all other thoughts from her mind. The subtlest of movements was amplified against the unyielding bar. Her sex had parted and her pussy-lips were being pinched between her thighs and the trestle's back.

'You have to try these,' the slave said firmly. 'You just have to try them.' She stepped past Jane, marching back to the shelves. With each step, her breasts flounced gently and a smile of mounting pleasure stole across her lips. She returned a moment later with a second pair of clamps and her grin even broader.

Glaring miserably, Jane made a muffled protest against the ball in her mouth. She could see the way the clamp's teeth bit against the slave. The dark pink nipple was squeezed between merciless jaws. Its tip had been bleached a painful white by the unrelenting pressure. The device looked cruel and exceptionally uncomfortable and Jane didn't dare to imagine the pain it would inspire.

Unhappily, she realised that her imagination wouldn't need to be tested if the slave did as she had threatened.

With a lunge, the slave grabbed Jane's nipple between finger and thumb.

Jane pulled herself out of the woman's grasp and was shocked by the agonising joy that jolted from her sex. Her labia were pinched against the horse's unmoving back. When the slave reached for her again, Jane held herself still, fearful of repeating that sickening delight.

'Don't pull away from me,' the slave warned. 'You'll make me cross by doing that, and you don't want to make me cross.' Her thumb and index finger tweaked Jane's nipple whilst she spoke.

The sensation was exhilarating. It was an unexpected pleasure in the torment of the evening but still Jane wanted it to stop. She tried beseeching the slave with a pained expression, but she knew the attempt was futile before she began.

The slave grinned, not bothering to conceal her sadistic satisfaction as she teased Jane's breast. Once the nipple was fully erect, she pressed one clamp against Jane with its jaws open wide. The metal was a shard of ice against Jane's areola but its discomfort was lost beneath the threat of pain about to be administered.

'You're making this worse for yourself by not relaxing,' the slave explained. 'But I don't mind that. You got a lot of pleasure from watching me suffer, didn't you?'

Before Jane could refute the allegation, the clamp had closed. An exquisite bolt of agony flared from the tip of her breast, sending her temperature high and instantaneously coating her body with sweat. She tried not to move away from the punishing grip but it was impossible to control her reflexive impulse. The need to distance herself from the clamp forced her to shift position. The wooden horse pressed against her and euphoria spasmed through her sex.

'It's good, isn't it?'

Jane stared down at herself and saw that the clamp was hanging from her orb. The jaws were fixed firmly against the sides of her nipple, pulling it downward with their weight. The teeth were buried deep into her sensitive bud and the pressure was an inescapable combination of pleasure and pain. Before Jane could convince herself that this was actually happening, the slave reached for her other breast. Jane managed to sob around the gag. The sound was tainted with anguish.

'It's better when you're wearing both of them,' the slave explained. She caught the nipple between her finger and thumb and squeezed. 'There's a completeness to the sensation when you're wearing both.'

Jane shook her head and tugged her hands against the manacles. It was an ineffectual attempt at escape, doing nothing more than pressing her body weight harder against the horse's back. Delicious tremors were evoked by the slave's squeezing fingers from the tip of her nipple.

'And it's even better when your nipple's at its most sensitive,' the slave went on. She moved her mouth over Jane's breast and began to suck. Her tongue teased the nub and she nibbled the tip between punishing teeth.

Despite the agony between her legs, and the pressure of the clamp, Jane was filled with a rush of arousal. She fought against enjoying the pleasure but her body seemed determined to take whatever comfort it could from this situation.

The slave moved her mouth away from the breast and smiled.

Jane was left panting. There was a battle of pleasure and pain fighting for control of her body and, for the first time since this torture had begun, Jane felt the balance fall in her favour. She knew there was no escape from the horse but the slave's ability to please her offered Jane a spark of hope. Regardless of how intense the punishment became, she saw that the slave was going to try and temper it with some measure of enjoyment. With their eyes locked on one another, and these optimistic thoughts cascading through her mind, Jane didn't notice the woman fixing the second clamp.

The sensation was far more profound than the first had

been. Her body had quickly grown accustomed to the pleasure it was receiving, even though the slave had barely suckled at her for half a minute. Now, the anguish seemed more poignant. Jane sucked greedy breaths around the ball gag, trying to cope with the tremors racking her body.

'Isn't it just wonderful?'

Jane couldn't hear the words. From the corner of her eye, she saw the slave teasing her own nipple clamps, shifting the weight and obviously rekindling the effects of the punishing pleasure. A giddy smile crossed her face and the slave chuckled salaciously. 'But these aren't the best toys in here. I'll go and fetch my favourite.'

This time, Jane heard clearly enough, but she wished she hadn't. The slave flounced back to the shelves before hurrying back with her latest acquisition.

After the nipple clamps, Jane had expected the slave to threaten her with something extremely torturous. There were dozens of whips and canes in the toy room and, at the least, Jane had expected the slave to be brandishing one of those. Instead, she held a rather innocuous pair of trophies in her hands and, for some reason, Jane found that more disquieting.

'It's an anal violin,' the slave explained. She was smiling proudly, as though this was a special treat she was extolling. 'This is the bow,' she said, holding up a thin strip of wood. 'And this is the catgut.' Raising her hand, she showed Jane the dangling thread. The curling length of catgut penetrated a polished wooden egg and Jane looked away, not daring to contemplate how the items worked together.

'Do you want to know what this does?' The slave was holding the egg in front of Jane's face. 'This holds the catgut in place,' she explained. 'Let me show you.'

Jane was in no position to refuse. She was unsettled when the slave stepped behind her but, as the device was called an anal violin, she wasn't overly surprised.

'Are you ready for this?'

If Jane could have responded, she would have screamed the word 'no'. The slave's hands were on her buttocks and she knew where the egg was to be inserted. The thought left her shivering with revulsion but she didn't bother trying to escape. Her body had already been taught the unpleasant futility of such attempts.

A finger pushed against her anus and Jane allowed it to enter. The exertion of holding herself still was taking a massive effort. To try and resist this inevitable degradation would only make matters worse.

'You feel more than ready for this. I'm not really punishing you here, am I?'

There was a note of disappointment in the slave's voice and Jane wanted to dispute her words. She couldn't imagine a more humiliating punishment than this and, if the gag hadn't been firmly in place, she would have told her that. The finger was squirming in the dark confines of her arsehole, stretching her anus and exciting the forbidden flesh inside.

The slave removed the finger slowly and Jane released a shuddering sigh. She knew that the punishment wasn't over – she realised that it hadn't properly begun yet – but the removal of the finger was a relief that needed to be acknowledged. Jane took a long breath around the gag and wondered if it was possible to prepare herself for the torment that was yet to come.

The wooden egg was pushed firmly against her anus and Jane groaned. She felt certain her body couldn't accommodate the egg and she dreaded the painful moments that lay ahead before the slave accepted this. It was impossible to relax as she dangled above the horse but she tried not to resist the threatening penetration, certain that would make the experience even more uncomfortable.

'You're very tight here and not very wet.'

The egg was snatched away and Jane was dizzied by a tidal wave of relief. Inserting the egg was clearly an impossible task and it hadn't taken as long as she had feared for the slave to realise this. Jane spent a silent moment thanking the gods who had deigned to answer her prayers for salvation.

'I think we need to lubricate you a little,' the slave decided.

Before Jane could groan, she felt the slave move close behind her. The caress of the blonde's hair tickled her back and Jane felt the pressure of the woman's cheek against her buttocks. A sickening mental picture of what was happening filled her mind and she tried to banish it from her thoughts. Before she could discard the idea as too obscene to be reality, she felt the tongue against her sphincter.

Her heart was pounding like thunderclaps. She couldn't properly call the feeling unpleasant. The tongue was warm and exciting, plunging deeper than Jane would have believed possible. The slave teased the rim of her anus, then pushed into the unexplored confines with a twisted French kiss. It was a passionate interlude, bringing a fullness to Jane's arousal and heightening the urgent need between her legs.

The slave stepped away, appearing briefly in Jane's line of vision. Her eyes were shining and her cheeks were flushed. Wiping the back of her hand across her smile, she looked at Jane and said, 'Now you're wet enough.'

Disgusted and sickened by her own arousal, Jane looked away as the slave walked behind her.

This time, the threat of the egg wasn't unexpected but it was no less intimidating. With her anus wet with saliva, Jane could feel its threat to intrude was made more forcefully.

'I think this will do it,' the slave exclaimed gleefully.

Jane hadn't needed the slave to speak to know that was true. Her tight sphincter spread wide open as the egg was forced inside. Her concentration was focused on the puckered muscles and she felt every moment of the egg's entry. The surface was beautifully smooth, allowing it to continue entering her even when her body protested that she could take no more. As the egg grew wider, Jane tried to scream around the ball gag. The sound only echoed in her own ears, never making it to the gloom of the toy room.

There was an instant when she thought it was going to be too much. She had been able to accommodate its widening girth up to that point but her muscles suddenly insisted that they couldn't take any more. In spite of the lubrication that the slave's wet kiss had given, the sphincter refused to open any wider. Jane held her breath, praying that the slave would realise the egg was too large.

And then it rushed inside her.

After passing the widest point, her anus relented and snatched the egg out of the slave's fingers. Jane could feel its degrading presence filling her backside and evoking the most disquieting sensations.

The slave was laughing softly. She stepped in front of Jane and said, 'You're really going to like this.'

Jane glared at her, blinking her vision clear from shameful tears.

'This is the bow,' the slave said, holding the strip of wood in front of Jane's eyes. 'Do you see that it's got a slightly serrated edge? That makes it better for playing the violin.'

Jane couldn't see what the slave was pointing at and she refused to contemplate the torture that was being implied.

'Feel how finely toothed it is,' the slave encouraged. She pressed the bow towards Jane's face and drew it lightly against her cheek.

Jane looked away, trying to make a last attempt at defiance now the opportunity was available to her. The wood grazed her cheek but its caress was a meaningless tickle.

Untroubled, the slave lowered the bow to Jane's breast. Its edge rested against a tiny bead of nipple that hadn't been caught between the clamp's jaws. 'Perhaps you'll be able to appreciate it more if you feel it here.' Steadily, she drew the bow downward.

Jane tugged her hands against the manacles. Her body was painfully responsive to every caress and the bow felt like a hacksaw against her nipple. She thrashed against her restraints, unmindful of the pain in her arms or the shifting weight that pressed on her pussy-lips. Her pelvis had been pushed forward so the slave could slide the egg into her anus and that meant Jane was resting on her clitoris. Each violent twist left her shivering. Even the subtler movements, like exhaling or simply bracing herself, incited Jane's body to further spasms. Repeatedly, she was battered by a rush of agonising pleasure but Jane was almost oblivious to the joy. Her attention was concentrated on the bow that rubbed against her breast.

'You look more than ready for this,' the slave giggled, stepping away.

Although she couldn't see the slave, Jane knew exactly what the woman was doing. She could feel the catgut being pulled taut. Her anus tightened greedily around its prize and, for an instant, Jane felt as though she was participating in the crudest tug-of-war imaginable. The pressure of the egg pushing to get out of her was a constant reminder of this moment's degradation. She steeled herself for whatever other unwanted treats the situation would offer, but she doubted that any preparation could be sufficient.

The slave pulled the bow along the taut catgut and Jane began to sob. Tingling vibrations – after-echoes of the violin's music – coursed upwards from her arsehole. There was no sound that she could hear but Jane didn't know if the violin was a silent instrument, or simply inaudible beneath the pounding in her temples.

Pulling the catgut tighter, the slave drew the bow back and forth as though she were playing an adagio. Jane could feel each ripple shuddering like a vibrator's buzz and it was impossible to deny the pleasure of the torment. She tried to tug away from the sensations, bruising herself against the horse in the process and evoking another scream from her labia. Her arms ached in the manacles but their dull discomfort was virtually forgotten as the unwanted joy overwhelmed her.

'This part feels even better,' the slave enthused. She tugged hard at the catgut. The egg felt as though it was on the point of being expelled and Jane was torn between a desire to release it and a need to hold on. She knew there would be relief in letting the egg slide away but that thought was unthinkably embarrassing. The humiliation of such an option would be mortifying and she didn't even entertain the idea after it had occurred. There was also the worry that the slave would simply push the egg back inside if she let go and so Jane resisted her natural impulse. She tightened her sphincter's hold on the egg, wishing that the effort didn't leave her at the mercy of so many exhilarating sensations.

The slave was playing the violin with the skill of a concert soloist. She allowed the bow to glide back and forth over the taut string, alternating her playing between long, searing sweeps, and short, staccato bursts. She plucked a blistering pizzicato close to Jane's backside, then drew the bow slowly away. Her pace began to quicken, as though she were building to a crescendo. She pulled the catgut tighter, inspiring a thrilling shiver, and then played out the final note with a furious flourish.

Jane wanted to scream.

'It's better than you were expecting, isn't it?' the slave gushed. 'The master had me in here two months ago, punishing me just like this when I neglected my kitchen chores.'

Hearing the words through a haze, Jane nodded. She was hoping that the punishment had ended now, but she doubted she would be so lucky. The slave had seemed determined to make her suffer when she was brought in here and Jane didn't think the woman had come close to doing half the things she intended.

'Do you know what the master did to me after the violin?'

Sniffing back a sob, Jane shook her head. The words 'after the violin' were making her hope that this particular punishment had reached its conclusion.

'Have you seen number three? Of course you have,' she said, answering her own question. 'You saw her do the dance of submission. The master's really fond of number three and he said it's because she's got all those piercings.' The slave was grinning at her and Jane swallowed thickly. 'He said that I might be better-behaved if I had piercings and he tried to get me to have some.' She reached for her badge and unfastened it from the strip of leather above her breast. 'I didn't think I could tolerate pain like that,' the slave continued. 'Do you think you could?'

Jane glared at her with tear-filled eyes.

The slave was holding her badge up, smiling thoughtfully at the pin as she reached for Jane's breast.

Jane tried to pull herself away from the woman's fingers. She was still wearing the nipple clamps but their punishing pressure was all but forgotten with the sensations of the violin and the terror evoked by the slave's threat. The slave caught hold of the clamp and managed to stop Jane's movements by tugging on it. Renewed pain shot from her breast, leaving Jane dizzy with its intensity.

'I'd been wearing clamps, too, at the time.' The slave spoke as though they were calmly discussing her entertaining afternoon from two months earlier and she treated Jane's fearful expression as silent encouragement. 'My nipples had been clamped, just like yours, and I expected them to be mega-sensitive: but the master said they wouldn't be. Are yours?' She snatched the clamp away from Jane's breast with a brisk motion.

Around the ball gag, Jane managed to release a shriek. Nothing had prepared her for a sensation like this one. The securing of the clamps had been painful and the anal violin had left her giddy. But this went beyond either of those experiences. The world became a sepia tint, faded and smoke-like at the edges as consciousness threatened to evaporate.

The slave was holding her nipple, pressing the badge's pin against her sensitive flesh. 'Yet the strange thing is, the pressure of the pin doesn't hurt, does it?' The slave pushed the point harder against Jane's nub to prove this.

Jane wanted to distance herself from the sensation but the evening had already taught her the folly of such actions. She might have tried to move away, regardless of that: but, as the slave pointed out, there was no discomfort involved. After being flattened between the biting jaws of the clamp, her nipple was totally unresponsive. She acknowledged this discovery with a shuddering sigh of gratitude.

'Afterwards, I told the master it didn't hurt, but he acted as though he'd known that before we started. I got the impression he'd tried it before because he said he could have made it feel a lot more intense if he'd wanted. Do you know what he said he could have done?'

Before Jane could think about the question, the slave was pressing her mouth over her breast. Her nipple had been unresponsive to the pressure of the pin but it began to harden beneath the slave's suckling lips. Feeling returned to the crushed bud, more intense than it had ever been. Memories of the jaw's teeth were rekindled as the slave teased her tongue against the tip. The sensations were a caress, compared to the extremes she had already endured, but they were still intensely pleasurable. Pressed hard against the back of the wooden horse, her pussy-lips began to tingle with a quickly welling excitement.

'See,' the slave grinned at her, wickedness apparent in the shine of her eyes. 'He was right, wasn't he? And, I think that now it's been made sensitive again, you'll feel this a lot more acutely.'

Jane glared at her, willing the slave not to carry out the threat. She watched the wicked tip move close to her nipple. Her breath came in laboured gulps as she tried to ignore the panicked hammering of her heartbeat and the irresistible impulse to drag herself away. The egg still nestled in her arsehole, its pressure filling her with a shameful pleasure. Her other breast remained caught between the unrelenting jaws of the second clamp.

And still, the slave moved the tip of the pin closer to Jane's breast. Like a sliver of evil, it sparkled in the torchlight before becoming lost in the shadow of her breast.

Jane groaned around the gag. She could feel the metal touching her nipple and she tried to shrink away from its threat.

A sound at the door startled them both. Jane felt a whisper of relief bristle through her when she saw McGivern step into the doorway.

The slave snatched the pin away and pushed it back into

160

her uniform. She fastened the badge with a quick, well-practised motion, as though this was something she had done on many previous occasions. As soon as she had done it, she glanced warily at her master and Jane could see that the woman was trying to decide if she had gone too far.

McGivern didn't look at the slave. His angry gaze was directed at Jane and the frown creasing his forehead was positively thunderous. The relief Jane had felt when he interrupted the slave was only a short-lived respite. Her hopes for salvation began to fade when she saw his fearsome mood. He took in the situation with a glance seeming untroubled by the torture Jane had been about to endure.

In a flat voice, McGivern said, 'Simon's submissive is ready to do the dance.'

Jane stared at him meekly, more chilled by his tone than the words.

'Your duplicity has cost me the challenge and this castle,' he growled. 'And I think I owe you something in return for that.' He stepped fully into the room and slammed the door behind him. Its heavy echo resounded in her ears.

Briskly, McGivern walked past Jane, and the slave, and snatched a riding crop from the wall. Standing behind her, he spoke in a voice made gruff with anger. 'Now that my slave's warmed you up a little, I think it's time I gave you a proper lesson in punishment.'

Nine

On the top of the west keep, Frankie smoked her cigar in the night's silence. She was naked, save for the biker's jacket draped over her shoulders, unmindful of the cold stone beneath her bare feet and the chill air around her. A stone gargoyle stared blindly into the night alongside her. Its twisted features and malformed body were a complete contrast to Frankie's figure of femininity, but their expressions shared the same menacing intent. Beyond the castle, the night's horizon was being slowly illuminated by the threatening dawn. A brightening edge on the canopy of blackness was enough to remind her that a new day would soon be starting. Unwilling to endure that sight, Frankie stared down into the bailey, glaring at the illuminated panes in the east and north keeps.

McGivern had told her that Simon's submissive was ready to dance and Frankie was still trying to come to terms with the news. It wasn't so surprising that Simon had won. Frankie was just amazed to discover that she had lost. Simon was a gifted master who worked with an irresistible combination of charm and authority. He deserved to win the bet, she thought, trying to convince herself that this was true. Not only was he likeable but he had proved his talents far more efficiently than either she or McGivern had managed. In less than twenty-four hours, he had transformed a woman from an unsuspecting uni student to the ultimate in servility. She knew that anyone capable of that sort of feat deserved to win the castle. But Frankie thought she deserved it more.

The proof of Simon's triumph was scheduled for dawn, in the north keep's banquet hall, and a part of her wanted to refuse to attend. She could have packed her bag, slipped off the island and gone home to try and rebuild the fortune she had just gambled away. It was a tempting idea because it would save her from losing face in front of the others: but she didn't entertain it for more than a moment. To sneak off the island would be an admission of failure, and that was something she had never done in her life.

Perhaps there were only two hours left, but past experience had taught her that a lot could happen in that time. Simon's submissive could have a change of heart, McGivern could find some way to wrangle them all out of the bet, or she could finally make number three relent. They were all possibilities and each one offered a small seed of hope.

She took a final breath from the cigar, then dropped it to the floor. As she ground the glowing embers beneath her bare foot, Frankie decided there was always hope, especially for those who were determined enough.

Marching briskly down the spiral staircase, she concentrated her thoughts on finally making progress and breaking the slave. The day had been an endlessly looped conversation, with Frankie asking number three to dance, and number three refusing.

'Say you'll do the dance for me.'

'I can't, mistress.'

'Now will you do the dance for me?'

'The master wouldn't want me to, mistress.'

'Dance for me.'

'No, mistress.'

In every other aspect, the slave had been more pliant than Frankie could have imagined. She tolerated caning, she accepted humiliation and she thrived on degradation. Frankie had tied weights to the woman's piercings and refused to remove them until the slave relented. The torment had left number three breathless, but not so breathless that she couldn't say the words, 'No, mistress.'

Frankie had chastised the slave, using a variety of

163

paddles, canes and whips. She had reddened the slave's backside and punished her breasts without bruising the slave's resolve. She had striped red lines so close to number three's labia, they looked like additional creases in her sex. And after that, when Frankie had asked if the slave was ready to dance, she still said, 'No, mistress.'

Straining her imagination to new realms, Frankie had humiliated the slave with watersports. The games had grown darker and more sadistic, forcing the slave to a point where she could do nothing but submit and say she would do the dance. And still she had turned to Frankie, defiance shining in her sultry brown eyes, as she said the words, 'No, mistress.'

Frankie had gone out of her way to make the day unbearable for number three, but it hadn't moved her any closer to making the slave agree to her one request. Bursting back into her bedroom, she decided it was time to try a different tactic. There was a saying about catching more flies with honey than with vinegar and Frankie supposed that, with only two hours left, it was time to see if there was any truth in the adage.

Number three was exactly where Frankie had left her. She stood with her back to the bedroom wall, her hands and feet secured to rings embedded in the stone. Weights, each one punishingly heavy, dangled from her piercings. The ones between her legs were suspended on long cords that swayed with each of the slave's tiniest movements. Frankie could imagine the constant pressure of those piercings, tugging at the slave's labia. It seemed like an unbearable torture but the slave had coped with it as though this was part of her daily routine. Her body was marked with the fading memory of earlier whippings and her flesh was coated with nervous sweat but, aside from that, she seemed unperturbed by her ordeal. Her face was an infuriating mask of composure.

'Are you ready to dance?'

'No, mistress.'

The denial made Frankie wanted to punish the slave again. A handful of whips and canes remained on the bed and Frankie could picture herself grabbing one and using it to stripe the slave's bare body. It was an exciting idea and it promised to vent some of the mounting frustration that welled inside her. She could picture the cane landing against the slave's breast and striping red marks beneath her areolae. The image was so vivid, Frankie could almost hear number three begging for release.

'Catching flies with honey,' Frankie reminded herself, muttering the words aloud.

Number three regarded her suspiciously.

Frankie ignored her, reminding herself of the tactics for this final gambit. 'You're catching flies with honey, this time,' she whispered. It was an uncharacteristic way forward, but Frankie could see little option other than to try it. Glaring at the slave's questioning expression, Frankie said, 'I think you've had enough of that, haven't you?' She started to unfasten the cords on the slave's arms and wrists, mindful that the woman's skin was probably still sensitive. 'Let's get you down from there, shall we?'

Number three studied her warily. 'Thank you, mistress.'

Frankie wondered if she should stop the slave from using the formal title. It seemed more in keeping with the 'flies and honey' tactic but there was something unthinkable about allowing a slave to use her name. It wasn't just that Frankie got a thrill from being addressed with such reverence, or that she disliked her given name being used by inferiors. Rationalising her own reluctance, she decided the slave would suspect a trick if she was told to, 'Call me Frankie.'

She released the slave's arms, then knelt down to unfasten the bindings at her ankles. Her face was close to number three's bare pussy and the fragrance of the slave's arousal lingered against Frankie's nostrils.

In all her years as a dominatrix, Frankie had never understood the excitement that submissives gleaned from their roles. How someone could extract satisfaction from humiliation and pain was a mystery that had always perplexed her. There had been times when she thought that some knowledge of a slave's psyche might help to break a more difficult submissive but determination and experience had always won the day for her. Those drivers who broke land-speed records seldom knew the intricacies of advanced mechanical engineering and, by the same token, she didn't need a specialised degree in submissive psychology to break slaves. She supposed that her own pleasure from domination was equally unfathomable to a slave and, while that paradox didn't make the situation any easier to understand, it evened the balance.

'These must have been intolerable,' Frankie said, releasing the weights from the slave's sex. She uncoupled all nine of the weights, tossing them to a corner of the bedroom where they landed noisily. Tracing her fingers over the piercings, she glanced curiously up and asked, 'You're not sore down here, are you?' The pussy-lips were slippery and coloured by a flush that looked more excited than uncomfortable, but Frankie thought the question would make her sound concerned. As she caressed the delicate folds, Frankie saw the slave's clitoris peep briefly from beneath its hood. It occurred to her that, regardless of how sore the submissive was, it hadn't hampered her arousal.

'I'm a little sore, mistress,' number three allowed. She sounded wary and, although she was trying to conceal her doubts, her forehead was creased with a suspicious frown. 'But these are more uncomfortable.'

She was pointing towards her pierced nipples and Frankie wasn't surprised to hear they had become burdensome. The rings through her breasts were each holding a quarter pound weight and they had been for the last hour. If she had been forced to endure something similar, Frankie guessed she would have been screaming by this point and she was struck again by the slave's phenomenal tolerance. Frankie unfastened the weights and put an arm around number three's waist.

'I've made today a complete misery for you, haven't I?'

Number three looked away.

Frankie made a sympathetic sound and started leading the slave towards the bed. 'Don't bother about embarrass-

166

ing me with the truth,' Frankie said. 'I know I've been a bitch and you have every right to call me one, if you want. I've just been determined to win this bet and I've been tackling it without any thought for the consequences. Now that it's all over, I guess I can show a little humility.'

Number three continued to regard her doubtfully.

'I've got some cream,' Frankie explained. 'You must feel sore after having those weights on you. Why don't you let me use it to make you feel better?'

The slave's expression remained sceptical and reluctant but she was too submissive to refuse. Frankie led her to the bed, pushing the whips and canes away with one hand. 'Lie there,' she told her. 'I'm going to try and make things up to you.'

'That's not necessary, mistress.'

Earlier, Frankie would have been excited by the slave's hesitancy. Reluctance was always a sign that a submissive was close to breaking point and Frankie was used to capitalising on its appearance. But time was against her tonight and number three's nervousness was an intrusion that she didn't have time for. 'I think it's necessary. I need to offer some atonement.' She swallowed and struggled to say something she had never said to a slave before. 'Please.' The word almost choked her as it came out.

'If you want to make things up to me, you could let me go back to the master, mistress.'

Frankie frowned and coughed back the harsh command she had been about to bark. 'Your master will be busy for the next couple of hours,' she began. 'And I think I owe you something.'

'I could just go back to my quarters, mistress.'

Frankie curled her hands into fists, then uncurled them before the slave could see. Trying valiantly to appear friendly, she exercised an uncomfortable smile and tried to say that forbidden word again. 'Please.' It felt more abrasive than the strongest tobacco smoke. 'Stay with me for a little while and let me make things up to you.' She contemplated using the hateful begging word for a final time, then decided she had already made enough sacrifices for one evening.

Number three was still studying her suspiciously, as though she expected Frankie to pounce at any moment. With a last wary glance, the slave gave a reluctant nod and climbed on to the bed. She looked as though she was still expecting a trick of some sort and Frankie found it impossible not admire the woman's shrewdness.

Although she was loath to admit it, thoughts like that had been spoiling her fun throughout the day. There was a dignity in the way that the slave held herself which Frankie found irresistible. Number three was wholly submissive, yet she had managed to remain defiant on the subject of the dance. It showed a strength of character that Frankie couldn't help but admire and she wished a submissive would give that sort of devotion to her. More than that, on several occasions, Frankie had caught herself wishing it was this submissive who was that devoted to her.

It was a facile thought, threatening to intrude on her plans to stay in with a chance of winning the castle. There was a lot of money at stake in the bet, not to mention the small matter of her pride. She badly wanted the castle, but she also wanted the prestige of winning it over Simon and McGivern. Those were the things that mattered and there was no time to start admiring the slave's servile disposition. Ignoring the twinge of guilt that nagged at her thoughts, Frankie shook her head and concentrated on the task ahead.

'Flies with honey,' she whispered. 'Flies with honey.' The words were sufficient to help her focus and she was able to forget the pangs of her conscience.

Not wanting to waste a moment as the dawn approached, Frankie joined the slave on the bed. She shrugged off her leather jacket and placed her bare body next to number three's. The slave stiffened when Frankie pressed close. It was a familiar sensation that Frankie still cursed, even though she had been expecting it. All day, number three had shown persistent reluctance when Frankie tried to become intimate. It had started with the woman's hesitancy from that morning. When Frankie had demanded that number three lick her pussy, the slave had come close to forfeiting McGivern's bet with her refusal. As the hours went on, she had continued to shy away from Frankie's touch. When her nipples were caressed before their canings, or when her sex-lips were teased open for some rude, undignified intrusion, the slave had made a small sign of her protest by either trying to pull away or whispering the words, 'Please, no, mistress.'

After the torturous day she had endured, number three was still suspicious and wary, Frankie reminded herself. Yet, if she was to have any hope of making progress in the bet, Frankie knew she had to win the slave's trust. It was a hell of a challenge to set herself but Frankie knew that if she didn't meet it, her hopes of owning the castle would be lost.

She studied the slave's body, rigid against the velvet bedspread, as though she was held there by invisible bindings. 'Relax,' Frankie said, reaching her hand towards the slave's breast. She drew her finger against one pierced nipple and number three shivered.

'You said you were going to use a cream, mistress.'

Frankie nodded. 'And I will. I just wanted to get to know a little more about you first.' The tattoo on the slave's breast begged to be touched and Frankie traced the ornate line of the number three with the tips of her fingers. She had been longing to caress it properly all day, intrigued by the artwork of the illuminated calligraphy. Her fingertips trailed over the embedded colour and she realised the skin was slightly raised beneath the ink. The slave's skin rippled, as though she had been brushed by a sudden chill, and Frankie wondered if the woman was responding to her. With rising hope, she glanced into the slave's face.

Number three glared at the canopy over the four poster.

'You used to work at a fairground,' Frankie remembered. 'That sounds like it was interesting.'

Number three blinked, still staring upwards.

'What did you do there?'

'I don't like to talk about it, mistress.'

Frankie bit her lower lip and resisted the urge to give the

slave's nipple a punishing tweak. 'No. Of course you wouldn't.' Frankie forced herself to sound calm and understanding. 'That's a lovely tattoo,' she tried.

Number three remained silent, still glaring at the bed's canopy.

'Did you design it yourself?' Frankie asked.

'No, mistress.' She paused for a moment before adding, 'The master selected the artwork for me.' There was a finality in her voice that said she didn't want to dwell on the topic.

Frankie wanted to sigh heavily but she resisted the urge, knowing that the sound would reveal her frustration. She racked her brains for a gambit that might get some sort of conversational response from the submissive. When the idea eventually came to her, she wondered why she hadn't had the insight to see it before. 'Could we talk about McGivern?' Frankie suggested. 'You seem very devoted to him.'

The slave glanced sideways. She still looked suspicious, but there was something in her expression that told Frankie this was a subject that she wanted to talk about. Her eyes were shining and her lips were parted into a shy smile. 'He's an adorable man, isn't he, mistress?'

Frankie blinked. 'It's not the word I would have picked for him,' she replied honestly. She could see that the slave was finally starting to relax and knew that she had to say something else to keep up the momentum. 'What is it that you like about him?'

Number three grinned. 'Everything.'

'Everything?' Frankie grinned back at her, hoping her smile didn't look too predatory.

'He's just so masterful, but considerate with it, and he has to be the most tremendous lover in the world. He has a way of saying things, a way of giving commands, and I don't just feel obliged to obey them. He makes me *want* to obey them.'

Frankie continued to tease the nipple between her thumb and forefinger, surprised by the glut of information that the slave had just given her. If she had suspected it could be this easy, Frankie would have adopted this tactic in the banquet hall and saved them all the trouble of the last day. She moved her hand to the other breast, pleased to see that the slave didn't stiffen beneath her touch this time. The button of flesh pulsed and its piercing trembled, but Frankie's discerning eye knew that this was a sign of arousal and not unease.

'You'd do anything for him, wouldn't you?'

Number three nodded. Her features bore the characteristic traits of infatuation. Her grin was wide, her eyes were smiling and her cheeks were coloured by a demure flush. The expression made her look younger and more vulnerable than Frankie had expected and she felt a rush of renewed hope for the challenge. Unexpectedly, she found herself needing to kiss the slave and she moved her lips over the woman's before the moment escaped her.

With their naked bodies pressed together and their mouths locked in a passionate kiss, number three made no attempt to resist. For one divine instant, Frankie felt sure the slave was wanting to take the kiss further. She could feel the gentlest pressure against her lips and knew that, if she had opened her mouth, she would have accepted the slave's tongue. It was a thrilling moment because, with that response, Frankie knew the slave was close to submitting.

Frankie broke the kiss, unwilling to rush the proceedings now that they were going so well. She moved her lips away but allowed her fingers to remain at the slave's breast. They studied one another with broad smiles and glassy eyes.

'What is it that makes McGivern so special?' Frankie asked. 'Is it his looks?'

Number three's cheeks flushed and she shifted her gaze away before meeting Frankie's eyes with a confidential grin. 'He's very handsome, don't you think?'

'I can see how he would appeal to some tastes,' Frankie allowed. 'Do you love him?'

Number three studied the velvet bedspread. Her cheeks had turned crimson and she refused to meet Frankie's gaze as she spoke. 'Slaves aren't supposed to love their masters.

171

They can be devoted to them, and they can worship them, but they aren't supposed to love them.'

'A lot of things happen that aren't supposed to,' Frankie said quietly. 'Bumble bees aren't supposed to fly. Scientists have decided they're so aerodynamically inefficient that they can't fly. Yet they still buzz around, making honey. You do love him, don't you?'

Number three nodded. She dared to gaze at Frankie as she made this silent admission.

Frankie made a soft, tut-tutting sound, continuing to roll the nipple between her thumb and forefinger. It was an awkward task to manage around the piercing but, with her fingers close to the tip, she was able to excite the bud without inflicting any discomfort. In a sad voice, she said, 'It's a shame that masters aren't as devoted to their slaves as the slaves are to their masters.'

'What do you mean?'

Frankie shrugged. 'Just what I say. I'm not talking about McGivern – not him specifically, anyway – I was just speaking from general experience.'

Number three was frowning. 'I still don't understand, mistress.'

Inwardly, Frankie cursed. Number three had stopped calling her 'mistress' for a brief moment and Frankie had seen it as a sign of the slave's developing trust. Hearing the word again sounded as though she had taken a backward step in the slave's affections. Determined to press on with her theme, Frankie forced her tone to sound reassuring. 'I was speaking generally. The majority of those masters and mistresses that I've known are an ungrateful breed.'

'Mr McGivern isn't like that, mistress.'

'Of course he isn't,' Frankie agreed. 'I was just telling you about those I've met before. Most of them would be very displeased by an adoration like yours.'

The slave was shaking her head, clearly puzzled. 'What master could be displeased by devotion, mistress?'

Frankie didn't need to act to make her tone sound cynical. 'You'd be surprised.'

'Are you talking about Mr McGivern?'

'You're fond of him. I wouldn't want to upset you by speaking against him.'

'It didn't stop you before.'

It was a defiant thing for a slave to say but Frankie was unperturbed. She felt pleased that the submissive had stopped calling her 'mistress' again. For this way forward to have a chance of working, Frankie knew that the slave had to believe that they were equals. And for number three to show some defiance was a sign that she was easing out of her role as an inferior.

'Before was different. Before, I was trying to force you to do my bidding,' Frankie reminded her. 'Right now, I'm trying to make up for some of the torment I've given today.'

Number three continued to frown doubtfully but Frankie could see she was half-convinced.

'I've been a worse bitch than is normal for me. I'm just trying to make things up to you.' Frankie eased herself away from the slave's side and placed herself over her. She stroked her hand down number three's body, over her stomach, and down to the shaved pubic mound. 'Let me make things up to you.'

'I thought you were going to use a cream,' number three reminded her.

Frankie smiled. 'I will, afterwards,' she said. 'But if you're covered with cream down there, I won't be able to kiss it better for you, will I?'

'But I don't . . .'

Frankie made no pretence of listening. She climbed between the woman's legs and lowered her mouth to number three's pussy. The scent of arousal was still strong and Frankie inhaled the aroma, surprised to discover that it awoke her own excitement.

'These piercings are beautiful,' she said honestly. She pushed her tongue forward, relishing the sensation of surgical steel and sensuous labia against her tongue. Number three quivered and her clitoris pulsed against Frankie's upper lip. Frankie teased her tongue through the piercing behind the bead of flesh and caused the nodule to pulse again.

Number three drew a long, shivering breath. 'There's really no need for you to do this,' she whispered.

'But I want to,' Frankie said. She teased the clitoris with the tip of her tongue and the slave responded with a sigh. Encouraged, Frankie lapped hungrily, savouring the taste of excitement.

The slave's cries deepened and her arousal grew more noticeable. She was obviously unwilling to just give herself over to the pleasure, but Frankie was determined to work against that reluctance. She knew she was close to breaking the slave's final barriers and the scent of victory felt as close as the aroma of pussy-honey.

'Where did you first meet the master?' number three asked.

Her words were husky and Frankie guessed that this was just an attempt to distance herself from the mounting arousal. She didn't mind the interruption, knowing that she could use the conversation to work on the slave's doubts. It was a manipulative way to think, but Frankie was used to absolving her conscience from any of the guilt that normally came with such thoughts. She just wished it was easier to rid herself of those feelings, this time. 'It's funny you should ask. I first met McGivern at a slave auction.'

It was a complete lie. Frankie had first met McGivern at an S & M bar. He had approached her table and told her that she was seated next to him and they were sitting in the non-smoking section. He had said that if she didn't extinguish her cigar he would extinguish it for her. She had told him to try it, and then try wiping his arse while both his arms were in slings. It had been an acrimonious beginning to their relationship and the years hadn't mellowed their mutual antipathy.

The mention of the slave auction had been another lie. Frankie had never been to one and she doubted the things existed outside the realms of torrid fantasies and sadomasochistic novels. She, McGivern and Simon all knew how to recruit new slaves for themselves and Frankie believed that if she had to find them at an auction, most of the fun would be bleached from the experience.

'What's a slave auction like?'

Frankie shrugged, still lapping at the dewy labia. The syrupy flavour was doing more than awakening her need. Now, it was fuelling her desires. She forced her mind to stay on the task of deceiving the slave. 'It didn't ring my bell,' she decided. She was trying to quickly compose a mental picture of a slave auction, hoping to slant her description so that it unsettled number three. 'The last one I went to was filled with a handful of crying slaves. There was a horde of lecherous businessmen, cursed with too much money and no real interest in the art of domination. The slaves were all chained and, although some of them seemed fairly happy, there were quite a few who looked sorry to be leaving their masters. I thought the whippings and beatings that went on seemed a little unnecessary: but then again, my tastes are quite puritanical.' Frankie stopped herself, wondering if she was stretching credulity too far with the dark picture she was painting, and her own supposedly pious response.

Number three didn't seem to have noticed Frankie's lapse in continuity. There was concern in her tone and her arousal seemed to be fading. 'Aren't potential owners vetted?'

Frankie thought quickly. 'They're credit-checked.'

'But . . .'

'The auctioneer doesn't need to do anything more than that,' Frankie broke in. She pushed her tongue against the clitoris but now it was unresponsive as the slave considered the bleak picture Frankie had drawn. Plunging her tongue deeper into the slave's wetness, Frankie realised she wasn't going to arouse any excitement while they were discussing this subject. It was an infuriating realisation because her own appetite had now become avaricious.

Trying to conceal her annoyance, Frankie said, 'I'll do that some more, once I've had a cigar.' She eased herself away from number three's pussy, giving the lips a final, parting kiss.

The slave smiled at her. There was a hesitancy in her eyes and, although she looked as though she was still contemplating the potential miseries of a slave auction, there was something else sparkling in her expression.

Frankie arched her eyebrows into a question as she retrieved a cigar from her jacket pocket.

The slave blushed. 'May I kiss you?' Her gaze flitted to the cleft between Frankie's legs, before she looked up again. Daring to hold Frankie's gaze, she added, 'You know. Like you just kissed me?'

Frankie grinned on hearing the words. When she had first dragged the slave into the bedroom, number three had refused to perform cunnilingus. Now she was asking to do it. The progress she had made in the last ten minutes was incredible. 'Do you want to?'

Number three nodded. With a shy grin, she whispered, 'I want to. I really want to.'

'If you really want to,' Frankie told her. 'I think I could enjoy that.'

Even if she didn't win the bet, Frankie had decided that this time at the castle had been worth the investment. She settled herself on the bed, a smouldering cigar in her mouth and the slave's lapping tongue nuzzling at her sex. It was a triumphant position – exactly how she had pictured herself when she first contemplated becoming the castle's owner. For the moment to be perfection, all she was short of was a bottle of beer for her free hand and heavy metal music as a backing track.

The only other thing she would have wanted was the removal of that nagging voice in the back of her head. Her conscience was telling her that she was wrong for deceiving the slave in such a calculated manner. While she knew that the voice was right, Frankie also knew that there was no other way forward that would give her any hope of success.

The slave's tongue was a delicious torture. She kissed, nibbled and lapped, making unspoken promises to the quickening tingle between Frankie's legs. Within moments of number three beginning, Frankie could feel herself heading towards a triumphant orgasm.

Glancing up from her position between Frankie's legs, the slave briefly stopped kissing. 'What was Mr McGivern doing at a slave auction?'

Frankie sighed, sorry that the enjoyment had been snatched away. Lying back and accepting the pleasure was a new experience for her and she was relishing it. She frowned to herself, trying to make sense of the slave's question as she toyed with the various answers. 'What do you mean when you ask, what he was doing at a slave auction? Did you think he might be there to sell ice-cream in the interval?'

Number three blushed and shook her head. She swallowed nervously before reiterating her question and Frankie guessed that it was an important point to the submissive. 'I meant, was he buying a slave, or was he selling one?'

Understanding crept over Frankie's face. She answered quickly, saying, 'He was doing both. He was buying and selling.'

'Do they allow both?'

Frankie nodded. 'McGivern was just trying to get a replacement for the slave he was selling on. We got to talking and he said his current submissive was boring him. She did everything he asked and he said there was no challenge any more.'

Number three studied Frankie, her eyes growing wider and more fearful as she considered this remark.

Frankie covered a wicked smile by drawing on her cigar. 'I thought it was just a sales pitch,' she went on. 'People say that sort of thing all the time at auctions. Even at car auctions, people don't say they're selling a vehicle because it's crap and won't do what they want. They say they're after something different and the one they're selling is more than worthy of the purchase price. But McGivern was telling the truth. The slave he was selling was truly obedient.'

'If she was truly obedient, why did he want to sell her?'

Frankie resisted the urge to sigh. She thought she had already explained things clearly enough, yet it seemed as though she was saying the same thing over and over again. Once number three had understood the subtle point she was trying to make, the slave could get back to her chore between Frankie's legs. For Frankie, that was a moment that couldn't come soon enough.

'He wanted the challenge,' Frankie explained. 'With the slave he had, he could say "do this" and "do that" and she'd do it. He's into CP and discipline and he needs a slave who will occasionally refuse, just so he can punish her.'

Number three considered this in silence, studying Frankie's face as though she was reading the depth of truth there. With a sullen nod, she moved her head back to Frankie's pussy and began to lap. Her tongue sparked tiny thrills from the tingling lips and Frankie shivered. She knew the slave was thinking things over and the realisation excited her as much as the squirming tongue. Her clitoris was teased to a frenzy and Frankie could feel herself moving closer towards a dizzying climax. The slave's fingers stroked at the folds of her labia and Frankie shifted her legs further apart. The lips of her sex were gently spread open and, with her clitoris revealed, the slave darted her tongue against the nub. Frankie drew a long breath, disturbed by the depth of her own excitement.

The slave's fingers were teasing her inner lips and Frankie wondered if the woman was going to slide a digit inside her. It was unusual to be with a lover and not know what was going to happen next. Since becoming a dominatrix, she had always taken control of every aspect of a sexual relationship, instructing her lovers exactly where and how to touch her. Common sense told Frankie that she couldn't start bellowing instructions at the slave now, as that would jeopardise the trust that had built between them. She considered making a gentle suggestion that the slave slip a finger inside her, but Frankie didn't trust her own tone to remain free from authority. With arousal blurring her thoughts, she knew it would be impossible to make any suggestion without barking it as a command.

Having to endure the slave's cunnilingus, when her body yearned for that little bit more, was an intolerable situation. For the sake of the bet, Frankie knew she had to make the sacrifice and allow the woman to continue at her own pace, even though her mind was screaming for a faster tempo. Under her commands, number three would have brought Frankie to a blistering climax by this point. She would have licked and finger-fucked her to a screaming orgasm, or suffered the consequences. But Frankie knew that, at this point, the mere mention of consequences would destroy her last hopes of winning the castle. She steeled herself against the relentless torment, sure that her body would soon be given the release it so desperately needed.

'Do you really think the master likes challenges?'

Frankie glanced down at the slave, her vision clouded by a haze of red. She was annoyed that the woman had stopped licking again and she wondered if the slave knew how much torment she was causing by breaking off to ask questions. If she had been paranoid, Frankie would have said the slave was bringing her to the point and then stopping as a deliberate act of revenge. It would be a fitting payback for the torture Frankie had given to her, but she doubted the slave had the capacity for that sort of manipulation. She knew there was only one bitch in the room who was cold enough for that degree of nastiness and Frankie had seen that woman's face in the bathroom mirror that morning.

Dismissing the idea of the slave being manipulative, Frankie blinked her vision clear and tried to focus on number three's face. She still felt dizzy with excitement and wondered why she had never experienced sex of this calibre before. She decided it didn't feel better, it was just different, and she thought the difference was her own lack of domination in the proceedings. Regardless of the reason for it, she knew that whether she won the bet or lost it, she was going to have to indulge herself in this new-found stimulus again.

Her wandering thoughts and escalating excitement made it difficult to keep track of the conversation and Frankie frowned at the slave, wondering what had stopped the woman from lapping at her sex. 'Say that again,' Frankie muttered.

The slave's lower jaw was hidden by Frankie's pubic mound but her words were clear enough. 'I was asking about the master. Do you really think he likes challenges?'

Frankie laughed, then stopped herself, hoping that her mirth didn't sound unkind. 'Do you really need to ask me that? If McGivern doesn't like challenges, what have you been doing in my bedroom all day? If McGivern doesn't like challenges, why have we all been dancing to his bloody tune since we arrived on the island?'

Nodding miserably, the slave lowered her head back to Frankie's sex and began to work her tongue against the folds.

'McGivern loves challenges,' Frankie told her, as another pleasurable ripple swept from between her legs. Knowing that this was the perfect moment to exploit the slave's growing doubts, she said, 'He loves challenges and he strikes me as the sort who likes them to be really demanding.'

The slave made a small sound and Frankie wondered if the woman was sobbing. Her tongue continued to lap daintily, and the tracing finger was moving ever closer to penetration, but her body undulated as though she was deeply unhappy. It was a sign of progress and Frankie felt more than a little guilty for gleaning so much pleasure from the slave's misery.

'Let's try this together,' Frankie suggested, shifting her position on the bed. 'I want to taste you again but I don't want you to stop kissing me.'

Number three's watery smile was tinged with gratitude. 'If you're sure,' she sniffed.

Frankie nodded, her crocodile grin calculated to look friendly. She dropped her cigar into an ashtray on the bedside cabinet and said, 'I think it's what we both want.'

Frankie remained with her back on the bed, allowing the slave to straddle her face. She had wanted to be on top but she didn't trust herself not to act like a dominatrix in that position. Being beneath the submissive was a reminder of the role she was playing and she consoled herself with the thought that it wasn't that unbearable. Number three's mouth was still able to reach her pussy lips and Frankie could tongue the slave's sex at her own leisurely pace.

The submissive's juices were honey-sweet with arousal. Frankie lapped at number three's labia, savouring the flavour as the slave continued to lick. She reached for the mounds of the slave's backside and pulled the cheeks apart so she could move closer. Her nose nuzzled deep between the pierced folds of flesh and the succulent aroma filled every breath.

Number three's fingers had slipped into the warmth of her sex and Frankie shivered as the tactile depths were teased. Her orgasm was sudden but no less satisfying because of that. A rush of elation swept through her body, tossing her back into the velvet bedspread.

Number three eased herself away, gracing Frankie with an unhappy smile as she lay down beside her.

Still giddy with pleasure, Frankie was oblivious to the slave's disheartened spirits. 'That was . . .' Frankie stopped herself, not sure there was a superlative capable of telling the submissive how tremendous the moment had been. She grinned down at her lover and watched as a solitary tear trickled down the woman's cheek.

'What's wrong?'

'What am I going to do?' number three whispered.

Frankie shifted herself up on the bed and tried to move closer.

Number three backed away, turning her face to hide her tears.

'What are you going to do about what?' Frankie asked.

'About the master,' number three explained. Her words were tear-choked whispers, but she still managed to deliver them as though Frankie should have known what she was talking about. 'I've done exactly as he asked me. He won't appreciate me any more. I know he won't.'

'I'm sure he'll appreciate you,' Frankie replied. Her voice was saccharine and motherly and she suddenly hated herself for deceiving someone who had given her so much pleasure. Reminding herself that this wasn't the way a slave-breaker thought, Frankie dismissed the voice of her conscience and said, 'You've followed his instructions to the letter.'

Number three wailed. 'Don't you see? That's what I'm saying. I've been truly obedient for him and now he's going to grow bored with me. He'll want to sell me and replace me with someone more challenging.'

'I'm sure he wouldn't do that,' Frankie said. She began to wish she could take back all the things she had said throughout the evening. More than that – if she could have backtracked on her conversations, she would have cancelled everything from the moment when McGivern asked her if she wanted to accept the bet.

'You know he'll sell me,' number three sobbed. 'You told me that he's done it before. You told me that he loves a challenge. I'm not so foolish as to think he won't do it again when he grows tired of me.'

Frankie cradled the woman in her arms and patted her back reassuringly. 'It can't be that bad,' she told her. 'Perhaps he'll sell you on to a nicer master, someone who you can love even more.'

'I don't want someone else. I don't want to *love* someone else. I couldn't love someone else.'

Now was the time to do the honourable thing, Frankie thought. If she wanted to retain a grain of self-respect, now was the time to tell the slave that she had been deceiving her. Then Frankie could go to McGivern and tell him she was withdrawing from the challenge. It was the only decent thing to do and if she hadn't invested so much money in the bet, Frankie knew she would have done it. If there wasn't the matter of her pride, Frankie told herself that she would have done it already. 'Perhaps you ought to start defying McGivern a little?' Frankie suggested. She held her breath, waiting for the slave's response.

Number three blinked her tears away and stared into Frankie's face. Her brown eyes were warm and filled with a helplessness that added to Frankie's guilt. Trying to ignore her conscience, Frankie continued to comfort the slave, drying the tears away from her cheeks.

'I could defy him,' number three decided.

'That should help bring you to his attention,' Frankie said carefully. She looked away, not wanting to meet the slave's eyes when she next spoke. 'If I ever visit you and McGivern again, will you tell me how it went?'

Number three shook her head. She wiped the last of her tears away and gave Frankie a watery smile. 'I won't have to tell you about it. You'll see how he responds to my defiance at dawn.'

Frankie tried to look as though she didn't understand what the slave was saying. Her expression felt contrived but she was sure number three hadn't seen the deception. 'What do you mean? What are you going to do?'

Number three swallowed and held her gaze. 'I'm going to defy the master. I'm going to defy the master and do the dance of submission for you.'

It should have been a moment of celebration, Frankie thought. After all her hard work, the slave's promise to relent should have made her feel triumphant. Instead, Frankie felt crushed beneath the weight of her own guilt. She tried to dismiss the feeling before it had properly settled but it was impossible not to suffer with it. Having lied to the slave and deceived her to get this far, Frankie wondered if she was paying too high a price to become the owner of the castle.

Ten

Jane swallowed around the ball-gag and stared at McGivern with terrified eyes. While the slave had been playing with her, Jane's naked body had become soaked with sweat. Now that sweat chilled her like ice-water and she shivered beneath McGivern's glare.

'I have the power to make you a very unhappy woman,' McGivern told her. He was brandishing a crop, his upper lip curled into a sneer.

Jane shook her head, her wide eyes watching as he stepped closer.

'I can hurt your career with my influence on your employer. I can hurt your future prospects by the same means. But, most importantly – and I think you should remember this – I can hurt you.'

Jane drew a ragged breath and rested her weight on her suspended arms. Her pussy lips pressed heavily against the wooden horse and she groaned as another shock of pleasure caught her unaware.

The blonde slave was grinning between them. Her eyes were shining in the orange torchlight and she switched her gleeful gaze from McGivern to Jane as though she was watching a tennis match. The nipple clamps still dangled from her breasts, forgotten and swaying gently as she turned from the master to his intended victim. Their polished handles sparked dazzling reflections into Jane's eyes, although the temporary blindness they inflicted was something of a respite. With her vision obscured, Jane couldn't see McGivern, or the crop he was carrying.

She screamed against the gag but the sound was muted to a pathetic whimper before it crossed her lips. Between flashes of light, she saw him raise the crop high in the air. Its black leather length was tinged with orange light from the torch behind him. His frown was sombre and he glared at her with the darkest loathing.

Even though it didn't strike her, Jane felt the blow of the crop as soon as it descended. The sound of leather slicing air rang in her ears. It was followed by the crisp crack of smacked flesh. Jane flinched away from the noise, sure that the blow had struck her somewhere.

The blonde slave gasped and turned to face McGivern. She wore an anguished expression and rubbed at her backside.

'You'll be dealt with later,' McGivern growled. 'I told you to entertain this one, not punish the life out of the poor bitch. Release her, take the remaining clamp off her tit, take the violin from up her arse and then go down to my bedroom and wait.'

The slave almost stumbled in her hurry to obey. She turned to face Jane, clearly uncertain as to which command she should be following first. Her hands darted out towards Jane's breasts, then she made as if to reach behind her.

McGivern broke in, grabbing one of the slave's nipple clamps and pulling.

She cried out, clearly winded by his brutal treatment. Her chest rose and fell with a nervous flutter and her eyes squeezed shut around the threat of tears.

'You'll do those things I've just said, and then you'll wait for me without removing these.' He yanked hard on the clamp, to show exactly what he meant.

What little breath the slave had managed to regain was tugged out of her. She nodded and mouthed a thank you to him before turning back to Jane. Her eyes were shining with glassy excitement and Jane saw that, inside the clamps, the woman's nipples were stiffer than ever. Although she was trying to conceal it from her master, the slave wore a grateful smile and her cheeks were flushed with excitement.

'Until dawn, at least, I remain the master of this castle.' McGivern's words were spoken directly to Jane but she realised he was speaking for the slave's benefit as well. 'That means my subordinates will do exactly as I say, exactly how I say it.'

Jane glared at him.

The slave nodded meekly, easing the clamp from Jane's breast.

It was an uncomfortable sensation. The jaws were lined with vicious teeth that had bitten into her nipple. The removal was a greater agony than the application had been and, since this remaining clamp had been secured, Jane's breast had become used to the torment. Admittedly, every little shiver reminded her it was there, but the relentless jaws no longer inspired the same reeling blows that they had initially. As the teeth gave up their grip, agonising pain flared from the tip of her breast.

'I'm very unhappy with you,' McGivern told Jane. 'I've lost this bet, I've lost my reputation and I've lost this castle. I blame you for all of that.'

Jane shook her head. She felt dizzy with the piercing bolts that were shooting from her breast and she was having difficulty concentrating on McGivern's words. Her breathing had deepened to a husky sigh and she braced herself for the final pain that would come when the slave pulled the clamp away.

'I can forgive you for having Simon's card,' McGivern said magnanimously. He was still wielding the crop, swiping it back and forth as though he was trying to perfect his stroke. 'I know what the faggot is like,' McGivern went on. 'And I suppose there could be an innocent reason for him wanting to employ your services in the future.'

The slave tugged the clamp away. The jaws weren't fully open and the serrated teeth scraped painfully at Jane's flesh. Jane bit into the gag and shrieked. The sound didn't make it into the room but her body needed to vent the air as a form of pain-killer. She believed she could have tolerated the discomfort more easily if the sensation hadn't had a sting in its tail. Along with the blistering pain, there was a rush of pleasure and that, more than anything else, left her breathless and panting. Her nipple was aflame with excitement and her arousal was now coloured by an unimagined richness.

'I can forgive you for trying to sneak into my bedroom,' McGivern went on, seeming unaware of her excitement. 'You're a solicitor and, with there being no ambulances for you to chase on this island, you must have been growing a little bored. Whatever drove you to try to sneak into my room, I can sympathise with it, I can understand it, and I can even forgive it.'

She glared at him through a misty haze. The slave had moved behind her and was starting to remove the violin's egg from her anus. The intrusive weight, like the pressure of the nipple clamp, had become almost tolerable. As the slave started to pull it from her rectum, Jane was torn between feelings of discomfort and humiliation. It was difficult to say which was worst to suffer, because she knew that neither was hampering her excitement. The pulse of her arousal continued to throb with a quickening beat. The egg made a slippery egress from her backside and Jane's inner muscles quivered unhappily as it slid away. In an attempt to appease her base appetite, Jane ground her pussy-lips against the horse's back.

McGivern tested the crop through the air. It whistled dryly, landing hard against the wooden horse. The tip was close to the lips of her sex and Jane felt the sting of hairs being snatched from her pubic mound. She sucked air and looked at him, her concentration suddenly focused on his words.

There was smouldering malice in his eyes. 'There's only one thing I can't forgive,' he told her. 'I can't forgive the way you've fought against me.'

Jane blinked, wishing she wasn't gagged so she could tell him to stop rambling and make his point. The slave was fumbling to slide a key into the manacles above her head and Jane didn't know whether she wanted to be released or not. Her position on the horse was unbearable, and she doubted her body could stand another minute of the torment, but she knew that her present situation had to be better than the fate McGivern was plotting. His eyes shone with the threat of retribution and she could see he wasn't simply going to let her go free, once she was released from the manacles. The way he was holding the whip, still testing it through the air now and again, left Jane in no doubt that his intended punishment was going to be merciless.

'You've fought me since you arrived here,' he said. 'And for no real reason.'

Jane shook her head. She was trying to deny the accusation and tell him she didn't understand what he meant. Seeing the anger remain in his eyes, she knew that neither sentiment had been conveyed.

'You were fighting against me when you said you didn't want to watch the dance – yet you watched it, and you got off on it. You were fighting against me when you said you didn't want to whip my slave's arse – yet you whipped her, and you got off on it. I can see that you want to do the dance for me. Your need to do it is shining in your eyes, and we both know that if you danced, you'd get off on it. Yet I know that if I suggest it to you again, you'll fight me and refuse.'

Jane looked away. Her hands fell from the manacles as soon as they were released and her entire body slumped heavily downward. McGivern stepped forward and collected her in his arms. He was surprisingly strong and he lifted her from the horse without making the effort look like an arduous task. Wordlessly, he carried her to the bed and lay her down. Behind him, as he towered over her, she could see her drained reflection in the mirrored ceiling. The ball-gag still filled her mouth, making her lips as wide as her scared, staring eyes. Her hair was bedraggled and sweat-soaked. The lank locks clung to her cheeks and forehead.

McGivern glanced towards the blonde slave and snapped his fingers. 'You have your instructions to go and wait for me. I shan't repeat them without losing my patience.'

The slave turned and ran for the door.

McGivern glared down at Jane. 'And what am I going to do with you?'

If the gag hadn't been in her mouth, Jane would have suggested several things. She groaned against the ball of the rubber but she already knew her words would be inarticulate gibberish.

McGivern reached for her breast and Jane allowed him to touch her. Her time on the wooden horse had left her drained and she couldn't find the strength to refuse his caress. She watched him tweak the tip of her nipple and was surprised by the crippling thrill that struck her. Glancing down at herself she saw that the clamp's teeth marks were imprinted in her skin and her nipple was standing erect for him. Miserably, she saw that her body was responding to McGivern with a need that defied all rational thought.

'It's still the same, isn't it?' he observed. 'Here you are, desperate for some satisfaction, desperate for me, yet you're still intent on playing the part of the pious innocent.' He shook his head wearily.

Jane opened her eyes in wide denial when he tightened his fingers around her bud. His concentration was fixed on his own introspective journey and she saw that he wasn't watching her face as she tried to tell him he was wrong.

'I should have started working on you as soon as you arrived,' McGivern told her. He rolled the nipple between his finger and thumb, ignoring her dull whimpering. Collecting the second teat with his other hand, he squeezed it artlessly. Discomfort spread from the areola, leaving Jane panting.

'Tell me you're not enjoying that,' McGivern growled.

If her thoughts hadn't been fogged with arousal, she would have pointed at the gag in her mouth and reminded him that she couldn't tell him anything. He had to know she was enjoying it but, with the rubber ball staunching her words, she had no way of confirming or denying his suspicions.

'Tell me you're not enjoying that, and I'll call you a liar. I'll bet it's the same with your cunt, isn't it?'

Before she could cross her legs, his hand had plunged down to the crease of her sex. She attempted to squeeze her thighs against him, but he broke her grip with an effortless flex of his knuckles. He pushed rudely between her aching pussy-lips and slid two fingers into her.

The penetration was an aperitif for the banquet that her body demanded. On the horse, her clitoris and labia had been stimulated beyond the point of pleasurable pain. The inner walls of her sex craved to feel something and, now that the moment was on her, she relished every millimetre.

'Like I thought,' he said, sliding his fingers out. 'Hot and dripping.' He held the fingers under her nose, allowing Jane to inhale the sweet scent of her arousal. 'You're as horny as a bitch on heat,' he growled. 'Yet still you're pretending to be the castle's resident vestal virgin.' He climbed from the bed and threw his crop to the floor in disgust. 'It's pathetic, Jane. You disappoint me.'

She tried to raise herself from the bed but she felt too weak for such strenuous exercise. Reaching for the back of her head, Jane started to work on the awkward clasp that fastened the gag. The straps had become entangled with her sweat-matted hair and her fingers were still numb from being trapped in the manacles, yet she struggled valiantly with the task.

'There aren't words to express my disgust,' McGivern said. He had his back to her, not watching as she released the fastening on her gag. 'I don't even think I have the interest to punish you. I know that you'd get off on it if I did, but I also know you'd pretend it wasn't what you wanted.' In a ponderous tone, he said, 'I think I'll just kill your career prospects.'

Jane snatched the gag away from her mouth and drew a long, heavy sigh.

He turned to face her, registering no surprise that she had removed the gag. 'I hope the prospect of unemployment doesn't upset you too much, but it's the best way I can think of punishing you.'

Jane lurched towards him. It took a tremendous effort – every movement of her thighs rekindled the agonising bliss

190

she had endured on the wooden horse. Her movements were unsteady; she fell towards him as soon as her feet touched the floor.

McGivern held out his hands and caught her but Jane didn't want to be caught. She knelt on the stone floor and brushed his arms away from her body. Determinedly, she reached for the belt around his waist and began snatching at it.

'What the hell are you doing?'

She couldn't have answered, even if he had tried forcing her. Although the gag was no longer between her lips, her lower jaw ached and she knew it would take a while before her mouth felt capable of managing normal speech. Besides, with her ferocious appetite dictating her actions, Jane knew there was no time for words. She tugged the belt from his waistband and began to pull the trousers from him.

'I asked you what the hell you were doing,' McGivern told her. His fingers caught her hair and he tugged her head back. It was a vicious movement, straining the muscles in her neck so harshly that tears welled in her eyes. Glaring down at her, he demanded, 'Answer me, woman. Tell me what you're doing.'

Jane drew a shuddering sigh. 'I'm going to suck you off,' she hissed. The words were agony to speak but she made sure he heard each one. 'Stop pulling my head away, and let me get my mouth around your cock.'

His hesitation only lasted for an instant. She saw the brief flicker of doubt in his expression, and then it was gone. His smile was wicked and he looked to be settling himself back in the position of control once again. 'Ask for it,' he told her.

Jane groaned. 'I want to do it,' she hissed. 'Isn't that enough?'

'It's not enough for me. I want you to ask for it.' His hard shaft was inches away from her face. The dark blue veins pulsed against the rigid length. His foreskin had peeled back to reveal his swollen dome and Jane knew she could have tugged her head forward and lapped at him.

McGivern held his shaft at the base and wafted his cock beneath her nose. 'Ask for it.'

'Let me suck you,' she whispered.

'Say please.'

She felt beyond arguing. She needed to take his shaft in her mouth and if that was the only condition preventing her, Jane was happy to relent. The scent of his excitement was infuriatingly close as he waved his shaft from side to side. 'Please,' she gasped. 'Let me suck you.'

He continued to hold her hair, tightening his grip so the follicles screamed as she strained to get her face closer to him. 'Say please, and call me master.'

She shivered and glared up at him. 'Isn't it enough that you've made me want this?' she demanded. 'I'm here on my knees, begging to suck you off, and I've said please, like you've asked. Isn't that enough for you?'

He pushed the tip of his dome over her upper lip. If she had pushed her tongue out, Jane could have lapped at him. Instead, she was treated to the slick smear of pre-come that he daubed against her skin. The smell of his seed was making her giddy.

'Say please, and call me master.'

His words were a fuel to the raging inferno of her desire. 'Please, master, let me suck your cock.'

His grin was triumphant. He started to ease his fingers from her hair and nodded permission. 'You may suck it,' he allowed.

She moved her head forward but he stopped her, tightening his grip viciously. Jane glared up at him, wondering what other condition he was going to impose on her.

'Make sure you do a good job,' he grinned. With the words spoken, he released his hold on her hair.

Jane fell on to his shaft. She opened her mouth wide, determined to accommodate as much as she could. She enveloped her lips around him, enjoying the feel of his shaft in her mouth. The head rested at the back of her throat and she rolled her tongue against the hard, pulsing flesh of his length. Greedily, she licked at the taste of arousal and clean, fresh sweat.

McGivern reached down to stroke her cheek and she flinched away from his touch, expecting him to pull her hair again. When she realised it was an affectionate caress, she smiled with her eyes up into his face.

'This is an unexpected turn of events,' McGivern told her. 'Once you've finished doing that, I want you to explain why you did it. I'm not complaining, or angry, I'm just curious.'

She nodded as she sucked him.

Each time she lowered her face on to him, the head of his cock pressed hard against the back of her throat. She wanted to feel him go beyond there, to deep-throat him properly. It was an act she had never performed for any previous lover and the idea only occurred to her now because she thought it would please him. Jane drew a deep breath and relaxed the muscles at the back of her mouth. She moved her head slowly down and allowed his dome to push further than it had before.

The bulbous end started to slide against the back of her throat.

Jane pulled away, gagging but delighted with the sensation. She felt sure that McGivern had come close to ejaculating and, although she wasn't certain, she thought he had muttered some grateful expletives. The pulse of his cock had been pounding so loudly that everything else in the room was inaudible.

She glanced up, delighted to see that he was studying her with renewed respect. His hand went back to her hair and he forced her on to his length. He was pushing deep into her mouth and she briefly wondered if he wanted her to try swallowing him again. It had been as awkward as she had anticipated, but no less satisfying because of that. She started preparing her throat muscles again, ignoring the shriek of her scalp as he pulled harder. His length was stiffening between her lips, and then she felt his climax.

She moved her face slightly away from him, so she could appreciate the full flavour of him. His seed spattered into her mouth in a hot jet. Before she could register it in her own mind, a second pulse was shuddering along his length.

She swallowed his come, continuing to work her mouth around him. The flavour was almost lost as she quickly gulped down his climax in a greedy attempt to suck more from him. He released his grip on her hair and started to take a step away from her. 'That was an unexpected turn of events,' he said.

Jane shook her head. He had pulled his shaft out of her mouth but she still wanted more from it. She could see his erection was beginning to wane and that sight inspired the threat of disappointment. Still on her knees, she lurched towards him and took his wilting length between her lips.

'There's no need to . . .'

Between her lips, she could feel his shaft pulse again. She couldn't decide if it was the last pulse of his fading erection, or the first stirring of his next. Whatever the cause, Jane knew that she had captured his interest.

'You were going to tell me what's driving you to do this,' he reminded her. He was trying to make his tone sound casual but Jane could hear the undercurrent of arousal that inflected his words.

She released him for a moment. 'I'll tell you when I'm finished,' she hissed, then resumed working her mouth up and down him. He was quickly stiffening as she rolled her tongue against him and now she was properly able to appreciate his taste. The salty flavour was cloying and intense and Jane savoured it with a growing warmth between her legs.

McGivern stroked his fingers through her hair, not pulling the strands but quietly maintaining the threat. 'I could make you stop and tell me,' he told her.

But you won't, she thought. She saw that she was close to enraging him with her defiance and she moved her mouth from his shaft so she could answer his anger before he vented it. 'You want me to suck you, as much as I want to do it. If you stop me now, I could change my mind.' She glanced slyly at him and said, 'I could change my mind about the other things I want from you this evening, so why don't you just let me finish?'

He was glaring at her, clearly unhappy with the demands

194

she was making. Jane doubted he was reluctant to enjoy the pleasures she was promising and she suspected his unease came from the challenge that she presented to his authority. Trying to coax him to her way of thinking, Jane licked the end of his shaft as though it were a treat. Holding his angry gaze, she said, 'Please let me suck it again, master.'

Her plea had the desired effect.

McGivern nodded grudgingly and said she could continue.

With permission given, Jane began to suck him again. She guided him towards the bed and, once he was sitting on its edge, she felt more easily able to satisfy him. The whole length of his shaft was accessible as he lay back and Jane made another attempt to swallow him fully. When the gag had been in her mouth, she had thought of screaming for release, and the only thing that had stopped her had been the knowledge that it would hurt her throat. Now, as she felt the pressure of his bulbous end against her tonsils, she was thankful that she hadn't tried screaming. Her throat was the only part of her mouth that didn't ache after the torment of the gag and the muscles relaxed easily to accept him.

'Too much,' McGivern growled, starting to raise himself from the mattress. 'You'll be bringing me off too soon,' he complained.

She snatched her mouth away from him and pushed him back on to the bed. It was easier to topple him than she had imagined and he simply lay there, staring expectantly up. 'I don't want you coming just yet,' she panted. 'I need to feel you inside me.'

'I've just been inside you.'

'Not where I need you most.' Without answering his questioning expression, she straddled him, took his shaft in her hand, and guided the head towards her sex.

He grabbed hold of her wrist, stopping her with a casual display of strength. 'Not so fast.'

She stared at him, uncertain and puzzled. She tried tugging his cock closer to the needy lips of her hole, but

195

his grip was resolute. 'Please,' she begged, unable to mask the mounting urgency. 'Please, let me.'

'Please, let me, master,' he corrected.

She glared at him, then smiled. 'Master,' she intoned. 'Please, let me, master.'

With a throaty chuckle, he nodded and released her wrist. Jane guided the head of his shaft to her bruised labia and nestled it against her cleft. As soon as he was in the right position, she squatted heavily down on him.

The pleasure soared through her like a rocket. His entry spread her sex-lips apart and forced his shaft deep within her. She could feel the head of his cock burrowing against the neck of her womb. It was the stimulus her body had been demanding all evening and she wished there was the time to revel in it. The frustrating time she had spent yearning for this as she dangled over the horse had taken its toll on her patience. He was inside her and all that mattered now was riding him to a climax.

She pulled away from him and then plunged back down. It was an artless form of lovemaking, barbaric and animalistic, but Jane knew it was going to satisfy her desires.

He reached up, his hands cupping her breasts. His fingers found her aching nipples and he squeezed them harshly.

Jane shrieked, putting her own hands to his chest and burrowing her nails against him. His length was filling her sodden hole and she could hear her labia slurping greedily with each thrust. Every downward plunge threatened to push her beyond the brink of orgasm and Jane quickened her pace, needing to experience that climactic thrill.

It took four thrusts to bring herself to the point. His punishing fingers at her breasts were helping. The combination of pleasure and pain was a pernicious aphrodisiac and Jane knew that a fifth and final thrust would give her the release she had been craving.

McGivern pushed her from his body and slid his cock from her hole. He twisted her to one side and threw her to the bed. Jane landed on her back, staring up at him with an expression of fury and hurt. She could see her own features reflected in the mirror above and the woman staring down looked like a wild thing.

'You want to come, don't you?'

She nodded.

'You're desperate to come, aren't you?'

She tried reaching for his shaft but he pushed her back to the bed.

'You're desperate to come, aren't you?'

'Yes,' she growled.

'Then we'll do it my way,' he told her. He was kneeling between her legs and he pressed his cock against her sex.

Jane groaned. McGivern wasn't inside her but the promise of intimacy was there. He dragged the moment out, rolling his bulbous dome over her sodden lips. The pressure was firm and intoxicating, but he managed to avoid actually sliding inside her. The need to have him began to well more intensely.

'Please, master,' she begged.

He grinned down at her and she could see that he was flattered by her use of his title. 'Master?' he asked, raising one eyebrow.

She nodded, trying to force herself on to him at the same time.

'Master,' he repeated thoughtfully. With a practised motion, he lifted her legs to his shoulder and pushed himself into her.

Jane screamed. The pressure of his entry seemed that much more fulfilling in this position. His length ploughed into her, rubbing sensuously along her inner walls. She had thought, when he moved her, that the moment of orgasm had been taken away. Now, she could feel herself hurtling towards the pinnacle of pleasure. Another thrust and she knew that the climax would be screaming through her body.

McGivern obliged, pushing himself fully into her.

There wasn't the time to savour it. He continued to force himself into her as the waves of jubilation sang through her. The climax was heightened by his continual thrusting.

Each movement of his cock intensified her pleasure and she realised that, after this moment's bliss, there would be plenty more to enjoy.

He showed himself as a masterful lover, taking control of her body as though she were his plaything. As the last echoes of her first climax began to subside, he slipped his cock from her sex and turned her over. The pleasure had weakened her to a point where Jane couldn't have protested, even if she had wanted to. She lay face down on the bed, preparing herself for whatever he had planned.

He took her from behind, pounding relentlessly between her arse cheeks.

Her pussy-lips responded to him with a blend of discomfort and delight that was too entwined for Jane to tell the difference. She buried her face against the bedspread and chewed on the velvet in an attempt to stifle her screams. From a distance, she heard herself shriek, not sure if she was in the throes of another climax or simply giving voice to the bliss that her body was receiving.

McGivern pulled himself out of her, then dragged her so that she was kneeling at the side of the bed. Before she could turn around to fix him with a questioning expression, he was plunging back inside. His shaft filled her, and this time there was no escape. He had trapped her between the edge of the bed and his relentless cock. Each forceful entry pressed her into the side of the bed and pushed her into dizzying realms of satisfaction. It didn't matter that he was now controlling the pace. His needs seemed in perfect rhythm with her own and she was happy to allow him to satisfy her. Another scream was building at the back of her throat and she buried her face in the bedspread, luxuriating in its velvet caress.

Before she could vent the sound, McGivern had tugged her from the bed and dragged her to her feet. She stood awkwardly in his embrace, allowing him to hold her tightly as he kissed her face and neck. His cock was back at the lips of her sex and he took her as she stood against him. This time, his shaft pressed unbearably against her clitoris.

The scream she had been about to release came close to

spilling from her lips. She deliberately stopped the sound, refusing to give voice to her pleasure. Jane wrapped her arms around him and pressed closer. Her bruised nipples were squeezed against his chest and the memory of their pain was the final impetus her body needed. The orgasm washed over her as the cry soared from her lungs.

His cock pulsed deep within her confines. The head shivered against the neck of her womb as he held her tightly. His own climactic grunt was lost beneath her wails but she saw his satisfied smile. His face was a dusty vision and she knew that her own gratified smile was weakened by tears.

Without saying a word, they collapsed on the bed together. Her heart was hammering in her chest and she was surprised to feel an ache in her sex, as though her body still craved more. Deliberately ignoring that sensation, Jane turned to him and wiped the tears from her eyes. She didn't dare to look into the mirrored ceiling above them, fearful of the bedraggled reflection that would stare down at her.

'Are you going to tell me now?' he asked.

He sounded as breathless as she felt and Jane wondered how much pleasure she had given him. His cool smile was faltering and his eyes shone with an appreciation that wasn't typical of the man she had first met in the banquet hall.

'What changed your mind?' he pressed. 'What fired that spark for you?'

She drew a long breath and tried to compose her thoughts from the maddening jumble that whirled inside her head. The flesh between her legs was still tingling and, although the last orgasm had been intensely satisfying, her body was beseeching her to try one last indulgence.

She sat up on the bed and fixed him with the sternest expression she could manage. After the intimacy they had just shared, it was difficult to be too firm with him, but she knew that she had to show some spirit if she wanted him to listen to her. 'All right, you bastard,' she gasped. 'If you want answers, then I'll give you answers, but you'd better listen to me, because I'm only going to say this the once.'

McGivern looked startled by her outburst and Jane supposed that his surprise was the only thing that stopped her from being punished again. She spoke quickly, fearful of the retribution that would be involved if she didn't make her point before he remembered to be angry.

'You terrified me when I arrived here yesterday. And the last day has been an eye-opener for me in so many ways that I couldn't begin to count them.' She glared at him, wishing she could conceal her reluctant admiration. 'But you've woken appetites in me, McGivern: appetites I didn't know I had, and appetites I'm still hesitant to acknowledge. But they're there. And you were the one who put them there.'

He continued to study her, his poker-face giving nothing away.

'For the sake of these appetites, because I want to find out more about the pleasures of submission and servility, I'm willing to propose a compromise.'

His upper lip curled. 'Submissives don't propose compromises.'

'Submissives don't usually have an absolute control over all your legal affairs, so you'll agree that this is an unusual situation which allows us a little leeway from what's considered normal.'

He nodded his agreement with obvious bad grace.

'I'm not happy about the way you misled your friends . . .' Jane started.

'They're not my friends . . .'

'. . . and I won't be a party to gaining money under false pretences,' she said, speaking over him.

'. . . was an honest bet.'

'You've been stringing them along by pretending you're not the owner,' Jane told him. 'You claim to have arrived here a couple of days before the rest of us, yet your slaves tell anecdotes about the punishments you inflicted in these rooms throughout the last year.'

He glared at her and she wondered if she had pushed him too far with this display of knowledge. She dared to hold his gaze and was surprised to see his features mellow into a sheepish grin.

'I guess you caught me red-handed,' McGivern admitted. 'I've actually lived here with my entourage for the last two years. When I decided it was time to sell, I thought the bet would be the ideal way of assuring a good return on my investment. It's a no-lose situation, really. If I had won the bet, I would have kept the castle and the money that those two had invested. With losing, I still get to keep the money they've used as their stakes and that amounts to nearly double the castle's value.'

Jane nodded solemnly, all her suspicions confirmed by his words.

He was still staring at her, but now his frown had developed a threatening sneer. 'So, what are you going to do about it? What's this compromise you're suggesting?'

'I want to do the dance.'

He stared at her with slack-jawed amazement. 'Excuse me?'

'I want to do the dance for you,' she repeated. 'And I will, providing you do one thing for me.'

'What's that?'

Jane grinned. 'You won't like what I'm about to suggest.'

Eleven

Dawn flooded into the banquet hall. The east window was ideally placed to catch the first morning rays as they climbed over the horizon. One moment, the room was trapped in ghostly shadows with the stone walls and ornate tapestries shrouded in gloom. And then it was swathed in glorious morning sunlight, the day's first beams picking out threads of gold from the drapes and upholstery.

'You may enter, my friends,' McGivern declared cheerfully. He raised his hand and slapped it heavily on to the bare bottom of the woman who knelt at his side.

Jane released a whistle of breath, the sound coming from some place between enjoyment and humiliation. She was dressed in the uniform of a slave, with strips of black leather wound around her bare body, exposing her sex and breasts as though she was on public display. 'That bloody hurt,' she gasped.

'It was bloody meant to,' he told her. 'You've got me over a barrel, you nasty little vixen, and if this is the only chance I get to pay you back, then you'd better prepare yourself for a lot worse.'

'If that thought didn't excite me so much, I'd take issue with it.'

'If that thought didn't excite you so much, you wouldn't be here.'

She glanced back over her shoulder, an action that any other slave would never have dared to do. McGivern met her cool stare with a questioning frown.

'As much as all this excites me, I'll nullify your contract

unless you do as you promised,' she warned him. 'I'm prepared to do a lot of things for you. I'm prepared to subject myself to a lot of things for you. But, rest assured, I won't sacrifice my principles.'

He glared at her and considered slapping her arse again. 'I've given you my promise. Stop gloating at me and start acting like a submissive.'

They studied one another defiantly before she nodded and lowered her gaze. McGivern contemplated smacking her backside once she was facing away from him, then thought better of it. He rested his hand against her cleft and gently teased her pussy lips. Jane's back broadened as she drew an excited breath. Her labia peeled open beneath his intrusive fingers and his hand was quickly soaked with her arousal.

'Enter,' McGivern called again. 'It's dawn. It's time. Let the challenge commence.'

The door opened and the guests marched slowly in. He guessed they had waited for him to call a second time as an act of defiance. Like him, they were masters in the art of domination and neither Simon nor Frankie took kindly to being summoned into a room.

Simon led the way, one arm linked with the woman he had been challenged to dominate and a fresh-faced young man dangling on the other. The young man was grinning inanely at Simon and the girl in turn.

McGivern's features hardened. Seeing the three of them grace each other with cheerful smiles, McGivern's frown resurfaced and his mood began to darken. 'Dear God!' He glared at Simon as he spoke. 'Aside from the gargoyles, is there nothing in this castle you wouldn't fuck?'

'Well, there's you.'

McGivern fell silent, stung by the retort.

Ignoring him, Simon gallantly pulled out a chair for the female student and then helped his male friend into a second seat. He kissed each of them before settling himself between the couple. Draping his arms around their shoulders, he whispered something to his lovers and their guffaws echoed merrily around the banquet hall.

Knowing that they were laughing at him, McGivern lowered his head to Jane's ear. 'Was there a rule in the contract that forbids him from having a guest here?'

'If there was, I didn't write it.'

McGivern slapped his hand against her arse. Before she had given release to her first cry of protest, he had slapped her for a second time.

'What the hell was that for?'

'The first was for not putting that clause in the contract.'

'And the second?'

He slapped her arse again. 'You forgot to call me master.'

Jane shivered. She released a guttural sound, thickened with the tincture of arousal.

McGivern pressed his fingers back to her sex and glanced up to see Frankie and number three walking into the room. The chance to insult Frankie cheered his waning spirits and he managed to shake off the feeling of nuisance that Simon had inspired. 'Ladies, and Frankie,' he called cheerfully. 'Come on in. We've been missing you.'

Frankie curled her lip as she glared at him. She reached for a cigar from her jacket pocket and held him with a disdainful expression as she lit it.

'I'd rather you didn't smoke that in here,' McGivern told her loftily.

'And I'd rather you didn't breathe,' she snapped. 'Why don't we both give up our annoying habits? You go first.'

McGivern pulled back the reins on his worsening mood. He forced himself to smile, incorporating number three with the grin. 'Enough unpleasantness. It's good of you both to come but I have bad news for you, Frankie. Simon isn't the only one whose submissive is willing to do the dance. Mine is ready to perform as well.'

Frankie blew a cloud of smoke in McGivern's direction. She glared at Jane and then dropped into a seat, facing Simon and his two companions. Number three stood dutifully beside her. 'And why is that bad news?' Frankie asked.

McGivern could feel his smile stretching like a lunatic's.

There was only one thing more satisfying than personal victory and that was rubbing an opponent's nose in their defeat. 'That means you'll be the only one who failed to meet the challenge. You're going to have the embarrassment of watching Simon and I prove our superiority over you.'

Frankie considered him nonchalantly. She glanced back over her shoulder, into the slave's face. 'Tell McGivern what you're going to do.'

McGivern's stomach muscles clenched uneasily. He frowned, not wanting to believe that Frankie could have broken number three. His slave's obedience was the one aspect of the bet he had never doubted. Number three was servile to him and to him only. To anyone else – including Frankie – she was indomitable.

Number three met his gaze. Her face was an inscrutable mask that hid any emotion she might have been feeling. 'I'm going to do the dance of submission for Frankie,' number three told him boldly. She glanced down at Frankie and asked, 'Do I have to call him a twat?'

Frankie shrugged and drew on her cigar. She was fixing McGivern with a wicked grin but speaking to the slave. 'Do you want to?'

Number three nodded. She glared defiantly at McGivern and, with their eyes locked, she whispered, 'Twat.'

McGivern blinked. His cheeks flushed an angry red colour and the need to vent his rage welled within him. He raised his hand and prepared to slap Jane's arse again.

'We've reached a stalemate,' Simon declared cheerfully. 'What do we do now? Call it off? Crawl away to our separate corners and wait for your solicitor to reclaim our investments?'

McGivern rounded on him. 'And when did we reach a stalemate? As I see it, we're in the same position now that we were yesterday morning.'

'But all our submissives have agreed to do the dance.'

'There was more to the challenge than that. They all have to perform before it becomes a stalemate.'

'You still want them to dance?'

McGivern nodded. 'Of course I still want them to dance. Isn't that what we're all here for?'

Simon glanced uneasily at the girl by his side.

Her reassuring smile made McGivern scowl. He glanced at Frankie and saw she was trying to lean closer to number three. She looked like she was trying to whisper something confidential and he sensed it was important to her that she do it discreetly.

'Is that what you're here for, Frankie?' McGivern barked.

There was a hint of guilt on her face when she turned to glare at him. 'Tell McGivern you're ready to dance,' Frankie told number three. 'And call him a twat again.'

McGivern raised a silencing hand. 'I've already got the message,' he said. 'We're all ready? We're all prepared?'

There was a general murmur of assent around the table.

'Very well,' McGivern said, slapping his hand against Jane's buttocks. 'Let the dance begin.'

Jane could feel herself growing dizzy with excitement. Her arse-cheeks were red and stinging from McGivern's repeated blows and the wetness between her legs was matching that furious glow for heat and warmth. She felt ashamed for being dressed in the way she was. Her breasts were openly displayed through the strips of leather and the lips of her sex were being publicly caressed by McGivern. Yet the shame was a catalyst for her arousal and her need to endure more humiliation was an undeniable force.

'Let the dance begin,' McGivern repeated. He snapped his fingers and pointed at two of the slaves that adorned the walls. After he had thrust his finger towards the girl at Simon's side, the two slaves escorted her from her chair.

Jane sensed the beginning of the dance was close and she held her breath. She glanced back over her shoulder and glared at McGivern. 'I want you to tell them,' she hissed. 'I want you to tell them now.'

He shook his head and spoke in the same lowered tone that she was using. 'I'll tell them when I'm good and ready.'

She sighed, wishing her husky tone didn't reveal her desperate need for him. 'I won't hear you if you tell them after the dance. I've seen what happens to dancers afterwards. Please, tell them now.'

Simon and his male friend walked around the table. By some unspoken agreement, the masters seemed to know they were to prepare each other's submissives. The two men went to Frankie's side and the trio mumbled quietly together. There was an intimacy between Simon and Frankie that defied the hostile mood McGivern emulated. The dominatrix no longer looked threatening as she laughed with Simon. She even teased her smile to incorporate Simon's male friend. The group enjoyed a moment's shared mirth and, although Jane couldn't hear what they were saying, she suspected that their laughter was directed at McGivern.

With a nod of approval, Frankie allowed the two men to lead number three away from her. They took the slave to the head of the table, where they patiently waited with the others.

Jane saw all this from the corner of her eye, her vision never leaving McGivern's severe face.

'I didn't agree to say it while you were listening,' he told her. 'But I've promised to say it. What's the matter? Don't you trust me?'

She sniffed. 'You don't really want me to answer that, do you?'

'Act like a good slave and stop questioning your master. I'll tell them in my own good time and you'll just have to accept that.'

Jane wanted to say something more. She wanted to insist that he tell them now, but Frankie was already approaching and Jane knew that to say any more while the woman was listening would usurp McGivern's authority. She glared at him and then turned to face the dominatrix.

'Are you ready to dance?' Frankie asked.

Jane smiled and eased herself from the floor. 'Probably not,' she conceded. 'But I'm willing to try it.'

'I'm sorry I included you in this bet,' Frankie told Jane.

'I think I was trying to get my own back for the nasty looks you were giving me yesterday morning.'

'Don't be sorry,' Jane told her. 'It's been an experience.'

Frankie shrugged and scowled at McGivern. 'It might have been a better experience if you hadn't had to put up with him.'

McGivern glared at her. 'You're taking her to do the dance, not chatting her up. Get on with it.'

Frankie blew cigar smoke at him. She held out her arm for Jane and turned her back on McGivern. 'Allow me to escort you,' she said quietly.

Jane took the offered arm and allowed Frankie to lead her towards the end of the table. As soon as they were two steps away from McGivern, the dominatrix moved her mouth close to Jane's ear. 'What was it that made you look at me with such contempt yesterday?'

Jane smiled to herself. 'You intimidated me,' she replied honestly. 'You were looking at me as though . . .' She shook her head and grinned, unwilling to say any more. 'It all seems so petty and long ago now.'

'Did I look like I wanted to kiss you?'

Jane nodded. Her arousal was already a potent force and Frankie's whispered words were a punishing torture. Each syllable was blown against the sensitive flesh of her neck like the promise of a kiss.

'You wouldn't have let me kiss you yesterday, would you?'

Jane shook her head, her cheeks flushing crimson. 'Of course not,' she gasped. 'Yesterday morning, I'd have screamed or died rather than endure that.' The tips of her nipples had stiffened with excitement and she wished her eagerness wasn't so obvious. They had both stopped walking and Jane turned to face Frankie. Their mouths were close and she could imagine the woman's lips against hers. The thought sent a searing shock through the lips of her sex. Her nipples tingled with unexpected pleasure and she shivered as her exposed breasts brushed against Frankie's jacket. The cool leather caressed her as she met the woman's gaze.

208

'Would you let me kiss you now?' Frankie asked.

Jane caught an excited breath in her throat. 'I'd let you,' she whispered.

She knew that McGivern was watching, but that only added to her arousal. She and McGivern were lovers, but they were in a relationship that she had never imagined she could be caught in. They weren't a boyfriend and girlfriend like the couple with Simon. There was no promise of betrothal or claims for undying love. She was simply his slave and, in assuming that title, she had agreed to become the plaything of superiors. With those thoughts colouring her excitement, Jane moved her mouth close to Frankie's and they kissed.

At the back of her mind, Jane knew that Frankie was only kissing her to annoy McGivern. The dominatrix manipulated herself into a position so she could glare over Jane's shoulder and stare back towards him as he watched. The realisation didn't trouble Jane. She wasn't bothered about showing her obedience to McGivern. She was too involved in the pleasure of being used by her masters.

They kissed deeply. Frankie's fingers found one of her breasts and the aching nub was squeezed.

Jane snaked her arm around Frankie's waist and pressed her near-naked body closer to the dominatrix.

'Hurry it up,' McGivern growled. He slammed his fist against the banquet table, making no attempt to conceal his growing annoyance. 'Once I've won this bet, I might let you play with her some more. But we still have to see if we've all met the challenge.'

Jane could feel herself shivering. Frankie's kisses, the impending dance and McGivern's threat of more abuse were all adding momentum to her arousal. Frankie gave her breast a final tweak, then guided Jane to the head of the table.

'I thought you weren't going to submit to him?' Simon said, greeting Jane with a kiss to her cheek.

Jane glanced at her feet, but he lifted her chin up so that their eyes met.

'I wasn't trying to reprimand you,' Simon explained. 'I'm just surprised. You seemed so determined.'

'I'm surprised, too,' Jane admitted honestly. 'But it's something I want to do.'

'As long as you're sure that it is what you want. I'm not saying this because it will help me to win the challenge, but if the dance goes too far for you, you have to stop yourself and leave.'

'It's what I want to do,' Jane repeated.

He nodded and reached out to touch the student he had dominated. She was still in the arms of her boyfriend, but she seemed happy to enjoy Simon's caress.

'I suppose Sally here feels the same way,' Simon told Jane.

'Stop trying to influence the dancers and start preparing them,' McGivern called. He sat alone at the foot of the table glowering at the group.

'Number three was right,' Simon told no one in particular. 'He is a twat.'

McGivern snapped his fingers and three slaves started from the walls towards the dancers. They each carried a pair of buckets with enema equipment dangling over the sides.

Jane studied them with growing apprehension. The enormity of what she was about to subject herself to weighed heavily on her mind.

'I need a quick word with number three,' Frankie said. Before anyone could stop her, she had grabbed the slave's arm and pulled her two paces away from the others.

'What the hell is going on up there?' McGivern bawled. 'This is well out of order. This goes against all the rules and conditions.'

They were all ignoring him.

Frankie had pushed her mouth close to number three's ear and, although the woman was struggling to keep her voice at a whisper, Jane could hear every muttered word.

'I wasn't being honest in the bedroom,' Frankie told the slave. 'I was lying.'

'Lying about what?'

'Everything. The slave auction, McGivern growing bored of you. Most of what I said was a lie. I was only saying those things so you'd agree to do this dance.'

Jane listened more intently, uncomfortable with the act of eavesdropping but intrigued by what she was hearing.

'Why are you saying this?'

'I don't want you to do anything you might regret. I know how important McGivern is to you and I don't want you to jeopardise whatever it is you think you two have.'

Silence fell between the two women. Jane strained her ears, wishing that she dared turn to see if they were still talking. The trio of slaves were now ready to start the preparations and they dropped their buckets with a clatter. Jane saw the waft of steam on the surface of one pail and her stomach lurched queasily.

'Are you going to stop priming your slave?' McGivern demanded. 'This contravenes all of the conditions I'd imagined when I set up this challenge.'

No one bothered to acknowledge him.

'It doesn't matter,' number three told Frankie. 'I'm still going to do the dance for you.'

'But you don't have to,' Frankie's voice rose insistently.

'I want to. I saw the way the master was glaring at me when I said I'd do the dance. I can see the livid way he's looking at me now and I know there'll be hell to pay for disobeying him.' She paused for an instant, then said, 'I'm looking forward to the punishments that he's planning.'

Jane couldn't see the slave's face, but she could hear the smile in her voice.

'Prepare the dancers,' McGivern called.

Frankie released her hold on number three's arm and guided her back to Simon's side. 'If you're sure,' she whispered.

Number three was struggling to contain her grin. 'I'm more than sure.'

'Are we all ready?' Simon asked.

Frankie said she was. Jane saw the other women nodding their assent and she tried to swallow her own nervousness, along with the lump in her throat. 'I'm ready,' Jane said. Her heartbeat hammered inside her chest.

McGivern seemed to relax in his chair. 'Then if we're all ready, I think it's time the submissives were prepared.'

211

Now the moment was upon her, Jane's growing doubts became more insistent. She glanced hesitantly at the others, wondering if there was any chance of putting off this humiliation. The tension had already become unbearable, and she didn't want to wait any longer, but her fears of the dance were screaming for her to use any delaying tactic she could think of.

Frankie didn't give Jane the chance to voice her fears. With a firm hand, the dominatrix pushed her over the banquet table. The polished oak was cool against her breasts and stomach and, as she noticed this, Jane also realised she was dripping with nervous sweat.

'What a shame you weren't my submissive,' Frankie whispered. 'You and I could have had a lot of fun together.'

With her cheeks glowing crimson, Jane said nothing. She had seen the fading marks that adorned number three's body and she was loath to contemplate how they had been administered. The punishments Jane had suffered had been cruel and bordering on the unbearable. Under Frankie's hand, Jane believed that torment would have been far worse. Briefly, she tried to picture herself being dominated by Frankie. It was a swift exercise which Jane cut short as soon as it had begun. She knew that if she dwelt on those images for any longer, her excitement couldn't be contained.

Frankie cupped a handful of soapy water and rubbed it against Jane's sex. The warm slippery wetness was a delicious frisson that sent thrills through Jane's pussy-lips. Frankie's vigorous fingers should have been a sexless caress but they worked against the pulse of Jane's clitoris. The stimulation left her breathless.

'Simon!'

Jane glanced towards the girl that Simon had introduced as Sally. She was writhing on the banquet table beneath the attention of McGivern's two slaves. Her smile was stretched into a shocked grimace.

'You never said it would be like this, Simon.'

Simon was soaping number three, his hand working

dextrously against the slave's sex. 'Should I have told you everything, and spoilt all the morning's surprises?'

Sally giggled. Her laughter had a throaty chuckle that Jane had heard in her own voice before now. 'If you'd told me it was going to be this good, I'd never have believed you.'

'This is just the beginning,' he laughed. 'It gets a lot better before it's over.'

Jane stopped herself from dwelling on that particular thought, wishing she could ignore Frankie's hand so easily. A pair of exploratory fingers had tested her sex and her body was responding eagerly. The ache of her bruised pussy-lips had been all but forgotten since she had agreed to do the dance for McGivern. At the back of her mind, as this moment had neared, Jane half-expected herself to be revisited by the pleasurable pain that had been the hallmark of the wooden horse. Instead, her labia sparkled with pure delight. Miniature lightning bolts coursed from her pussy-lips, leaving her drained and shivering.

Frankie tested a thumb against the rim of her anus and Jane gasped. The tip was held firmly over her sphincter and Frankie gently increased the pressure.

Jane squeezed her buttocks together in a defiant attempt to stave off the entry. Her cheeks were glowing crimson and she dreaded the obscene penetration as much as she craved it. Before she could tighten herself impenetrably, the thumb entered in a slippery rush. The intrusion was a shameful embarrassment – a sensation heightened by the presence of the others. Even though she knew they were suffering the same humiliation, and not the least bit interested in her, Jane could imagine the weight of their disapproving frowns as she submitted herself to this indignity. A mortified tear trailed down her face.

To make it all worse, Jane's arousal was spiralling.

'Are you ready for the brush?'

Jane couldn't draw enough breath to manage a response. She wondered how she could have forgotten about the scrubbing brush, then closed her eyes and shook her head. She might have considered herself prepared for many things, but the scrubbing brush wasn't one of them.

For her own reasons, Frankie took the gesture as a nod of assent. She dragged her fingers from Jane's anus and, from the corner of her eye, Jane saw the dominatrix reach into the bucket.

Her throat was thickened by a hateful excitement and Jane tried to hiss her denial. The sound came out as a whispered sibilant, cut short as she snatched a startled breath.

Her sex was treated to the harsh caress of a stiff brush. The bristles douched her with a surprise of warm water before scouring at her sensitive flesh. The pleasurable sensations she had been tolerating were scrubbed away from her pussy-lips. As Frankie attacked her with renewed vigour, flecks of warm, soapy water spattered against her thighs.

Sally groaned. She was leaning over the table and banging her fists against it as she told Simon how marvellous this experience was. The two slaves attending to Sally seemed oblivious to her enjoyment and they carried out their duties like impartial technicians.

On Jane's other side, number three was immobile as she accepted her fate beneath Simon's hands. Her gaze was focused towards the foot of the table, where McGivern sat alone. Simon worked the scrubbing brush briskly between the tops of her legs but the slave ignored him. Her fingers had curled into fists but, apart from that, she showed no outward signs of involvement. She kept her gaze fixed on McGivern and graced him with an enigmatic smile.

Jane glanced from number three to McGivern and saw that the master and slave were locked in a staring contest. McGivern still appeared incredulous and unable to comprehend that his slave had agreed to do the dance. Number three looked as though she was savouring his potential wrath. If Frankie hadn't been distracting her, Jane would have loved to study the pair further.

'You're all scrubbed up and ready to dance,' Frankie whispered. 'What a shame I haven't got a corsage for you.'

'Why are we still going through with this?' Jane asked. She pushed herself on to her elbows and glanced from

214

Simon to Frankie. She tried to ignore the pressure of Frankie's finger at her sphincter. The inquisitive tip was promising to enter her again and her inner muscles were yearning to relent. 'Why are we still subjecting ourselves to this humiliation when we've all said that we'll dance?'

'Your word isn't enough,' Simon reminded her. 'McGivern wants proof.'

'And the dance isn't that easy,' Frankie added. 'You have to manage it without embarrassing yourself.'

Jane blushed, able to picture the scene that Frankie was alluding to. She drew a deep breath, preparing to tell the dominatrix she had changed her mind. Before she could give voice to the thought, it was all happening. The tip of the enema slid into her arse.

With a firm hand, Frankie pushed Jane back to the tabletop. She used the other to force the enema pipe deeper.

Number three was suffering the same violation and she grunted quietly.

Jane glanced at her and saw that the slave's face remained impassive. Her gaze was still locked on McGivern's and the same sly smile still twisted the corners of her mouth.

'Jesus! Simon! Jesus!'

Jane turned to glance at Sally as the student shrieked her delight. Her cheeks had flushed to an orgasmic purple and her lips were curled into a sneer of elation.

'This is divine,' Sally sobbed.

'I told you you'd enjoy it,' Simon reminded her.

'Hold still,' Frankie whispered the words in Jane's ear.

Jane started to say that she couldn't. She had wanted to stop her involvement before but now more than ever she needed to distance herself from this perversity. She glanced back over her shoulder to tell Frankie that she was withdrawing.

A flood of warm water hurtled through the pipe. There was an instant before it hit when Jane could feel the enema pipe being warmed from within. The sensation pierced her with the shameful sting of excitement. Before she could relish the moment, a barrage of soapy water was filling her bowel. With a soft growl, the air was forced from her lungs.

Number three whimpered. Jane didn't hear the noise but she saw the slave's mouth part to release the cry. Sally's elated shrieks had turned into screams as she thrashed against the table, but her excited tirade was also inaudible to Jane. The sound of her own shrill screech echoed around the banquet hall.

The spray erupted again and again, filling Jane to a point of impossible fullness. Twin urges fought for control of her body. There was a need to release and a need to hold on, each one arguing its point with an unswaying force. Jane balled her fists, started turning to glare at Frankie, then changed her mind and hugged the banquet table. The swirling waters were already churning inside her and the slightest movement made their presence more threatening. Her embarrassment was tremendous and nearly as crippling as the rush of arousal it inspired.

'Are the dancers prepared?' McGivern called.

Simon told him they were.

McGivern snapped his fingers and music began to play. 'Slaves. Return to your places,' he barked. 'Frankie, Simon.' McGivern sounded as though he was trying to be genial to his guests, but his gruff voice still made the request grate like a command. 'Take your seats and let us watch the dance.'

Jane shivered against the squirming of an internal spasm.

The music began with a maniacal flurry of drum rolls, followed by an abrupt fanfare.

Jane eased herself from the table and tried to stand straight. It occurred to her that she had no idea what dance she was meant to perform, or how long it was meant to go on for. When number three had been dancing, the previous day, Jane's gaze had been everywhere except on the naked slave. Rather than watching the dance of submission, Jane had been trying to distance herself from the room. She had caught glimpses – her horrified mind wouldn't allow her to ignore all of it – but the little she had seen was barely remembered now. The music was unfamiliar and, for a brief instant, as the opening crescendo closed, Jane wondered if the tape had stopped playing.

She glanced at number three and saw the slave was wrapping her arms modestly around herself. Jane guessed this was a part of the dance and covered herself in the same way. From the corner of her eye, she saw Sally was following suit. As the music began to whisper its first wary rhythms, number three took a step forward.

Jane drew a deep breath and copied her.

It was almost impossible to concentrate on the dance. Her bowels screamed for release and the soapy water inside her was swelling to a burdensome weight. Her cheeks were burning and her body was oiled with sweat. To make the whole exercise even more humiliating, the pulse of her arousal was beating louder than *Salome's Dance of the Seven Veils*.

Jane mimicked number three's steps, performing each movement with the same rigid posture. As she raised her legs, and twisted and turned, she was clenching her buttock muscles. Her bowels were churning at a rapid rate and she was fearful of allowing herself any opportunity for release. Her hands covered her breasts but she splayed her fingers so the thrust of her nipples could be seen. The pressure against her areolae added impetus to her arousal and she fought against its thrill. Turning and writhing, she allowed the masters to watch as she slowly revealed herself to them.

McGivern's grudging smile widened. The redheaded slave with the number eleven badge had taken Jane's place at his side and McGivern's hand rested on her rear. Jane could see his fingers were sliding in and out of the woman and the slave was struggling to remain sanguine as he casually frigged her.

She glanced at Simon and saw he was momentarily ignoring the dancers. His mouth was locked on to his male friend's and the two men seemed oblivious to everything else in the room. Their hands were exploring each other as they savoured their kiss.

Frankie grinned at Jane. She was sitting behind the table, with the lower half of her body lost to Jane's vision. She held a cigar in one hand but the other had disappeared beneath the table. Jane didn't need to read the dominatrix's sly smile to know that Frankie was touching herself as she watched the dancers, and that thought darkened her excitement.

The music built up speed and number three began to twist and turn more furiously. Jane attempted to copy the slave's athletic grace, but she felt like a clumsy amateur in comparison. Her high kicks and graceful poses were tempered by the swirling chaos in her stomach. The constant holding of her buttock muscles was making each step feel forced and mechanical.

Sally was managing to perform with an artfulness that defied her studious appearance. Her lithe, naked body was paraded splendidly before the voyeuristic guests and what she lacked in skill, she made up for with enthusiasm. Like Jane, she was drenched in sweat and occasionally she lost step with the others as she tried to contain herself against the enema's irresistible impulse. However, her dance was only made more attractive because of that.

Following number three's example, Jane stepped towards the foot of the table. She could see that the slave was trying to position herself in front of Frankie, while Sally was directing her steps towards Simon. Following the mad logic of this insanity, Jane knew she would have to perform her ultimate humiliation beneath McGivern's fearsome gaze. All three of the masters were accepting short, stubby maces from the attendant slaves and Jane swallowed uneasily at the sight. The music was building to a frantic climax and she knew that the most dreaded moment of the dance was almost upon her. She drew a deep breath and prayed that she possessed whatever strengths were needed for the finale of this degradation.

As the music reached its abrupt end, the three submissives dropped to their knees.

McGivern studied her, one hand still working against the redheaded slave at his side. He held the mace in the other and clutched the implement to his chest.

He only held it there for an instant but, as that long second passed, Jane could see the pleasure he was extracting from her humiliation. In this punishing hour, he was teasing her with the threat of withholding the mace and it wasn't until he pressed it into her hand that she realised how desperately she needed the implement.

'Pleasure yourself,' he whispered.

She hadn't needed the instruction. She snatched the mace away from him and pushed it towards herself.

Sally was screaming euphorically, her elated cries echoing from the walls. Jane guessed that number three was holding herself with her typical, distinctive composure but she couldn't see and she didn't care. She was under McGivern's gaze now and all that mattered was doing as he had instructed. The relentless demands of her bowel, and her arousal's need for satisfaction, were unimportant whispers beneath the need to do his bidding.

Eagerly, she pushed the mace against her sex-lips. Her body quivered as the polished wood touched her. Her labia had been ignored during the dance and the pleasures of the last day had made them greedy for attention. With the mace rubbing hard at her, Jane could feel herself shooting towards a blissful utopia.

'Pleasure yourself,' McGivern repeated.

Jane glanced at him, blinking her eyes free from shameful tears to focus on him more clearly. The slave by his side was panting heavily and Jane could see the redhead was close to attaining her own pinnacle. The slave's eyes met Jane's and her groans grew deeper.

Trying to dismiss the pair of them, and concentrating on her own satisfaction, Jane pushed the mace between her sex lips.

It was as broad as she had anticipated and she wondered if its girth was greater than she could accommodate. Glancing down at herself, she saw that her pussy-lips were already over-stretched and the head had barely begun to nuzzle inside. The gnarled carvings were a marvellous annoyance that had been designed to inflict maximum pleasure and Jane wished she could desensitise herself to their stimulation. She felt sure that, with a firm hand, she could slide the whole thing inside but her sphincter was urging her to be cautious. The soapy waters of the enema were still churning and she knew she couldn't resist their demands for ever. Forcing herself to endure the orgasm too quickly, before her body was prepared for it, was bound to have a catastrophic result.

Even with that thought screaming inside her mind, Jane knew that she needed the orgasm. She edged the head of the mace deeper, easing it inside with a slowness that was agonising. Every millimetre was a voyage of discovery and the sensations were too new for her to decide if they were pleasure or pain. Each ridge of the carved head inspired a ripple that threatened to push her beyond the realms of orgasm.

While she had danced, Jane had held her buttocks rigid and the effort had left her aching. Now, she steeled herself against the pleasure, not knowing whether to revile it or revel in it. The exertion left her acutely conscious of the penetrating mace and the sensations it evoked were stronger than she could deal with. The humiliation was a constant torment and the torture of her bowel grew stronger. And all the time, the need of her arousal became more insistent. When the head of the mace was finally inside her, Jane knew she was close to orgasm. She longed for her climax and dreaded it in the same instant. She was pushing the shaft deeper, daring to allow the head to stretch her inner muscles. Her body was rewarded with a pleasure that was too extreme to be enjoyable.

Sally's screams had tapered to guttural sobs and Jane could hear Simon and his friend cheering her to the brink of climax. Frankie was mumbling words of praise as number three spat bitter words of elation, but all those voices were a background noise to the scream of Jane's own fury. Rubbing her index finger over the pulse of her clitoris, Jane braced herself for the flood of the orgasm. She was unable to simply give in to the pleasure, and that made it all the more punishing. The first ripple left her breathless but she resisted the urge to let the wave sweep through her. She stiffened the muscles of her arse, and was treated to a body-blow of euphoria. The second orgasmic ripple shuddered from the lips of her sex and went to every nerve-ending.

There was no air left inside to scream but a shrill voice echoed in her mind. As the multiple climax soared through her, Jane's inner muscles squeezed frantically and the mace was pushed from her pussy-lips. It was automatic to try and hold the implement inside, the way she had been trying to hold everything else inside. The effort accentuated each gnarly bump on the mace's head.

'Tremendous,' McGivern muttered, raising from his seat. His grin was wide and maniacal. He started clapping his hands as he glanced at the others and he roared the word again.

'Tremendous.' McGivern was happy to begin the applause, truly delighted by the performance. Everything had gone better than he had expected: and if this really was going to be his last day as the castle's owner, he thought it was one hell of a way to relinquish his position.

Admittedly, to make things slightly more perfect, Simon and Frankie's submissives could have embarrassed themselves. Such a display would have lost them the challenge and left him victorious, and that would have really been the best outcome: but, as performances went, McGivern thought the one he had just witnessed was as good as any.

Frankie and Simon joined his show of appreciation and McGivern allowed the submissives a moment to bask in their glory. It was only a brief moment because he could see they were anxious to visit the garderobe. With a snap of his fingers, he summoned his slaves from the wall to help the dancers.

The youth from Simon's side was already rushing to his girlfriend and McGivern scowled as he saw the pair kiss hungrily.

'Take them away,' McGivern said. 'They've done well. They've all done well.'

Jane glared up at him. Her cheeks were still flushed. Her hair was plastered to her forehead and her eyes were shining madly. 'Tell them, McGivern.'

He mouthed nonsense words, refusing to meet her gaze. He caught the eye of one slave and nodded in Jane's direction. 'Take her away,' he told the slave.

'Tell them,' Jane bawled. She started trying to raise herself from the floor and almost collapsed in the attempt. Despite the obvious pains of her pleasure-weary body, Jane's gaze was fixed firmly on him.

McGivern graced her with a disdainful smile as two of his slaves tried helping her from the floor. He thought she looked like a wild animal and, although he could see she was preoccupied by the threat of the enema, her ferocious glare never left his face.

'Tell them,' Jane wailed. 'Tell them. I want to hear you tell them.'

He remained silent, smiling benignly until Jane was led from the room. 'What a tremendous dance,' McGivern said, settling himself back in the seat. The three of them were alone. His slaves had departed with the submissive dancers and Simon's male friend had accompanied Sally to the garderobe. The silence between them wasn't companionable but it lacked the antagonism that their first morning together had harboured. 'I have to say, as much as it galls me, you two are almost as good as I am.'

'Rare praise indeed,' Simon mumbled.

'What did she want you to tell us?' Frankie asked.

McGivern glanced at her and then looked away. 'Maybe later. We have other things to discuss first.'

'Such as?'

'Such as the ownership of this place.'

Simon leant forward. 'And what do you suggest we do now? We've each managed the bet. Do we pack up, go home and wait for your solicitor to extricate us from this co-operative purchase? Or is there time for another challenge?'

McGivern grinned. 'You really are a game one, aren't you?'

222

'Another challenge?' Frankie sounded doubtful.

'There won't be another challenge,' McGivern said flatly. 'Not with my involvement, anyway. You two can do what the hell you want, but I'm leaving.'

'Leaving?'

Simon looked as startled as Frankie sounded.

McGivern nodded and eased himself from the seat. 'Claim back your investments, if you like; Jane will be able to sort that out. If you want, you can share the place. I think I can persuade the owner to accept your monies without including my substantial contribution. There are four keeps here and that's enough room for the pair of you. You can do whatever the hell you like, but you can do it without my involvement.'

Silence returned between the three of them as Simon and Frankie considered McGivern's words. McGivern saw them exchange a wary glance and knew they were both contemplating joint ownership. He guessed that either of them would be happy to share the building with a second person, as long as that second person wasn't him. It was a realisation that would have knocked the confidence of a lesser man.

'It's an idea,' Simon said thoughtfully. He glanced at Frankie and told her, 'I could impose on your slave-breaking skills whenever I encountered a trouble-some initiate.'

She sniffed disdainfully and drew life back into her cigar. 'And I could borrow your nail polish and lipstick if I ever decided to dress like a schoolgirl.'

McGivern could sense that she wasn't won over by the suggestion, but he was already dismissing them as he made for the banquet hall's door.

'Why are you pulling out of the deal, McGivern?' Frankie asked.

McGivern paused with his hand on the wrought-iron door handle. Meeting her gaze, he shook his head and said, 'I don't think you'd understand. I've had a pang of conscience.'

Frankie looked away, her cheeks colouring.

'I understand,' Simon broke in. 'But I'm not sure I believe it. You're more likely to start menstruating than have a pang of conscience.'

McGivern and Frankie ignored him.

'I can accept that,' Frankie said. 'And if you're determined to pull out, then Simon and I will make our own arrangements. The idea of sharing isn't so unappealing. But, before you leave, I need to ask you something.'

He raised his eyebrows, silently encouraging her to continue.

'Number three,' Frankie whispered.

McGivern grunted. 'You did well to dominate her. I felt sure she couldn't be broken.'

Frankie shook her head. 'She wasn't broken. I just misguided her a little. But I want to ask a favour concerning her.'

'You can ask,' McGivern allowed.

'This conscience of yours. Is it a short-term malaise, or does it look likely to be a long-term condition?'

'Why do you ask?'

She drew on her cigar and allowed smoke to shape her words. 'If it's still affecting you in the future, when you've grown weary of number three, give me a call and let me know.'

McGivern nodded, a smile of understanding crossing his face. Without another word, he left the room.

'Did you tell them?'

McGivern found it difficult to believe that Jane had made it from the garderobe so quickly. She was standing outside the door as he left the banquet hall and he could see she had been about to burst in. She was still dressed in the slave's uniform and he thought she looked more exciting than ever. It was certainly an improvement on the dowdy office-girl image that she had projected the previous morning.

'I withdrew myself from the bet,' McGivern told her. 'Does that satisfy you?'

She stared at him with a look of genuine surprise. 'I

thought you'd have bought them off or given them their money back or something else.'

McGivern shook his head. 'There was no point, really. I've grown rather bored with living in this place and I'm looking for pastures new.'

Jane seemed doubtful. 'Really?'

'Really,' he assured her. 'The weather is too cool for me and the rot that started in the south keep is likely to spread to the other buildings. Do you know, if Frankie or Simon had decided to purchase this place properly, a good surveyor's report would have told them it wasn't worth the investment.'

Jane glared at him. 'You bastard,' she whispered. 'You planned all of this from the beginning, didn't you?'

McGivern shrugged. 'I planned most of it,' he conceded.

Jane shook her head, treating him to a smile that was torn between loathing and admiration. 'And what are you going to do now? Where are you going to take your entourage, once you've left the castle?'

'Funny you should ask,' he grinned. 'There's another castle, just off the coast of Crete. It's a remote location and the local authorities seldom visit to enforce their jurisdiction. The weather is particularly clement and, since I've just made a healthy profit on the sale of this place, I think I might be able to afford it.'

Her lips were curled into grudging sneer. 'Will you be needing the services of a solicitor, to help sort out the paperwork?'

McGivern laughed and placed an arm around her shoulders. Feeling her mellow in his embrace he said, 'I'll be needing the services of my solicitor for a lot more than that.'

NEW BOOKS

Coming up from Nexus, Sapphire and Black Lace

Confession of an English Slave by Yolanda Celbridge
September 1999   Price £5.99   ISBN: 0 352 33433 9
Introduced to the joys of bare-bottom discipline by lustful ladies,
naval cadet Philip Demense, posted to the far east, painfully learns
true submission from the voluptuous dominatrix Galena. Escaping
from her lash, he is kidnapped to serve in an English school of female
domination, transplanted to the emptiness of Siberia to escape do-
gooding restrictions on corporal punishment. His male arrogance
utterly crushed, Philip gladly submits to total enslavement by women,
with unlimited flagellant discipline of naked males – and females . . .

The Rake by Aishling Morgan
September 1999   Price £5.99   ISBN: 0 352 33434 7
Henry Truscott is a dissipated rake even by the standards of the late
eighteenth century. When his eye catches the beautiful Eloise he
expects either to be thrashed by her footman and dumped in a ditch
or to take his full pleasure in her magnificent curves. He gets more
than he had anticipated, in every way, trading seduction and revenge
and finally using her and her maids in an increasingly perverse
manner as they are pursued across France by bloodthirsty
revolutionaries.

Citadel of Servitude by Aran Ashe
September 1999   Price £5.99   ISBN: 0 352 33435 5
Tormunil: the mysterious citadel of erotic mastery from which there
can be no excape. Sianon is the beautiful love-slave whose breasts
weep milk; Josef the outlander who tries to save her, only to be drawn
ever deeper into a vortex of perverse desires. In the Citadel of
Servitude, every avenue of sexual love must be tested, every strange
pleasure explored, and every taboo broken. The eighth in a series of
Nexus Classics.

Giselle by Jean Aveline

October 1999   ISBN: 0 352 33440 1

Aside from her extreme beauty, Giselle appears to be an ordinary country girl when the English photographer Charles discovers her in Northern France. Yet when he takes her to Paris to recreate her as a model, he discovers that she has a history. On an island in a flooded quarry in Avignon, boys and men have already reached her and corrupted her. All Charles can do is feed her appetite for perverse sex, and the higher she rises in the world of fashion the lower she falls in her sexual games with strangers.

House Rules by G.C. Scott

October 1999   ISBN: 0 352 33441 X

When Richard meets Helena in Hamburg's red light district, he isn't prepared for either the forwardness with which she seduces him or his imminent involvement in her curious business dealings. For Helena is a designer of fetish clothing, and her colleagues have very forceful ideas about how a man should be treated.

Bound to Serve by Amanda Ware

October 1999   ISBN: 0 352 33457 6

Caroline West is facing up to the absence of her master, Liam, as he battles to save himself from bankruptcy. When the cruel and manipulative Clive offers her a means of helping him, on condition that she becomes his slave for three weeks, she does not hesitate, and is soon signed over to him. She is then handed over to Lynne, her former mistress for further, more severe training – treatment which Caroline soon finds is more and more to her liking. A Nexus Classic.

A new imprint of lesbian fiction

Sweet Violet by Ruby Vise
September 1999   Price £6.99   ISBN: 0 352 33458 4
Violet is young, butch and new in town, looking for a way to get over her childhood sweetheart Katherine. And there are plenty of distractions in 1980s London, as the rarefied big-city dyke scene is both politically and sexually charged – full of everything from cosmic mother-earth worshippers to sexy girls in leather.

Getaway by Suzanne Blaylock
October 1999   Price £6.99   ISBN: 0 352 33443 6
Brilliantly talented Polly Sayers had made two big life shifts concurrently. She's had her first affair with a woman, and she's also stolen the code of an important new piece of software and made her break, doing a runner all the way to a seemingly peaceful coastal community. But things aren't as tranquil as they appear in the haven, as Polly becomes immersed in an insular group of mysterious but very attractive women.

BLACK
lace

Out of Bounds by Mandy Dickinson
September 1999   Price £5.99   ISBN: 0 352 33431 2
When Katie decides to start a new life in a French farmhouse left to her by her grandfather, she is horrified to find two men living there already. But her horror quickly becomes curiosity as she realises how attracted she is to the two men, and how much illicit pleasure is to be had by becoming involved with them. The world in which they live knows no rules, and for the first time she can explore her darkest desires to the full.

A Dangerous Game by Lucinda Carrington
September 1999   Price £5.99   ISBN: 0 352 33432 0
Jacey, tired of the opportunities available to her at home and deciding to push her boundaries, takes a job as a doctor in a hospital in Guatamàl, South America. It's the ideal environment for experimental sex, and she soon finds herself loving the kinky medical games she can play. But Guatamàl is not a safe place to play around with men – how soon will it be before Jacey realises she is playing a very dangerous game? By the author of *The Master of Shilden*.

The Ties That Bind by Tesni Morgan
October 1999   Price £5.99   ISBN: 0 352 33438 X
When Kim meets devilish stanger Jack Loring at a fancy-dress party, her comfortable world turns upside down. For a start, Jack might have some family ties to Kim, which only makes their mutual attraction all the more problematic. As he demonstrates some kinky new ways of loving her, she's torn between his amoral lust for life and her love for her husband – which will she choose?

Sleepless Nights by Zoe le Verdier
October 1999   Price £5.99   ISBN: 0 352 33439 8
Zoe le Verdier's first collection of stunning short stories, *Insomnia*, pushed the boundaries of women's erotica – but this collection looks set to be even hotter. The author's never been afraid to explore the most explicit female fantasies, from kinky fetishism to sex with a stranger, and her unashamed, powerfully erotic style shows these situations as you've never seen them before.

NEXUS BACKLIST

All books are priced £5.99 unless another price is given. If a date is supplied, the book in question will not be available until that month in 1999.

CONTEMPORARY EROTICA

THE ACADEMY	Arabella Knight	
AMANDA IN THE PRIVATE HOUSE	Esme Ombreux	
BAD PENNY	Penny Birch	
THE BLACK MASQUE	Lisette Ashton	
THE BLACK WIDOW	Lisette Ashton	
BOUND TO OBEY	Amanda Ware	
BRAT	Penny Birch	
DANCE OF SUBMISSION	Lisette Ashton	Nov
DARK DELIGHTS	Maria del Rey	
DARK DESIRES	Maria del Rey	
DARLINE DOMINANT	Tania d'Alanis	
DISCIPLES OF SHAME	Stephanie Calvin	
THE DISCIPLINE OF NURSE RIDING	Yolanda Celbridge	
DISPLAYS OF INNOCENTS	Lucy Golden	
EMMA'S SECRET DOMINATION	Hilary James	
EXPOSING LOUISA	Jean Aveline	
FAIRGROUND ATTRACTIONS	Lisette Ashton	
GISELLE	Jean Aveline	Oct
HEART OF DESIRE	Maria del Rey	
HOUSE RULES	G.C. Scott	Oct
IN FOR A PENNY	Penny Birch	Nov
JULIE AT THE REFORMATORY	Angela Elgar	
LINGERING LESSONS	Sarah Veitch	

THE MISTRESS OF STERNWOOD GRANGE	Arabella Knight		
ONE WEEK IN THE PRIVATE HOUSE	Esme Ombreux		
THE PALACE OF EROS	Delver Maddingley		
PENNY IN HARNESS	Penny Birch		
THE PLEASURE CHAMBER	Brigitte Markham		
THE RELUCTANT VIRGIN	Kendal Grahame		
RITES OF OBEDIENCE	Lindsay Gordon		
RUE MARQUIS DE SADE	Morgana Baron		
'S' – A JOURNEY INTO SERVITUDE	Philippa Masters		
SANDRA'S NEW SCHOOL	Yolanda Celbridge		Dec
THE SCHOOLING OF STELLA	Yolanda Celbridge		
THE SUBMISSION OF STELLA	Yolanda Celbridge		
THE SUBMISSION GALLERY	Lindsay Gordon		
SUSIE IN SERVITUDE	Arabella Knight		
TAKING PAINS TO PLEASE	Arabella Knight		
A TASTE OF AMBER	Penny Birch		
THE TEST	Nadine Somers		
THE TRAINING OF FALLEN ANGELS	Kendal Grahame		
VIRGINIA'S QUEST	Katrina Young	£4.99	

ANCIENT & FANTASY SETTINGS

THE CASTLE OF MALDONA	Yolanda Celbridge		
THE FOREST OF BONDAGE	Aran Ashe		
NYMPHS OF DIONYSUS	Susan Tinoff	£4.99	
TIGER, TIGER	Aishling Morgan		Dec
THE WARRIOR QUEEN	Kendal Grahame		

EDWARDIAN, VICTORIAN & OLDER EROTICA

ANNIE	Evelyn Culber		
ANNIE AND THE COUNTESS	Evelyn Culber		
BEATRICE	Anonymous		
CONFESSIONS OF AN ENGLISH SLAVE	Yolanda Celbridge		Sep
THE CORRECTION OF AN ESSEX MAID	Yolanda Celbridge		

THE GOVERNESS AT ST AGATHA'S	Yolanda Celbridge		
THE MASTER OF CASTLELEIGH	Jacqueline Bellevois		Aug
PRIVATE MEMOIRS OF A KENTISH HEADMISTRESS	Yolanda Celbridge	£4.99	
THE RAKE	Aishling Morgan		Sep
THE TRAINING OF AN ENGLISH GENTLEMAN	Yolanda Celbridge		

SAMPLERS & COLLECTIONS

EROTICON 4	Various		
THE FIESTA LETTERS	ed. Chris Lloyd	£4.99	
NEW EROTICA 3			
NEW EROTICA 4	Various		
A DOZEN STROKES	Various		Aug

NEXUS CLASSICS
A new imprint dedicated to putting the finest works of erotic fiction back in print

THE IMAGE	Jean de Berg	
CHOOSING LOVERS FOR JUSTINE	Aran Ashe	
THE INSTITUTE	Maria del Rey	
AGONY AUNT	G. C. Scott	
THE HANDMAIDENS	Aran Ashe	
OBSESSION	Maria del Rey	
HIS MASTER'S VOICE	G.C. Scott	Aug
CITADEL OF SERVITUDE	Aran Ashe	Sep
BOUND TO SERVE	Amanda Ware	Oct
BOUND TO SUBMIT	Amanda Ware	Nov
SISTERHOOD OF THE INSTITUTE	Maria del Rey	Dec

Please send me the books I have ticked above.

Name   ....

Address   ....

            ....

            ....

            .... Post code........................

Send to: Cash Sales, Nexus Books, Thames Wharf Studios, Rainville Road, London W6 9HT

US customers: for prices and details of how to order books for delivery by mail, call 1-800-805-1083.

Please enclose a cheque or postal order, made payable to **Nexus Books**, to the value of the books you have ordered plus postage and packing costs as follows:

UK and BFPO – £1.00 for the first book, 50p for the second book and 30p for each subsequent book to a maximum of £3.00;

Overseas (including Republic of Ireland) – £2.00 for the first book, £1.00 for the second book and 50p for each subsequent book.

We accept all major credit cards, including VISA, ACCESS/ MASTERCARD, AMEX, DINERS CLUB, SWITCH, SOLO, and DELTA. Please write your card number and expiry date here:

....

Please allow up to 28 days for delivery.

Signature ....